THE MANNEQUIN HOUSE

In this intriguing historical mystery, Detective Inspector Silas Quinn investigates one of the strangest cases of his career...

London, 1914. Called out to investigate the murder of a fashion model employed by the House of Blackley, a prestigious Kensington department store, Detective Inspector Silas Quinn of Scotland Yard's Special Crimes Department is thrown into the bizarre: the chief murder suspect is a monkey. He may be sceptical, but how will Quinn ever get to the truth when faced with the maelstrom of seething jealousy, resentment, forbidden desires and thwarted passion that is the mannequin house?

THE MANNEQUIN HOUSE

A SILAS QUINN MYSTERY

R. N. Morris

Severn House Large Print
London & New York

This first large print edition published 2014
in Great Britain and the USA by
SEVERN HOUSE PUBLISHERS LTD of
19 Cedar Road, Sutton, Surrey, England, SM2 5DA.
First world regular print edition published 2012 by
Severn House Publishers Ltd., London and New York.

British Library Cataloguing in Publication Data

Morris, Roger, 1960- author.
    The mannequin house. -- Large print edition. -- (A Silas
    Quinn mystery ; 2)
    1. Quinn, Silas (Fictitious character)--Fiction.
    2. Murder--Investigation--England--London--Fiction.
    3. London (England)--History--1800-1950--Fiction.
    4. Detective and mystery stories. 5. Large type books.
    I. Title II. Series
    823.9'2-dc23

ISBN-13: 9780727896810

Severn House Publishers support the Forest Stewardship Council™
[FSC™], the leading international forest certification organisation. All
our titles that are printed on FSC certified paper carry the FSC logo.

Printed and bound in Great Britain by
T J International, Padstow, Cornwall.

Author's Note

Benjamin Blackley is a fictional character. However, certain aspects of his story were inspired by the life of William Whiteley, the founder of Whiteleys department store, as described in Linda Stratmann's fascinating account, *Whiteley's Folly: The Life and Death of a Salesman* (2004, Gloucestershire: The History Press).

London, April, 1914

The House of Blackley

'Numéro sept! Numéro sept! Vite, vite! Allons! Numéro sept, s'il vous plait!'

Inside the House of Blackley department store, a fashion parade was in progress.

The audience was highly exclusive. In fact, there were just two women watching, the countess, Lady Ascot and her daughter, the Honourable Caroline. They were seated beneath the Grand Dome, which formed the centrepiece of the recently remodelled building. Through the stained-glass cupola high above, a flood of colour-softened light suffused the vast space with a sense of promise.

Monsieur Hugo, the head of the Costumes Salon, called out numbers in French, each number corresponding to the next costume to be modelled. But there was a problem. *Numéro sept* had failed to appear.

'Excusez-moi!' said Monsieur Hugo, bowing sharply. He turned and poked his head through the curtain at the rear of the podium.

Backstage, six mannequins were in various stages of undress. Cries of protest met the appearance of Monsieur Hugo's male face, which was now a shade of pink that matched the last dress modelled: cerise.

'*Où est numéro sept?*'

'What's he saying?'

'He's speaking that funny lingo again.'

Monsieur Hugo rolled his eyes. '*Ce n'est pas un* funny lingo. *Je parle français. N'oubliez pas, vous êtes toutes des françaises!*'

'What's he say?'

'I said don't forget you're all supposed to be bloody French!' Monsieur Hugo spoke English with a strong and surprisingly authentic south London accent. 'We've got a real live *Your Ladyship* in today. Mr Blackley is hoping for great things from this showing. If Lady Ascot likes what she sees, she might spread the word among her upper-class friends. So it's important to make the right impression. Speaking of which, where is Amélie? This isn't like her. She's normally so reliable. She is a *veritable* Parisian model. So professional. So slender. So beautiful.'

'Well, she ain' here!' snapped a tall, wide-faced girl in her underwear.

'*Elle n'est pas ici* is what you say, Marie-Claude,' insisted Monsieur Hugo.

'My name's Daisy, not bleedin' Marie-Claude.'

'You'd better not let Mr Blackley catch you talking like that! You know the penalty for profanities. It's in the rules.'

Marie-Claude pulled a face that suggested she didn't care what Mr Blackley caught her doing and cared even less for his rules, all 462 of them. This was far from the truth, as everyone knew. On the wages Blackley paid even the

8

favoured mannequins, the sixpence fine he levied for any infringement was a serious blow.

A scrawny, moon-eyed girl in a pink slip followed the exchange closely. 'You don't think anything's happened to her, do you, Monsieur Hugo?'

'There's nothing for you to worry about, Albertine.' But Monsieur Hugo couldn't quite keep the anxiety out of his voice. He clapped his hands as if to dispel it. *'Allez, allez! Giselle, porte-toi numéro sept! Maintenant!'*

'Come again?' said Giselle, her brow creased in confusion.

'I said you can wear number seven! Gawd, give me strength!'

Meanwhile, on the floor of the Costumes Salon, in front of the stage, Mr Blackley himself did his best to pacify his very important new customers.

'May I offer Your Ladyships some refreshment? A cup of tea, perhaps?' Despite being the son of a farm labourer, Blackley's Yorkshire accent was of the genteel, almost effeminate kind. He had served his apprenticeship in a drapers' store in Harrogate, learning to blend in by emulating the softer vocal tones of the ladies who frequented the shop. It was here that he had first discovered himself to be a profound, if not pathological, lover of women. His adoption of their speech patterns was just one expression of his love. It was here, too, that he had learnt how closely the arts of selling and seduction were related.

9

An aristocratic moue of displeasure appeared on the countess's lips. And yet her eyes were lit with an enthusiastic fire as her gaze passed over Blackley's head, taking in the full height of the Grand Dome. She let out an involuntary gasp at the sight of the great cupola. It seemed to float above six storeys of promise and desire, pulling the viewer ever upwards in an ascent of consumption.

Blackley allowed himself a self-satisfied smile. It would seem that the expense of the cupola at the time of the store's reconstruction had been a good investment.

'Vulgar,' said Lady Ascot, suddenly remembering herself. She gestured a hand in the direction of one of the upper galleries, which was decorated with umbrellas and parasols of every size and colour. The bulbous canopies were like a line of overweight bottoms sticking out. Perhaps it was this that had provoked her judgement.

'But Your Ladyship, the costumes we have for you today are very far from vulgar! On the contrary, we have for your delight only the very latest fashions, direct from Paris. The height of sophistication, I assure you.'

For all his charm Blackley was a hard-headed realist. He knew well enough that Lady Ascot would not normally be seen dead in an establishment like his. But like many aristocratic families, the Ascots had fallen on hard times. Buying her couture from a department store that had a reputation for value was just one of the economies she had been forced to con-

10

template, after her credit had been politely declined at a number of the more prestigious establishments.

But where these older stores saw a credit risk, Blackley saw a valuable marketing and publicity opportunity. He was composing the advertisement in his head as he bowed to his seated guests: The House of Blackley, Couturier to the Aristocracy.

Benjamin Blackley was a man of prodigious talents, as well as impressive facial hair. His distinctive mutton-chop whiskers framed a permanent expression of bland affability. Indeed, his ability to maintain this expression, even under trying circumstances such as the present, could be counted as one of his greatest talents. His most impressive creation was this face, utterly without guile or guilt. To look upon it, it was impossible to conceive that ambition had played any part in his rise to commercial pre-eminence. The face declared that Providence had surely smiled on Mr Blackley, undoubtedly because Providence found him to be a thoroughly amenable fellow.

'Well, get on with it then!' commanded Lady Ascot. 'We don't have all day.'

'There has been a slight delay, Your Ladyship. To compensate you for which, I hope you will accept a complimentary item of millinery of your choice. That is to say, a hat.'

The countess's eyes narrowed in calculation. 'Only one?'

'And one for Lady Caroline, of course.' The old crone drove a hard bargain.

Lady Ascot gave a terse nod – but no thanks – to accept the deal. 'This doesn't give you licence to keep us waiting all day, Blackley.'

'I will see what can be done, Your Ladyship.'

With his imperturbable smile in place, Blackley mounted the platform and extricated Monsieur Hugo from behind the curtain. 'Well?'

'*C'est Amélie. Elle a disparu.*'

'English, you ninny.'

Monsieur Hugo cast a nervous glance over his employer's shoulder. His voice dropped to a conspiratorial whisper. 'I thought you said I was to speak French at all times in front of our guests.'

'I don't have time for that now,' whispered Blackley. 'What's going on?'

'It's Amélie. She's missing.'

For a moment, Blackley's calm exterior was ruffled. His brows descended, partially concealing his eyes. 'Amélie?' he said almost reverentially.

'I'm getting one of the other mannequins to model her costumes,' said Monsieur Hugo. 'She should be ready in a moment.'

But Blackley hadn't heard him. He was lost in contemplation of something private and precious. 'Amélie?' he murmured her name again, a half-appeal and half-complaint on his lips.

Then Blackley blinked once. A look of calculation came over him. His old equanimity was restored.

Waiting to go on in costume *numéro sept*,

12

Giselle looked through a gap in the curtain to see Blackley's uncharacteristic loss of composure. She turned to the other mannequins with a vindictive smile that suited her pinched face. 'Amélie is in trouble now! Monsieur Hugo just told Mr Blackley.'

'Do you think he'll fine her?' asked Minette with an anxious shudder.

'Fine her? I shouldn't be surprised if he gives her a good beating,' said Marie-Claude.

'He wouldn't do that, would he?' said Albertine, her eyes wide with fear.

'You read what it said in *The West End Whisperer*,' said Michelle. The girl appropriately dropped her voice to a cowed whisper. The latest edition of that scandalous magazine had been passed around the employee dormitories and lodging houses. Its *exposé* of what life was really like inside the House of Blackley was not news to any of the six hundred people who worked there, but still it was shocking to see it printed in black and white. What had been rumour and gossip was now elevated to the status of fact. 'He took a stick to a fellow just for yawning in front of him!'

Albertine gasped in horror. She raised a hand as if to ward off a blow. A half-cry, half-moan escaped from her. It could have been a name. *Amélie*.

'I heard about that,' said Giselle. 'But I never knew it was true.'

'Well, now you do,' said Michelle. 'They wouldn't have printed it if it weren't.'

'Who told them? That's what I want to know,'

13

wondered Minette.

'Oh, Mr Blackley has no shortage of enemies,' said Marie-Claude with a grim smile. 'There's plenty who want to destroy him. One day he'll go too far, you mark my words. Then the whole rotten House of Blackley will come falling down around him.'

'What's going on, Blackley? It may be All Fools' Day, but I will not be made a fool of like this!'

The countess's sharp tone did not seem to perturb Blackley. He bowed deeply, employing the full serenity of his smile. 'I do apologize, Your Ladyship. It seems that one of our mannequins has gone missing. I shall look into it myself, personally.'

Lady Ascot gestured impatiently with her hand. 'You will do no such thing! So a girl's gone missing? Good riddance to her, we say. Have one of the other girls model her costumes. It's all the same to us. You can chastise the miscreant later. We don't have all day, you know. We have a lunch appointment with the Duchess of Brecknock at twelve. When you do catch the idle hussy, be sure to remember the inconvenience she has caused us. We trust you will deal with her with the utmost severity.'

'You may count on me to take all appropriate action.' Blackley straightened himself. He signalled to Monsieur Hugo. 'On with the show, Monsieur Hugo. We must not keep Her Ladyship waiting.'

Monsieur Hugo clapped his hands and called

14

out *numéro sept.*

With Lady Ascot distracted by the next costume, Mr Blackley moved discreetly away. He signalled to one of the sales assistants. 'Arbuthnot, isn't it?' Blackley's voice was an urgent whisper. 'I want you to do something for me.'

A look between terror and pride showed on the young man's face. This curious expression betrayed how Blackley's employees felt towards the great man more eloquently than any article in *The West End Whisperer.*

Young Arbuthnot had been chosen for a commission. More than that, Mr Blackley knew his name. This was undoubtedly an opportunity to be noticed. If things went well there could be a bonus – even a promotion – in it. If not, his life, it might reasonably be presumed, would not be worth living.

He listened to Mr Blackley's words with a look of such intense concentration that it was close to panic.

'You understand,' said Mr Blackley, when he had finished explaining the mission, 'the importance of discretion in this matter? I trust that my confidence in you will not prove to be misplaced.'

Young Arbuthnot gulped and nodded nervously. Mr Blackley's mouth was formed into the same affable smile as ever. But in his eyes, there was the glint of ice.

The House of Blackley was a sprawling establishment occupying a considerable length of the south side of Kensington Road. It had grown organically over the years, as Blackley had snapped up the leases and freeholds of all the adjoining properties; all of them, that is, apart from the Roman Catholic church of Our Lady of the Sacred Heart. And so the store had mushroomed up around the church, a temple of Mammon surrounding one of God.

The church was only accessible through a narrow entrance passage that gave on to Kensington Road, a kind of tunnel through the House of Blackley. The church's location seemed to give its name an extra significance: was it the sacred heart at the centre of Blackley's commercial empire? An emblem of his conscience, perhaps?

A thorn in his side, more like.

The complete destruction of the original store premises in a fire some years ago had afforded Blackley the opportunity of radically remodelling the site (although he was still unable to do anything about the presence of the church, which had stubbornly survived the fire intact). However, apart from the addition of the Grand Dome, and the transference of the Menagerie from the fourth floor to the ground floor close to an exit, he chose to retain most of the store's original haphazard design.

The result was a veritable warren of consumerism, in which it was possible even for regular visitors to lose their way. But that was part of the pleasure of shopping at Blackley's: to be lost, and yet to find precisely what you were looking for, even if you didn't know you were looking for it.

Even members of staff were not immune to this spirit of disorientation, especially those like young Arbuthnot who had only recently started working there. As he hurried across the floor of the Grand Dome, he had no clear idea of where he was heading. He was impelled only by a sense of urgency. He had been charged with a task by Benjamin Blackley himself. There could be no delay, not the slightest hesitation or uncertainty. The situation clearly called for him to be eager and brisk; for rushing about, in other words. If he could not be purposeful, then at least he would be energetic.

It was only when he was out of sight of Blackley that Arbuthnot paused to take his bearings. He had come out of the Grand Dome into the Frills and Fripperies department, in the eastern wing of the store. Or was it the western?

Arbuthnot caught the attention of Mr Dresden, an old commissionaire who had been with the store since the beginning. Indeed, his presence was so permanent that it seemed probable his spectre would walk the floors of Blackley's for all eternity. 'I say, Mr Dresden, sir. Is this the right side for the Abingdon Road exit?'

'You're on the wrong shide here, shonny,' said Mr Dresden, his dentures whistling sibilantly. 'You want the other shide of the Grand Dome.'

The commissionaire moved on, giving Arbuthnot no opportunity to explain that he could not possibly go back into the Grand Dome and risk being seen by Mr Blackley.

17

Arbuthnot hurried on through Boots, Shoes and Waterproof Articles into Locks, Clocks and Mechanical Contrivances.

The arrangement of departments in Blackley's might have appeared curious at times, or even random. But there was always some subtle logic behind the juxtapositions.

To take Arbuthnot's journey so far as an example: the Costumes Salon in the Grand Dome naturally led on to Frills and Fripperies. Mr Blackley's instinctive understanding of the female psyche told him that any woman who had indulged her passion for the Fashionable would before long seek to redress the balance by striving towards the Practical – without, however, going too far in that direction. Hence his placement of Boots, Shoes and Waterproof Articles nearby, a department in which the Fashionable and the Practical were harmoniously combined.

Waterproof Articles keep out the rain; Locks keep out unwanted intruders. Thus, one form of protection leads to another. Put so crudely, the connection may seem contrived. But in fact it revealed a sophisticated grasp of psychology. If the relationship between one department and the next was not consciously perceived, so much the better. The subconscious association was always felt. An almost dreamlike state of existence was conjured up. And as the Viennese doctors will tell you, the wellspring of dreams is wish-fulfilment.

And so the visitor to Blackley's found herself not in a shop, but in a dream and, more precisely, in the kind of dream where every desire is capable of satisfaction. She only had to reach out and ... purchase.

For a moment, Arbuthnot, too, felt like a figure in a dream, though in his case it was a nightmare. Surrounded by a perplexing assortment of locks, he suddenly found himself incapable of movement. It was as if the idea of imprisonment in the department was so strong that he himself was fixed in place. His sense of the urgency of his mission did not diminish. On the contrary, he felt it all the more intensely. And the more intensely he felt it, the more powerfully was he immobilized.

'What do *you* want?' The voice was charged with antagonism and suspicion, which was not unusual among Arbuthnot's colleagues. In fact, it was Spiggott, one of the sales assistants for this department, who made the enquiry.

'I want to get out of here.'

'Then go. I am not detaining you.'

'Yes, I shall. Just as soon as I...'

'What's wrong with you?' Disgust rather than concern showed on Spiggott's face.

'I can't ... move my feet!'

'Don't be ridiculous. Of course you can. I saw you run out of the Costumes Salon a minute ago.' Spiggott looked past Arbuthnot back into the Grand Dome where the fashion show was still in progress.

'This is terrible,' protested Arbuthnot. 'Believe me when I say that I am trying with all my strength to move my feet.'

'Well, you can't stay here. You'll get us both

into trouble.'

'You don't understand! I don't want to stay here! Nothing would give me greater pleasure than to leave! I have been charged with an urgent commission by Mr Blackley himself! I must *not* delay!'

At that moment, quite unexpectedly, a customer made his presence felt. It was impossible to say if he had been there all the time, unobserved by the two young men, or if he had just stepped into the department of Locks, Clocks and Mechanical Contrivances. The former seemed improbable because he was a man of considerable bulk, dressed in a voluminous Inverness cape – a veritable mountain of tweed. And yet, he must have been there for some time, for he demonstrated a complete understanding of Arbuthnot's predicament.

The man, who was wearing a monocle, stared fixedly into Arbuthnot's eyes, raised his right hand and moved it in front of Arbuthnot's face in a mysterious manner. At the same time he murmured something softly to Arbuthnot.

To his amazement, Arbuthnot felt himself instantly released. He was aware that the stranger had spoken to him, but had no memory of what he had said. And now he was gone, as suddenly and inexplicably as he had arrived.

'How strange,' said Spiggott. But then he began to berate Arbuthnot. 'If it hadn't been for you, he would have bought something. You'd better go before you scare away any more of *my* customers.' But there was no conviction in his complaint.

Even so, Arbuthnot needed no further encouragement to be on his way. He put his head down and ran through the shrieks and howls of the Menagerie into the stockroom at the back of the store. From here, he could exit to the street via the delivery entrance.

A warehouseman in a brown coat was sweeping the floor, stirring the scents of cardboard and boxwood into the air. He stopped to light a cigarette, watching Arbuthnot's progress with a dark, envious glare. But what was there to envy about Arbuthnot? Only his urgent sense of purpose, perhaps.

The Locked Door

Arbuthnot shot out on to the street like a pea expelled from a peashooter.

The air had a resentful edge to it, as if to say he had no business being at liberty. But he was *not* at liberty. He had no time to appreciate the strange, unearned licence of being out of the store during trading hours. He must put his head down and hurry.

But he was only human. To expect him not to lift his head and take in his surroundings, not to breathe deeply of that air, however sharp, however chill, not to be diverted by the passing of a pretty face, or the gleam and growl of a polished motor car, was to expect too much.

Naturally he did not allow such distractions to waylay him from his course, but he did allow a certain jauntiness to enter his step. He did not go so far as to attempt a whistle. Somehow he could not quite shake himself free of the impression that Mr Blackley was watching him. Or if not Mr Blackley himself, then his spies. Arbuthnot imagined that Mr Blackley must have any number of spies. He glanced nervously at the shops on the opposite terrace, then up at the windows of the apartments above them. No sign of anyone lurking, but still, you could never be too careful.

Whistling during working hours was forbidden under Mr Blackley's rules. For a young man of ambition such as Arbuthnot, it was not just the sixpence fine that had to be borne in mind; more serious was the black mark against his name. These things were noted down, he knew. If he hoped to progress, it was important to keep a clean sheet.

The turning into Caper Street – the street of his destination – was opposite a public house. For a moment, Arbuthnot was tempted to stop off there, for a quick dose of Dutch courage. But then the absurdity and horror of what he had just contemplated struck home. He had rigorously been on his guard against whistling in the street, and yet had come this close to casually wandering into a public house for a furtive snifter. It was not that Arbuthnot was a toper, far from it. The example of his father had been enough to immunize him against that particular vice.

He and his six siblings had grown up with the old man's drunken rages. Booze made him a fighter, but he was too much of a coward to take on any of his cronies at the Dog and Whistle. He'd stagger home and pick a fight with Ma, pulling her from the bed by her hair. She always took her beatings stoically, silently. It was Pa's snarling curses that would draw them from their beds, not any sound from Ma. They cowered behind the washing that Ma took in, taking their lead from her, keeping mum, mute witnesses to the violence. Was that where the expression came from?

Then came the day when young Arbuthnot could keep mum no longer. He rushed out from behind a hanging sheet and threw himself at his father. The state Pa was in, together with the element of surprise, worked in Arbuthnot's favour. It was shockingly easy to overpower the old man. And in that moment, the moment of his father's befuddled toppling, young Arbuthnot grasped the full extent of the degradation and shame that alcohol wrought. A grown man knocked off his feet by a scrawny twelve-year-old kid.

His father never hit Ma again. At least not in front of the children.

And so Arbuthnot had never felt the allure of the public house. Not until this day. To have felt the pull now frightened him. So he was a chip off the old block, after all? Was his father's weakness at last asserting itself in him?

The north side of Caper Street was a row of three-storey Georgian houses. The ground storey was neatly rendered in cream-coloured stucco, with rather grand arched windows in the *piano nobile* above, and plainer windows on the top floor. The row presented a unified facade of primness and propriety. And yet Arbuthnot felt the thrill of transgression as he approached number seven, the house where the mannequins lodged. Under normal circumstances the mannequin house, as it was known, was barred to male employees – to all except M. Hugo and Mr Blackley, that is. This had naturally led to much speculation as to what went on behind its door. Some even referred to it as 'Blackley's harem', with M. Hugo in the role of eunuch, no doubt. Now, here was Arbuthnot, about to cross the threshold and discover the secrets of this forbidden precinct.

The door was opened by a woman who was evidently the housekeeper. She was dressed in a black skirt and high-necked white blouse. Her tightly bundled black hair was streaked with white. Arbuthnot guessed she was aged somewhere in her forties but had kept herself well. Her figure was stocky: muscular rather than corpulent. Her arms and upper body appeared fashioned by hard work and hefting. Her complexion was clean and fresh, as if she had been recently polished; but as Arbuthnot peered into her face, he noticed a lattice of fine lines, a palimpsest of woe beneath the untroubled surface.

There was the smell of cleaning fluids about her. She regarded Arbuthnot with a calm curiosity that was perhaps a little too controlled and calculated. For some reason, she reminded him of the Mother Superior of a particularly austere order of nuns.

Arbuthnot was reassured by the thought that she did not appear to be a woman who would stand for any nonsense. Whatever rumours about the mannequin house he might have heard were suddenly and conclusively dispelled. 'Miss Mortimer? My name is Arbuthnot. Mr Blackley sent me.'

The housekeeper began to brush invisible grains of dust from the sleeve of her blouse.

Arbuthnot suppressed a smile. She was almost like a bird preening itself. Suddenly her eyes narrowed as if she was angry that he'd seen her moment of weakness. Her expression became suspicious. 'Mr Blackley, you say?' Her voice was loud, almost a shout.

Arbuthnot thought she was probably a little deaf and raised his own voice to answer her: 'Yes.'

'Mr Blackley usually comes himself. He doesn't like the men to know where the mannequins live.'

'He couldn't come.' He spoke slowly, making allowance for her presumed deafness. 'He's with an important customer. Obviously he felt that he could trust me, otherwise he would not have chosen me for the errand.'

Miss Mortimer looked Arbuthnot up and down before glancing past him down the short street. 'You'd better come in.'

As the door was closed behind him, Arbuthnot breathed in deeply as if he expected to detect strange, intoxicating scents in the air. Instead there was just the homely smell of wood polish.

The hall itself was narrow. A bold, floral wallpaper, which bore the influence of William Morris, gave the impression of entering a kind of bower, faintly medieval and altogether fantastical. A rich carpet of Turkish design ran over the floorboards.

A mirror was placed just inside the door, presumably for the girls to check their appearance as they left for work each morning. Beyond that on the wall hung a couple of framed prints showing a variety of Parisian scenes rendered in what Arbuthnot presumed to be a modern style. A third picture was propped up against the seat back of a chair which partially obstructed the hallway. A bent nail projected from the wall ready to receive it. A hammer lay on the chair seat.

Miss Mortimer pushed the seat out of the way, causing the picture to fall over on to its face. There was a sharp crack as the glass hit the hammer head. When Miss Mortimer righted the picture, a jagged line of fissure ran across one corner. 'Now look what you've made me do! Mr Blackley will be furious. I was to hang these up today. I shall have to get the glass replaced now.'

'I'm sorry but I hardly think...'

'What's this all about?' demanded Miss Mortimer. Her voice was still loud and abrupt.

More than a little deaf, thought Arbuthnot. 'He's sent me to find out what's happened to Miss Amélie. She didn't appear for Lady Ascot's costume showing.'

'I'm sure I don't know where she is.' Miss Mortimer frowned as she considered the broken picture glass. She propped the damaged picture against the back of the chair again and turned her frown on Arbuthnot.

'Perhaps she's unwell. Did you see her at breakfast this morning? Did she not leave with the other mannequins?'

'I cannot be expected to keep tabs on them all.'

'Mr Blackley has asked me to see if Miss Amélie is in her room. He wishes me to convey his solicitude to her.'

'I do not believe she is there,' pronounced Miss Mortimer with an air of finality.

'He was very precise in his instructions. I was to knock on her door and deliver a message to her.'

'You may give me the message,' said Miss Mortimer. 'I will see that she gets it.'

'It is a verbal message,' said Arbuthnot.

'Then you may tell it to me.'

Arbuthnot was firm. 'It is for Miss Amélie's ears only.'

Something like a smile twitched on Miss Mortimer's pinched lips. 'She's not in her room, I tell you.'

'At any rate, I must try her door.' Arbuthnot drew himself up self-righteously. 'That is what Mr Blackley instructed me to do.'

With an impatient nod of her head, Miss Mortimer turned to lead him into the house. 'Be careful,' she snapped over her shoulder. 'I don't want you doing any more damage.'

As he progressed deeper into the bower-like hallway, the sense that he was penetrating a forbidden interior increased. And yet there was nothing so extraordinary about his surroundings. Looking in on the drawing room through a half-open door, Arbuthnot saw that it was furnished in the manner of a respectable middle-class home, more Basingstoke than Baghdad. A pair of enormous Chinese-looking vases was the only hint of the Orient that he could detect. And there was something familiar, as well as homely, about the comfortable furnishings. Of course, he realized – everything had come from Blackley's.

He had to admit that the place did not exhibit the decadent luxuriousness that he had been imagining. However, it certainly provided a different level of comfort to the Spartan unisex dormitories where the rest of the live-in employees were obliged to sleep. He wondered if the mannequins were also forced to vacate their rooms every Sunday, eating solitary meals in cheap restaurants to pass the time. Somehow he doubted it.

Miss Mortimer stopped at a door on the first floor. Before Arbuthnot could prevent her she knocked and called out: 'Amélie? Are you there?'

'Mr Blackley specifically directed that *I* should knock on her door,' protested Arbuthnot.

The housekeeper gave a disdainful snort. Even so, she stood aside. Like all of Blackley's employees, it seemed she had learnt the importance of obeying the letter as well as the spirit of his law.

Arbuthnot rapped briskly. 'Miss Amélie?' He pressed his ear to the door. And pulled it away instantly as a piercing scream sounded from within.

'What the devil?' Arbuthnot's eyes widened with horror. He tried the handle and pushed his shoulder into the door. It didn't budge.

He turned to Miss Mortimer. 'Do you have a

key?' The housekeeper appeared to be in a state of shock. No doubt it was the effect of the scream, thought Arbuthnot. He had never heard anything like it, except perhaps in his dreams. To describe it as inhuman would not have been an exaggeration. 'I say, Miss Mortimer,' he prompted.

She looked at him as if she had no idea who he was or how he came to be there. 'Did you hear that?' Her voice was a terrified whisper.

'Yes.'

'What was it?'

'We must open the door to find out. I assume you have keys to all the rooms?'

From beneath her apron, Miss Mortimer produced an enormous bunch of keys on a long chain. She selected one and inserted it into the lock, or at least tried to. After a series of frustrated attempts, she stood up straight and turned to Arbuthnot. The door remained closed. 'There appears to be something blocking it.'

Arbuthnot put his eye to the keyhole. 'There's another key in the lock. On the other side.'

'The silly girl has locked herself into the room.'

Arbuthnot knocked on the door again. The fearful screaming had stopped, but he could hear movement from within. 'Miss Amélie, are you all right? I have a message for you from Mr Blackley. If you will only open the door.'

'Amélie! Open this door right now!' Miss Mortimer seemed to be restored to her former

30

self. And yet there was something quivering and uncertain beneath her composure.

'Perhaps she cannot,' suggested Arbuthnot. 'She may be incapacitated in some way.'

The horrible screaming started again.

'My God, what is the matter with her?'

'I don't think that is Miss Amélie,' said Arbuthnot.

'Who is it then?'

'*Who* is it? Or *what* is it?'

'What do you mean?'

But before Arbuthnot could answer, they heard the key on the other side begin to turn.

The effect of this on Miss Mortimer was striking. She began to shake her head in fierce denial. 'No! No! No!'

The unseen presence struggled with the key, stopping occasionally to scream in frustration.

Then, all at once, the key turned fully in the lock.

But the door remained closed. There was no further attempt to open it from the other side.

Arbuthnot interpreted this as an invitation. He reached out a hand tentatively towards the handle, looking for encouragement from Miss Mortimer. But that lady's expression was far from encouraging. Still shaking her head, she was now murmuring incomprehensibly to herself. Arbuthnot could not understand all that she was saying, but he seemed to hear: 'This cannot be!'

He had not pushed the door more than a few inches when he saw a flash of silver speed out from the opening at ground level, brushing

31

against his trousers as it hurried past him. 'A monkey!' he cried. The tiny shrieking macaque scurried down the stairs, a diminutive Turkish fez attached to its head.

'But that's not possible!' cried Miss Mortimer, her habitual loud volume at last justified. 'The girls are not allowed to keep animals. Wait till I see Amélie! The rules are quite clear. No animals in rooms! Mr Blackley will not stand for it.' She shook her head somewhat self-consciously, it seemed to Arbuthnot.

Arbuthnot pushed the door completely open and stepped in.

The missing girl lay fully clothed on top of the bed. She was as still and lifeless as a plaster – rather than a human – mannequin. But unlike the inanimate white dolls that populated the windows and displays of the Costumes Salon, her face was swollen and purple.

Her eyes were open. Arbuthnot's attention was drawn by the vivid bursts of red that showed in the corneas. As a salesman in the Costumes Salon, he couldn't help observing to himself that the colour of these flecks matched perfectly the silk scarf around her neck.

The Usual Misunderstanding

Sir Edward Henry received the bulging file from Silas Quinn with a disapproving glower. He signalled curtly for Quinn to sit down.

From time to time, Sir Edward winced as he read. The detective hoped that it was the commissioner's old gunshot wound playing up. That was not to say that he wished actual bodily pain on Sir Edward, but it was better that than the alternative: that his wincing was due to the contents of the file. In Quinn's defence, Sir Edward was rather given to wincing, and the cause usually was the bullet he had taken in the belly two years ago.

Quinn knew very well what was in the file. He had compiled it, and written the report that tied together all the statements, interim reports, post mortem reports, forensic analyses and crime scene photographs. The file, in essence, was the justification of Quinn's conduct. If the file was causing Sir Edward pain, it was the same as saying that Quinn was causing him pain.

Now and then, Quinn craned his neck to look across Sir Edward's desk to see where he had reached in his perusal. Once or twice he attempted to venture an explanation, but Sir Edward would cut him off peremptorily, raising his hand and barking forbiddingly. Sir Edward kept Irish Wolfhounds and it seemed that he viewed members of the Metropolitan Police Force and his dogs as being somehow equivalent. In both cases he evidently saw barking as the most economical way of asserting his dominance.

Certainly, after a couple of such attempts, Quinn was deterred from interrupting again.

Sir Edward replaced the last sheet with trembling hands. He closed the cover of the file and peered across at Quinn. His head seemed to rise out of his winged collar and extend towards Quinn, giving him something of the appearance of a moustachioed turtle. 'Was it really necessary?'

'I beg your pardon, sir?'

'Was it really necessary for him to die?'

'Who, sir?'

'Who? He asks who! The fellow you killed, that's who.'

'Ah, sir, it was a matter of self-defence.'

'He was naked. And unarmed.'

Quinn appeared startled by this information. 'I could not be sure, sir.'

'You could not be sure he was naked? Could you not tell by looking at him?'

'It was dark in that cellar, sir.'

'There was a lamp, I believe.'

Quinn threw up his hands evasively. 'The man was clothed when we went down into the cellar. I didn't know he had undressed. I couldn't take any chances. I knew he had killed five times at least. Possibly more. There was a member of the public there.'

'Whom you had coerced into accompanying you. Whom you had endangered.'

'No, not coerced. He came willingly. He wanted to help.'

'But was it necessary, Quinn? Was it really necessary? Could you not have overpowered him? You had access to chloroform, I believe. You had already administered it to the other one, after all.'

'Ah, but you see, the problem was, sir...'

'What?'

'He wanted to die.'

'And so you obliged him?'

'I could not have prevented it, even...' Quinn broke off.

'What? Eh? What were you about to say? You could not have prevented it, even if you had wanted to?'

Quinn flinched under the force of Sir Edward's snapping rebuke. He said nothing for a moment. At last, without lifting his head to look Sir Edward in the eye, he ventured: 'I had no choice. That is what I meant to say.'

' "Ye did not hear; but did evil before mine eyes, and did choose that wherein I delighted not." Isaiah, chapter sixty-five, verse twelve. You had a choice, Quinn. You always do have a choice. And always you make the same choice.'

'Not always, sir. With respect, I feel that is rather overstating it, sir.'

'Have there been any whom you did not kill?'

'I feel there must have been, sir.'

'Can you name them?'

'My mind's gone blank, sir. But if you were to look back over the files I am sure you would find some whom I did not kill.'

'Oh, if they were not killed by you they were killed by your men, Inchball and Macadam? Men acting under your command.'

'That's unkind, sir. Sergeant Macadam only once killed a suspect and that was by accident. It was before he had fully got the hang of the motor car, sir. It wasn't his fault the fellow ran out in front of him.'

'You make no defence of Inchball?'

'Sergeant Inchball is a first-rate police officer.'

'His methods are brutal.'

'His methods are effective, sir.' Quinn paused a beat before adding, 'As are mine, sir.' So confident was he of this assertion that he repeated it. 'As are mine.'

'You cannot keep using that argument as your licence to do what you will. You must exercise more control, Quinn. That's an order.'

'You don't understand,' said Quinn. Even to his own ears his voice sounded pathetic. 'In those situations...'

He was almost grateful when Sir Edward cut him short: 'You cannot set yourself up as judge, jury *and* executioner. Does the Bible not say, "Judge not, that ye be not judged." Matthew, chapter seven, verse one. It has similar prescriptions against the taking of life.'

'I found the killer.'

'Well, that's another thing, isn't it? We only have your word for it that this fellow confessed to the crimes.'

'You doubt that he was the killer, sir?'

'Oh, I'm not saying that. It all adds up. You've tied it all together very neatly. But the fact remains: the man you say confessed to the crimes is no longer alive to confirm his confession, which was made only to you.'

'I cannot help that, sir.'

'But it is a failing. A lamentable failing. If you are not careful, this sort of thing will be held against you.'

'By whom, sir?'

Sir Edward pulled out some press clippings that had been included in the file. 'I see the papers are no longer calling you "Quick-Fire Quinn". No, now it's "Cut-Throat Quinn"!'

'That's just the *Clarion*, sir. I think we both know what lies behind that. The *Clarion* has not been our friend since you threatened to arrest its editor. They see me as your man, so they attack me to get at you.'

'What? Eh? Allow me to enlighten the eyes of your understanding, Quinn.'

Quinn suspected there was a biblical allusion behind Sir Edward's choice of words but he was unable to place it.

'You cut this fellow's throat. You cut his throat! With a razor!'

'There was nothing else to hand.'

'That is not how you bring in a suspect. That is not consistent with self-defence. The *Clarion*

37

is even hinting that you are the Exsanguinist yourself, and that you killed this fellow to divert suspicion away from yourself.'

'Libellous!'

'Oh, they are very clever in the way they word it. But that is clearly the inference.'

'He was the killer. The forensic evidence was conclusive. There were traces of human blood in the back of his van. And then there was the young man whom he had drained in his cellar.'

'Yes. I had wanted to talk to you about that, too. A civilian employee of the Met. You had no business involving him in your hazardous enterprises either.'

'He volunteered to help.'

'You should have refused.'

'With hindsight, of course, I wish that I had.'

'Too many deaths, Quinn. That's the long and the short of it. Too many deaths.'

'I'm sorry, sir.'

Sir Edward shook his head sternly. 'I don't know how much longer I can carry on protecting you, Quinn.' After a moment, he added: 'This must stop. *Repent therefore and be converted.* Acts, chapter three, verse nineteen. No more deaths, Quinn. Do you understand?'

'Yes, sir. I understand. The Home Secretary...'

'There is a higher authority even than the Home Secretary. We must think of your eternal soul, Quinn.'

'I fear that it is already too late for that, sir.'

'Nonsense. It is never too late. Do you attend church, Quinn?'

Quinn mumbled something in embarrassment.

'As I thought.' Sir Edward's turtle head nodded in his stiff collar. 'My life changed, you know, that day Alfred Bowes took a pot shot at me. You may find it hard to believe, but Bowes did me a great favour. I would go so far as to say it was the best thing that ever happened to me.'

'But you nearly died, sir.'

'Exactly, Quinn. And that was what it took for me to see things as they really are. I nearly died, but I was reborn. The scales fell from my eyes. Do not wait for the same thing to happen to you before you open your eyes to God. It may be too late.'

'I will bear that in mind, sir.' Quinn bowed his head as if he intended to pray. Then remembering himself, he sat up sharply. 'Will that be all, sir?'

'What? Eh? No. Not quite. Have you seen the papers this morning?'

Quinn shook his head. He had seen enough of the papers these last few days.

'They're full of this business over at the House of Blackley. You know, the department store. Lady Henry is a great devotee of the place.' Sir Edward's voice was laden with disapproval and regret as he made the pronouncement. It was almost as if he was accusing his wife of being a devotee of the Goddess Shiva. 'One of the mannequins has been found dead. Murdered, it seems. The house where it happened – a house owned by Benjamin Blackley

39

for the purpose of lodging the mannequins – is not far from our home. Lady Henry is rather upset about the whole affair. She believes she knows the girl in question. She once had a costume modelled by her.'

'And so you wish the Special Crimes Department to look into it?' It was Quinn's turn to introduce a note of disapproval into his voice.

'No, no, no, Quinn. That's not the reason why I want Special Crimes involved. In fact, the suggestion that you take over the case did not come from me. It came from the Home Secretary himself.'

'But I thought the Home Secretary wanted to close us down?'

'When did I say that, Quinn?'

Quinn's brows drew together in confusion. 'Why does the Home Secretary want us involved, sir?'

'The local bobbies are out of their depth. They've already turned themselves into a laughing stock. According to the newspapers, they're pursuing a theory that the murder was committed by a monkey.'

'What sort of monkey, sir?'

'A monkey in a hat. A fez, at that. It's clearly preposterous.'

'I meant what *species* of monkey, sir.'

'I don't know what species!' cried Sir Edward impatiently. 'It doesn't matter what species. The monkey clearly had nothing to do with it. I want you to get over there and put them straight. We want it wrapped up quickly too. The papers have already dragged in Lady

40

Ascot's name. She and her daughter were attending a costume showing at the store at the time the body was discovered.'

'I see. And her husband, I suppose, is a friend of the Home Secretary's?'

'That has nothing to do with anything, Quinn.'

'Are there any other unusual aspects to the case that I ought to know about?'

'Oh ... not really,' said Sir Edward, suddenly subdued, his eyes flicking evasively to one side and his head receding towards his winged collar, as if it would disappear inside it. 'I dare say you'll find out all about it when you talk to the local CID.' He opened the file on his desk and began shuffling the papers uselessly.

Quinn knew when he was being lied to. The interesting question, of course, was *why*? 'Sir Edward?'

But the commissioner would not be drawn. He closed the file and handed it to Quinn. 'Take this away.'

Quinn obeyed. He would find out what Sir Edward was holding back soon enough.

Outside Sir Edward's office his secretary, Miss Latterly, was at her desk. Her fingers worked tirelessly to produce a stream of angry clatter on the typewriter.

Quinn paused just in front of her. As always when he encountered Miss Latterly, he experienced a strong urge to speak to her, but was utterly at a loss as to what to say. At last he settled for: 'I am to go to the House of Blackley.'

The frenzy of clatter intensified. He watched her fingers, fascinated.

She broke off and looked up at him. 'Why are you telling me this? Does Sir Edward require me to provide you with anything?'

'I was merely making conversation.'

'I was under the impression that we had agreed to confine our exchanges to matters related strictly to our work.'

'I beg your pardon. I had forgotten.'

'It was only a few days ago when we made this agreement.'

'I know, but a lot has happened to me in the meantime.'

'You are not going to talk to me about *that*, are you?' Miss Latterly went so far as to put her hands over her ears.

'Of course not. I wouldn't dream of it.' This was true. He had sworn to himself that he would never reveal to anyone what had really happened in that blood-damp cellar in Limehouse. 'I thought perhaps you might wish me to bring you something from Blackley's.' This was not, in fact, what Quinn had been thinking. And to hear himself make the offer caused the heat of duplicity to flood his cheeks. But he was trying to extricate himself from any accusation that he wanted to engage her in a lurid conversation about murder. He knew how little she enjoyed such discussions. Perversely, however, that had not in the past prevented him from initiating them.

'You are going on a shopping expedition? I had imagined you were going there in connection with the poor girl they found murdered.'

'Yes, that's true. But I thought, while I was there...'

'While you are there, I trust you will focus all your energies on finding her murderer.'

'Naturally. However, if the opportunity arises...'

'I have no money to spend on fripperies.'

'I was thinking of a gift. To make amends for the misunderstandings that have arisen between us.' Quinn added hastily: 'For which I am solely responsible.'

'No, that's out of the question. I cannot allow you to buy me a gift.'

'It need not form the basis of any understanding between us.' As soon as the words were out of his mouth, he regretted them.

'As if there could be!'

'You are quite right to insist on that. As if there could be. There is no question that there could ever be. I understand that.'

'I am very disappointed that we are having this conversation, Inspector Quinn.'

'As am I. I blame myself entirely.'

'If there is nothing else you require from me...?'

Forgiveness? Quinn came close to saying.

Speak of the Devil

'Here we are, sir,' said Sergeant Macadam as he drove the car slowly along Kensington Road. 'The House of Blackley.'

Quinn looked out of the window as they passed the front of the great emporium. The vast white structure extended across a whole block of the main street. Window after window in hypnotic monotony. Its architecture possessed a whimsical, almost dreamlike quality. It was like a pavilion, but on a vast scale, as if a garden folly had been infinitely stretched in every dimension. A series of caryatids punctuated the top storey, obscure mythical females bearing the burden of the roof between them. A central dome seemed to hover above the whole fantastic edifice, on the verge of shooting upwards into the clouds. The building's facade contained within its design a capacity for multiplication. Look away for a moment and it would have taken over another ten yards of the high street. Quinn had the vertiginous sense that it would one day possess the whole world. No doubt that was its proprietor's dream.

The car glided along the length of the store, so slowly they were overtaken by more than

44

one pedestrian. Their funereal pace drew inquisitive glances, as well as horn-toots and oaths from more impatient road users. But it gave Quinn time to notice that the unbroken uniformity of the frontage was not all that it seemed. It was interrupted at one point by an opening in the wall, a vaguely ecclesiastical arch through which could be glimpsed a short path leading to an ogee-arched door. A squat, brickwork tower rose above the door, peeping over the top of the store's facade, which was merely an empty screen at this point.

There was something inviting about the entrance, Quinn felt. He was aware of a desire to find out what lay on the other side of it.

Sergeant Inchball was next to Quinn in the rear of the Model T. Quinn felt the press of Inchball's considerable bulk as he leaned over to get a better look at the view. 'What's tha'? A bleedin' church?' Inchball sounded outraged by the possibility.

'The church of Our Lady of the Sacred Heart,' said Macadam from the front. 'Blackley has never been able to get rid of it – unlike all his other neighbours, or anyone else who has got in his way. So he has been forced to build his empire around it.'

'How comes you know all this?' Inchball's tone was resentful, as if he took Macadam's knowledge as a personal affront.

'Don't you read *The West End Whisperer*?'

'Wouldn't wipe my arse on it.'

'There was a piece about Benjamin Blackley in there the other day.'

Quinn had seen the article. There had been a copy of *The West End Whisperer* left in the lavatory at his lodging house. He had glanced idly at the scurrilous exposé. He did not feel inclined to admit to it, however. In truth, it was not the first time he had read about goings-on at the House of Blackley. He remembered being mesmerized by the graphic accounts of the fire that had destroyed the store several years ago. It was possible that he had seen them in the same publication.

Macadam evidently felt the need to justify his choice of reading matter. 'Mrs Macadam is a frequent visitor to the House of Blackley. I have accompanied her on more than one occasion, for my sins.' The driver craned his neck to direct his remarks more to Quinn. 'You would not believe it, sir – to see the change that comes over her. Most unseemly, it is. Generally speaking, I would say she is a quite sensible woman, is Mrs Macadam. But the moment she walks inside that store it's like she loses her wits, Lord help me. It's a frenzy comes over her. *Berserk*, she goes. Berserk. You are familiar with the word, sir?'

'I am, Macadam.'

In the back of the car, Sergeant Inchball rolled his eyes and mouthed an oath.

'So anyhow,' continued Macadam, oblivious to Inchball's silent abuse. 'I was curious to read about the man who exercises such a hold over my wife. Normally I would not bother myself with the tittle-tattle of such a low publication.' He slowed the car to a virtual standstill. 'Speak

46

of the devil.'

There he was, Benjamin Blackley, in position at the main entrance, welcoming shoppers with a cheery shake of the hand. He was recognizable from the pictures of him that had appeared in the newspapers over the years. The mutton-chop whiskers, the affable smile, the clear air of confidence and command ... it couldn't be anyone else. And of course, it was well known that whenever possible he liked to greet visitors to his store in person, the humblest and the most elevated alike.

Quinn studied the famous commercial genius closely. He pondered the question that he always asked himself whenever he encountered someone new: could this person be a murderer?

Seeing the unshakeable smile on the man's face, Quinn felt himself stirred by an emotion somewhere between admiration and horror. 'After what has happened? After a girl has died?'

'Begging your pardon, sir?' said Macadam.

Inchball watched his guv'nor closely, his expression guarded, anxious.

'Take us round to the house where the girl was found, Seven Caper Street. You can drop Inchball and myself off there. Then come back for Mr Blackley. Bring him to us at the house.'

'Very well, sir.' After a moment, Macadam added: 'Sir, you will be careful, won't you?'

'What are you talking about, Macadam?'

'We don't want any unfortunate accidents, do we, sir?' said Macadam warily.

47

'If by *unfortunate accidents*, you are referring to the criminals who are alleged to have met their deaths in the course of my investigations, I will remind you that these were for the most part ruthless and desperate men. We may be sure that the overwhelming majority of them would have died on the scaffold anyhow. It must be assumed they preferred to fight to the death than surrender.'

'Must it, sir?' asked Macadam a little sadly.

'Yes, it must,' insisted Quinn. 'Besides, you need not worry. I shall have Inchball to keep me on the straight and narrow.'

'That is precisely what worries me, sir.'

'Cheeky bugger!' came from Inchball.

'I wasn't supposed to tell you this, sir,' said Macadam, 'but the commissioner had me in his office.'

Inchball sniggered.

Macadam pressed on earnestly. 'He asked me to keep an eye on you. For your own sake, was how he put it, sir. He intimated that if there were any further incidents such as ... well, I think we all know the kind of incidents we are talking about. At any rate, he said that if there was any more of that kind of thing ... any more...'

'Spit it out!' cried Inchball.

'Well, sir, he said that the command of the Special Crimes Department would be taken away from you. You would still be on Special Crimes, but he has it in mind to bring another officer in over you, sir. A safe pair of hands was how he described the fellow.'

48

'I see. I am grateful to you, Macadam. And did Sir Edward divulge to you whom he had in mind for this post?'

'No, sir, he did not. And he was most insistent that I should not say a word to you. He did not wish it to put you off your stroke.'

Inchball sniggered again. Quinn flashed a warning glance, which prompted a *well-what-do-you-expect* shrug.

This was a disturbing development. In the first place, he did not expect the Commissioner of the Metropolitan Police to speak directly to his sergeants. Without telling him, it should be said. It just wasn't done. Second, why had Sir Edward not warned him about this at their *tête à tête* earlier? It was all very well dropping dark hints, but he could just as easily have given it to him straight.

It could only be because he *wanted* Quinn to come a cropper. In that case, why tip the wink to Macadam?

Perhaps Sir Edward himself had been caught in a cleft stick: told by those above him (which could only mean the Home Secretary and his faceless civil service mandarins) that Quinn was to have his authority usurped if he slipped up again; warned also not to say a word about it to Quinn. Being an honourable man, Sir Edward could not disobey a direct order. Quinn wouldn't put it past them to make the commissioner swear an oath on the Bible. They knew every man's weakness.

And so Sir Edward had found a way to stick to the letter of the command, while at the same

49

time putting Quinn on alert. First there was the talking-to this morning. Then the word in Macadam's shell-like. Sir Edward must have counted on Macadam's fierce loyalty to his guv'nor. He knew that telling Macadam was the same thing as warning Quinn.

Quinn had to accept that there were other less comforting ways of looking at it. It was possible that he had lost even Sir Edward's confidence, and that Sir Edward was now on the side of those who wished to see him fail. These latest manoeuvrings were designed to unsettle him, making it more likely that he would stumble.

Even if the more positive interpretation were true, it was worrying. The last thing he wanted was a by-the-book stickler brought in over his head. He had encountered enough of those in the course of his career. Worse would be the kind of egoist who always believed he was in the right. It would be bad enough for Quinn to have his every move questioned, but to have some pompous idiot telling him what to do didn't bear thinking about. And the man would be an idiot, that was a given.

The simple fact was that there was no better detective in the whole of the Metropolitan Police Force than Silas Quinn. Sir Edward knew that. Why else would he have put him in charge of the Special Crimes Department, a unit that at times seemed to have been created purely to accommodate Quinn's unique talents and idiosyncratic methods?

But whichever way you looked at it, what it

came down to was that there were powerful individuals out to get him. On balance, he felt that he could trust Sir Edward. He had to believe that the commissioner was looking out for him. The important thing was not to let Sir Edward down. This case – everything hinged on how he handled this case. He would crack it quickly, without any serious mishap.

Quinn turned in his seat to continue watching Blackley through the rear window of the car as Macadam accelerated away. 'Is it a sign of guilt or innocence that he continues as if nothing has happened, I wonder?'

The question went unanswered. Either his sergeants had not heard or they knew from experience when not to intrude on the governor's musings.

Hear No Evil

A uniform on guard at the front door marked out the house. He watched suspiciously as Quinn and Inchball got out of the Model T, then stiffened and bridled at their approach, as if readying for a fight. But when Quinn introduced himself, the uniform relaxed. They were his kind. Coppers. He touched his helmet in salute. 'We've had some journalists sniffing round, sir,' he explained distastefully. 'You can't be too careful.'

'Indeed,' said Quinn. 'Who is the senior CID officer on the case?'

'That's DCI Coddington, sir.'

'*DCI?*' Quinn was thrown by Coddington's rank. He immediately began to speculate whether this was the man earmarked to be his boss. But Sir Edward had said that the locals were turning themselves into a laughing stock. It was hardly likely that they would put someone they knew to be a fool over him; or that they would prepare for it by having Quinn go in to sort out the aforementioned fool's botched case. Unless it was all part of a strategy to unnerve him, and their ultimate plan was to close down Special Crimes completely. 'Where is he?'

'He's already inside, sir. Like a bloodhound off the leash, he is. We couldn't hold him back if we wanted to.' The constable paused momentously, as if he was remembering the one time they had tried to hold DCI Coddington back and how much they had all regretted it. 'Going over the crime scene with a fine-tooth comb, he is, sir.'

'A bloodhound with a fine-tooth comb? What an arresting image!'

Quinn's irony was lost on the constable. 'That's right, sir. He has a terrific record for arrests. I'll ring the bell for you. The housekeeper will let you in.'

A primly dressed middle-aged woman opened the door, blocking the threshold with her solid frame. She regarded Quinn and Inchball with an expression of imperturbable calm. Quinn was reminded of Blackley's determined cheerfulness outside the store.

'You will take these gentlemen to Chief Inspector Coddington.' Quinn noticed that the constable raised his voice to a shout to address her. It seemed unnecessarily rude. But then the bobby confided out of the side of his mouth: 'She's deaf as a post, sir.'

At the whispered aside, Quinn thought he noticed an involuntary contraction of the woman's brows. He could not say for certain what it signified. One possibility was that she was not as deaf as she liked to appear.

She indicated Quinn and Inchball with a curt nod. 'I cannot admit just any Tom, Dick or Harry to this house. Mr Blackley is very particular.' Her own voice was raised to the stifled shout of the deaf.

'I am Detective Inspector Silas Quinn of the Special Crimes Department, Scotland Yard.' Quinn enunciated the words clearly, moving his mouth with exaggerated precision. 'This is Sergeant Inchball.'

'Policemen?'

'Yes, of course.'

'We've got more than enough policemen inside already.' This was as if to say she hadn't ordered any more policemen. Her gaze was strangely unfocused; either she was not quite all there, or she was working hard not to meet anyone's eye. Perhaps it was simply the stress of recent events, although 'stress' was not quite the word that came to mind looking at her. Far from it. Stolid, that was the word for her. Quinn felt she lacked the imagination – or any empathetic faculty – necessary to suffer stress. But behind her stolidity he detected an air of suppressed excitement.

'This is a very grave case,' said Quinn. 'As you can see, we're taking it very seriously.'

'It's hard enough keeping this place tidy without all you lot clomping through with your big boots on.'

'I quite understand. Regrettably, however, after a crime such as this it is necessary for a certain amount of clomping through of police-men. We will do our best to minimize the inconvenience.'

'It is too late for that!' cried the housekeeper. 'The damage has already been done.'

'Damage? I am very sorry to hear that there has been damage. I shall speak to DCI Coddington about it. What exactly has been damaged?'

'A girl is dead!'

Quinn was about to object when he thought better of it. There was no logic to her complaint, and yet he felt it would be futile to point that out to her.

The flicker of a smile: he could not dismiss the possibility that she was playing with him.

She turned abruptly and led the way inside. Quinn took off his bowler hat as he entered and gestured for Inchball to do the same.

Somehow the house had a soulless feel to it. From his cursory glance he could see that everything was smart and well-maintained. No expense had been spared. But it seemed to lack the loving touch. Perhaps this was to be expected of a lodging house. But when he compared it to the lodging house where he lived, which bore the imprint of his landlady, Mrs Ibbott's personality, he found Seven Caper Street strangely wanting. There was too much calculation, he decided, in the choice of furnishings and decor. Who was responsible for the calculations, and what result they were intended to achieve, he could not yet say.

As they walked the length of the narrow hall, a cracked glass in a picture frame caught his eye.

Miss Mortimer caught him looking at it. 'Oh, that was that young man's fault.'

'I beg your pardon?'

'The young man Mr Blackley sent round. Mr Arbuthnot, I think his name was. I was in the middle of hanging these pictures for Mr Blackley – he had expressly asked that they be put up. It was very inconvenient to have him coming round here asking for Amélie when I had work to do.'

'I don't quite understand. How did Mr Arbuthnot break the picture?'

'He knocked it over. I hadn't hung it up yet. He was very clumsy.'

'You've hung it now? Broken?'

'I thought it was best to get it out of the way, with all these policemen clomping about.'

On cue, Quinn heard the unmistakeable tread of policemen's boots above. The sound acted as a spur, reminding him of the presence of that other detective, his senior in rank, against whom he already saw himself as pitted. Coddington had a head start on him. He had better not waste any more time.

The housekeeper had turned to lead on. 'So it was you and Arbuthnot who found the body?' he enquired of her back. She carried on without answering. Quinn reached forward and tapped her on the shoulder.

The woman turned sharply. 'What's that?'

'Who found the body?'

She repeated the question back to him. 'Who *found* her?'

Perhaps the woman was stupid, after all. It was a simple enough question. It was possible that she could be both stupid and deaf. 'Yes, who found her? I presume it was you and

56

Arbuthnot?'

'If you presume that then you would be correct. And I don't see the need to go around tapping folk on the shoulder.'

Her eyes had a glazed detachment. But he decided she was not stupid. Far from it. She was undoubtedly cunning. Her repetition of his question had simply been a delaying tactic to give her time to formulate her answer. But why would she feel it necessary to do that unless she had something to hide?

Perhaps he was being unfair. He knew that he had a tendency to over-analyse. The simplest explanation often proved to be the correct one. Quite possibly the woman was still in shock after discovering the victim. What he had taken to be a hint of enjoyment might have been something quite different. Terror was a form of excitement. He must not underestimate the emotional bonds that existed between the housekeeper and the girls in her protection. To some of the younger ones, she would have been like a mother. She would have felt the girl's death severely, especially as she had found her.

And yet, somehow, looking at her calm de-meanour, he had trouble imagining her feeling anything. Was that the secret she guarded – an unimagined depth of feeling in the most pri-vate part of her being?

Quinn himself was no stranger to buried secrets. His police work was the camouflage he used to conceal them, from himself as much as from others. This realization brought him back to the task in hand. 'Where is Mr Arbuthnot now?'

'Back at work, I should imagine. Mr Blackley would not countenance his remaining idle for no reason.'

'Doesn't the intrusion of death into the working day constitute a reason?'

'Not as far as Mr Blackley is concerned.'

'Yes, I saw him myself, standing in front of the store, greeting his customers as if he hadn't a care in the world.'

The housekeeper made no comment. At that point, a man with an undersized bald head and oversized moustache appeared at the top of the stairs and peered down. Quinn was dismayed to see that he was wearing a herringbone Ulster. *That's what I wear!* was his first thought. Naturally he had left the garment at home today as it was shaping up to be fine, with not a drop of rain in sight.

If this was Coddington, Quinn was not impressed. No doubt he thought the herringbone Ulster made him look more of a detective. Why else would he insist on keeping it on inside? Perhaps he had even heard that it was something of a trademark garment with Quinn, and was seeking to emulate him. Quinn was surely not flattering himself to think that he was known for his herringbone Ulster, at least amongst the detectives of the Met. But this was ridiculous. They could not both wear herringbone Ulsters. If it should happen to rain one day and they were working together, they would look like a couple of idiots.

'Inspector Quinn, I presume? DCI Coddington. Come on up – we've been waiting for you.'

So this *was* Coddington. Quinn felt immediately that he had nothing to fear.

'You won't be needing me anymore, then?' said the housekeeper.

'We may have some questions for you later.'

'I've already spoken to the other one.'

'Yes, of course. But in an investigation such as this it is often necessary for us to interview witnesses a number of times as we go over their evidence and make new discoveries.'

'I'm not a witness. I didn't see anything.'

'You found the body. You knew the deceased. You may have witnessed something significant without realizing it. Please don't go anywhere without letting us know.'

'Where would I go? *I* have work to do.' Her resentful emphasis suggested that the policemen, on the other hand, were merely engaged in some kind of idle horseplay. She nodded tersely and disappeared towards the back of the house.

Quinn looked up at Coddington, who was waiting expectantly at the top of the stairs. That great drooping moustache dominated his face, at the same time as sapping it of any intelligence or energy. Quinn presumed there was a mouth beneath it because he had heard the man speak. Facial hair was all very well; it might even be considered necessary on a man. But one mustn't let it get out of hand. That, at any rate, was Quinn's position, whose own moustache was so minimal as to be hardly worthy of comment.

It looked far too much as if Coddington had grown the moustache in another attempt to look the part. It was his bid for a trademark feature of his own. And yet he evidently lacked confidence in it, because he had felt the need to appropriate Quinn's use of the Ulster.

'Very glad to have you on the case,' said Coddington, extending his hand as Quinn reached the first landing. But the shifty flicker of his eyes belied his welcome. Quinn suspected that DCI Coddington was one of those who were capable of saying the precise opposite of what they meant, if they felt it would serve their ends better than the truth. 'Of course, your reputation precedes you.'

Quinn nodded tersely as he shook Coddington's hand; there was more than one way to take that remark. 'Are you not hot in your coat?'

Coddington frowned in confusion as he led the way along the first-floor landing. He kept his head half-turned back towards Quinn. He managed a deferential expression, or perhaps it was simply wariness. It couldn't have been easy for him, as the higher rank, to have Quinn catapulted in to take over his case. 'I ... uhm ... I had not really thought about it. We have been so busy, you see. I had no time to hang up my coat.'

Quinn decided to let it go. 'What have you discovered so far?'

'The dead girl is a professional mannequin at the House of Blackley. A French girl by the name of Amélie Dupin. It appears she was strangled. We're still waiting on the ME's full report but Doctor Prendergast, who examined the body at the scene of crime, confirmed that the facial appearance was consistent with strangulation. There was blood in her eyes. And a red silk scarf around her neck, which we assume to be the murder weapon.'

'Do we have a time of death yet?'

'Doctor Prendergast was able to offer the opinion that death occurred sometime during the evening or night of this Tuesday, March thirty-first. That is consistent with witness statements. She was last seen returning to the mannequin house that evening. She locked herself in her room and did not take her evening meal with the other mannequins, which apparently was nothing unusual. She failed to turn up for work yesterday morning. Mr Blackley sent someone round from the store to find out what had happened to her and her dead body was discovered.'

'I hear you are pursuing the theory that the murderer is a monkey?'

There was a derisive snort from Inchball.

Coddington dipped his head in embarrassment. 'Well, no, I ... obviously not. That would be ... absurd. I merely happened to make a jocular remark to a colleague to the effect that I wouldn't be surprised if it turned out to be the monkey. Unbeknownst to me, there was a journalist in earshot.'

'But why that particular attempt at jocularity? What is the monkey's part in all this?'

Coddington's demeanour became guarded.

'You haven't been told?'

'I have been told nothing. Other than that a girl is dead.'

'You haven't read the newspapers?'

'I prefer not to. I would rather hear the details myself from the senior officer of the local CID. I know from first-hand experience how the gutter press can twist things round.'

Coddington smiled tentatively and even risked an appreciative nod. 'The case has a number of extraordinary features. The door was locked from the inside.'

'From the inside? How can you be sure?' So this was the detail that Sir Edward had deliberately kept back. He was sending Quinn to investigate a locked-room mystery. No wonder Coddington was out of his depth.

'Amélie's key was still in the lock.'

'I see.'

'Making it impossible for anyone to have locked the door with another key from the other side. The windows were fastened too. The room was sealed, in fact. There was no way the murderer could have made his escape. However, the dead girl was not alone in the room.'

'The monkey?'

'Yes!' Coddington appeared unduly impressed by Quinn's guess. After all, the animal had to fit into the jigsaw somewhere. Quinn was beginning to doubt the man's sincerity. He couldn't possibly be as stupid as he appeared to be. 'When Arbuthnot and Miss Mortimer knocked on the door, the monkey calmly turned the key. The door was opened and the beast ran off.'

'I see. And so, it was natural to presume that the monkey...'

'I made no such presumption, I tell you!' The force of Coddington's insistence suggested that this was precisely the assumption he had made.

Quinn attempted a conciliatory tone. 'I was merely going to say that it was natural to presume that the monkey must be involved in some way. If not as perpetrator, then as accomplice. He could have locked the door after the murderer had got away. At the very least, he is a witness.'

Coddington frowned. His oversized moustache twitched as if it was a small dog sniffing out a scent. 'Are you serious?' A look of almost cunning came into his eyes as he scrutinized Quinn.

'Are you familiar with the works of Edgar Allan Poe? There is one story, *The Murders in the Rue Morgue*.'

'But that is fiction...?' Coddington's objection was tinged with a touching hope that Quinn might be able to persuade him to the contrary.

'I believe it was based on a real case.'

Coddington's moustache became suddenly enlivened; his eyes took on a dangerous gleam. 'Yes!' The DCI suddenly clamped one hand over his moustache, as if he was afraid that in its excitement it would bolt from his face. 'I confess, it was that story that gave me the idea.'

'If it could happen once...'

'It could happen again!'

'And did Sherlock Holmes not say something along the lines of, "Eliminate the impossible, and whatever remains, however improbable, is the truth." '

'The Sign of the Four!' Coddington held out his hand for Quinn to shake again. 'I have a feeling you and I are going to get along just fine, Inspector Quinn. Just fine!'

Quinn caught Inchball's scornful glance. And now it was his turn to give a *well-what-do-you-expect* shrug.

The Weeping Mannequin

The sound was animal and raw, a constant stream of small, emotional explosions, each somewhere between a sob and a yelp. Quinn thought of something tender and blind being pulled from deep within a bed of pain. Repeatedly.

He held up his hand to halt Coddington.

'That's Albertine,' said Coddington. 'One of the other mannequins. She was very close to the deceased. The only one of the girls here that was, apparently.'

Quinn rapped quietly on the door and opened it.

A single bed practically filled the room. It sat on top of a zebra-striped rug that took up what little floor space there was. The girl sitting on the edge of the bed, framed by the doorway, was the physical embodiment of the sound he had just heard, a sound which was shockingly amplified now that there was nothing between Quinn and its source. She was wrapped in a rather tatty rust-coloured dressing gown several sizes too large for her. Either it belonged to somebody else, or it had once fitted her and she had shrivelled inside it. The damp pallor of her face was reminiscent of a plate of tripe; or perhaps of something even more unseemly: his own flesh after he had lain too long in the bath. Her frail body appeared to be twisted together from pipe cleaners. How it supported her enormous doll's head was a mystery.

She barely acknowledged Quinn's intrusion. The heavy swivel of her eyes was devoid of all curiosity; no room for anything but anguish there. If she looked at Quinn at all, it was not to take him in but to transmit her suffering. This was done involuntarily, of course. The savage, raucous gulps that convulsed her did not abate. How could they? She had no power to control them.

'I wanted to look at her grief,' said Quinn as he closed the door on her.

Coddington nodded as if what Quinn had just said was standard procedure. 'All the other mannequins are at the store. Clearly she is too distressed to model clothes successfully.'

'You have taken statements from the others?'

'Of course.' Coddington took out a notebook from the inside pocket of his Ulster. 'I took them myself. Given the seriousness of the crime, I thought it best. Would you like to read them now?'

'I'll have a look round first, I think.'

Coddington pocketed the notebook. 'Whatever you think best.' Was there a hint of resentment at Quinn's rebuff? It was clear that Coddington was proud of the statements he had taken, and was eager to share them. He gestured to the door next to Albertine's. 'This is the dead girl's room. Her body has been taken to

66

the morgue, of course, but everything else has been left as it was found.'

Quinn crouched down and peered into the keyhole. 'The key is still in the lock, I see. Have you examined it?'

'It has been dusted for fingerprints.'

'And?'

'It was wiped. The only imprints found are thought to be the monkey's. They are too small to be human.'

'Wiped, you say?'

'Yes.'

'Presumably *not* by the monkey,' observed Quinn drily as he stood up.

'Well, no. Obviously not. That is to say, we don't know who wiped the key.' Coddington appeared wounded by the quip.

The talk of fingerprints reminded Quinn to don the white cotton gloves that Macadam insisted he wear when examining crime scenes.

'Ah, yes, of course,' said Coddington, following his example. 'You can be sure that I ordered my men to take scrupulous care in preserving the integrity of the crime scene.'

Quinn gave a non-committal nod. In truth, he disliked the gloves and often forgot to wear them. He valued the direct touch of his skin against some object that the victim, and quite possibly the murderer, had handled. In his mind, a kind of communion took place. Of course, he would never admit it to his eminently rational and scientifically-minded sergeant.

Quinn realized that he would have to play it by the book this time. He couldn't afford a single slip-up. Besides, he no longer believed that the insights he gained through his finger-tips were more valuable than any information the forensic boys could provide. The last case had cured him of that particular delusion. He knew that if he was going to survive as the Head of Special Crimes he would have to change his methods. But if he changed his methods, would he still be able to do the job?

The art of detection was a strange combination of evidential analysis, ratiocination and instinct. A delicate balance. For it to work, all three elements were required in equal measure. But the problem with instinct was that it did not come when bidden. To summon it, he relied on superstitious rituals such as handling vital evidence with his bare hands. Putting on the cotton gloves was to create a barrier between Quinn and the part of himself that solved crimes, or so he believed.

Quinn began to examine the outside of the door, lightly running his gloved hands over its surface. He got nothing back, of course. The cotton layer sealed him off from the world he was investigating. He stood back and considered the door as a whole. 'Did the monkey open the door itself?'

'I don't know. Is it important?'

'If it had the strength to open the door ... What kind of monkey is it, do we know?'

'A small monkey, the witnesses said. The kind people keep as pets. Silver grey in colour. A macaque, we believe.'

'Did it belong to Amélie?'

'No. Not that anyone knew. The girls are not allowed to keep pets. Mr Blackley is very strict about that, apparently. However, we found a cage in her room. Hidden in her wardrobe.'

'So the monkey first escaped from the cage and then the wardrobe, before unlocking the door to the room?'

'I suppose he must have,' said Coddington.

'Clever monkey,' said Inchball.

Quinn gestured for Coddington to open the door, with the forlorn air of someone relinquishing a long-coveted privilege.

The first thing that he noticed was the smell, a mixture of disinfectant and faeces.

'Apparently, there was quite a lot of monkey shit about the place when they opened it up,' explained Coddington. 'According to the housekeeper, there was even some on the walls. Presumably, the animal threw it about when it became agitated. Naturally – though perhaps regrettably – the maid cleaned it all up before the police arrived.'

'I thought you said the room had been left untouched?'

'Well, apart from that, yes. I made sure of it myself.'

'So, apart from it being completely cleaned with chemical disinfectant, it was untouched?'

'Yes.'

'And so the chances of us finding any significant clues are wiped away at the stroke of a cloth?'

'I understand your frustration, Quinn.' Coddington's omission of Quinn's rank in addressing him was a pointed reminder of his own superiority, his pretended deference for the other detective's superior powers momentarily forgotten. He sounded tetchy. 'But there was nothing we could do about it. We gave strict instructions that nothing was to be touched...' Coddington appeared to remember himself; his tone became more conciliatory. 'But you know women. It was done before we got here.'

The room was larger than its neighbour, and contained more in the way of furnishings. It was full of a vaguely feminine clutter: knick-knacks on shelves, clothes spread across a chair, framed artistic prints on the walls. They were of a similar style to the prints in the hallway, though of rural scenes, rather than Parisian.

The key was still in the door. Quinn took it out to examine more closely. It was a basic design, a cylindrical shaft with teeth at one end and a bow for gripping it at the other. The bow was a rounded trapezium, with the narrower end towards the shaft, and a hole in the middle for attaching it to a key ring. But there was, in fact, no ring linked to it. This in itself struck Quinn as unusual. 'This is the key that was found in the door?' He wanted to be sure.

'Yes, that's correct.'

Quinn handed the key to Coddington. 'I would like it sent to the forensics boys at New Scotland Yard. Could you arrange that, please?'

'Of course.'

'Have it marked for the attention of Charlie Cale.'

Quinn picked up a small fabric-covered box with a key sticking out of one side. He wound the key and sprang the lid. A tiny porcelain ballerina pirouetted to a twinkling melody.

Quinn sensed Coddington watching him closely as he waited for the music box to wind down. He couldn't be sure whether the other man's scrutiny was critical or merely interested. Quinn did not quite trust the eagerly expectant gaze that met him when he turned back to Coddington. 'The theme from *Swan Lake*,' said Quinn as he replaced the object on the shelf.

'Is it important?'

'It could be. At this stage, anything and everything could turn out to have a vital significance. Or none at all.'

'You don't know what a wonderful opportunity – indeed, what an honour – it is for me to be able to work alongside you, Inspector.'

Quinn frowned. He couldn't work out what Coddington's game was. Quinn had never encountered a DCI so completely devoid of egotism as Coddington would have to be to mean what he said. Perhaps he was simply trying to recover ground after his slip-up over the crime scene. He wanted to ingratiate himself back into Quinn's good opinion. If it wasn't that, it was something more sinister. One thing was certain: the soft-soap act was designed to hoodwink him in some way.

Quinn turned to the bed, single like the one in the next room, though in fact it appeared smaller, lost in the larger space surrounding it.

The mattress dipped in the middle, as if it bore the imprint of the dead girl's presence.

'That was where she was found,' said Coddington.

The room's monumental wardrobe drew Quinn's attention, a looming mausoleum of dark wood tucked against one wall. 'Was this where the monkey was confined?' asked Quinn. He opened the wardrobe door and saw the gilded cage in the bottom, the flimsy door hanging open.

'Yes. Presumably Amélie was worried about the pet being discovered.'

'It's not much of a life for the poor fellow.'

'Motive, sir?' asked Inchball mischievously. 'Monkey becomes dissatisfied with its life in the gilded cage, hidden away in the dark of the wardrobe. Escapes and murders his gaoler?'

Quinn indulged his sergeant with a half-smile. He began rifling through the hanging garments. Quite an array. Not that he knew much about ladies' fashions. Well, nothing – it had to be owned. But he could sense the fineness of the fabrics even through the cotton gloves. His hands delved into a black well of evening glamour, yieldingly inviting. The sparkle of sequins flashed here and there, glistening like dark promises. He had to suppress a desire to bury his head in the sheaths of enticement he uncovered between the garments. He settled instead for inhaling the frail, fleeting scent that clung to them. It was overpowered by other smells – mothballs and the aftermath of monkey faeces.

In amongst it all he found one full-length fur coat and a silver fox stole.

'How much do mannequins get paid?' he asked, lifting out the fur coat and turning it to show Coddington and Inchball.

'Knowing Benjamin Blackley, I shouldn't imagine they get much in the way of a salary,' said Coddington. 'He operates on the principle of paying his staff just enough that they can survive, but not enough that they can escape. It is a form of bonded servitude.'

'How could she afford these then?' asked Quinn, returning the coat to the rail.

'Having spoken to the other mannequins, I very much doubt she could,' said Coddington. 'They do not seem particularly happy with their lot. Unless she was paid significantly more than her peers she would not have been able to run to such expenditure.'

'Maybe she nicked 'em,' suggested Inchball, with a certain amount of relish.

'Or they were gifts,' said Quinn. He crossed back to the shelf where he had found the music box and picked it up again.

'You think that was a gift too?' asked Coddington.

Quinn shrugged.

'From who?' said Inchball abruptly.

Quinn nodded his approval of the question. 'This room is bigger than the other girls',' he observed.

'Yes,' said Coddington. 'It's the largest in the house, apart from Monsieur Hugo's.'

'Monsieur who?'

'Monsieur Hugo. He is the head of the Costumes Salon. And he lives in the house with the mannequins.'

'Frenchy, is he?' said Inchball suspiciously.

'He pretends to be a Frenchman.'

'Pretends to be a Frenchman!' It seemed that as far as Inchball was concerned, this was an even greater offence than actually being one. He gave Quinn a look that suggested the case was surely closed. 'Why in the name of Jesus would anybody do that?'

'For professional reasons. All the mannequins do it too. Apart from Amélie. She was the only real French native among them.'

'Who else lives in the house besides Monsieur Hugo and the mannequins?'

'Just the housekeeper, Miss Mortimer, whom you have met. And the maid, an Irish girl called Kathleen. She's as dumpy and plain as the other girls are pretty and slim.'

'Was she the one who cleaned the monkey shit?' Inchball's tone was disapproving.

'She can't be entirely blamed. She's not the brightest of creatures. A little bit simple, if you ask me.'

'So Monsieur Hugo is the only man?' asked Quinn.

'That's correct.'

Quinn and Inchball exchanged a glance. 'Lucky bleeder,' was Inchball's comment.

'Having interviewed him, I rather think the prerogative is wasted on him,' said Coddington.

Inchball rolled his eyes. 'Not another one of

74

them blasted queers, is 'e? We 'ad enough of them with the last case.'

'It's true to say that he appears more interested in ladies' costumes than in the ladies who wear them,' said Coddington. 'That said, he was very fond of Amélie. And is the only one who appears genuinely cut up over her death – apart from Albertine, that is.'

'Where is he now?'

'At work, of course. Blackley would not permit him to remain absent for long, no matter how upset he was. I dare say it was only because Albertine's distress would repel customers that he has allowed her to stay here.'

'What else do we know about the dead girl?' said Quinn.

'The housekeeper describes her as a good, quiet girl. She said she never had any trouble from her. I got the impression that this was another thing that set her apart from the others. Most of them, that is. I don't think anything bad can be said against the poor wretch next door, either.'

'Any enemies?'

'No one would admit it, but my sense is that most of the other girls hated her guts. Albertine excepted, once again. Miss Mortimer dropped hints to that effect. She said she liked to keep herself to herself. Which perhaps led the other girls to believe she was something of a snob. Saw herself as a cut above them.'

'What about admirers?'

'I dare say everyone who saw her admired her. She was a looker, all right.'

'But no one in particular? No beau?'

'According to the housekeeper, Blackley wouldn't stand for it. He was very strict with them. The front door was locked at nine o'clock every evening and only opened in the morning when it was time for them to go to work. They were only allowed out with Miss Mortimer, or another of the older female employees, as chaperone. They lived like nuns. It might have suited Amélie, but it didn't suit the others.'

'Nuns? Or prisoners?' said Quinn.

'It ain' natural,' said Inchball.

'Sergeant Inchball is right,' said Quinn. 'When you impose conditions like this on healthy young people, you are asking for trouble. Mr Blackley may think he can control the lives of his employees, but they will find a way to evade that control. The monkey in the wardrobe is one example. We may be sure that there are other secrets that this young girl kept locked away somewhere.'

Quinn dropped down on to one knee and peered under the bed. He retrieved an object that looked like a short wooden knitting needle.

'We saw that,' said Coddington quickly. 'It's a hairpin. Girls like this are very untidy. They drop things on the floor.'

'There was nothing else under there,' said Quinn.

'It's hard to see how it could have anything to do with her death. She was strangled, not stabbed. And there doesn't appear to be any

76

blood on it.'

'Although it could have been cleaned up by the girl who cleaned the monkey faeces.' Quinn handed the hairpin to Coddington. 'Something else for Charlie Cale.'

'I shall see to it now,' said Coddington. 'Unless there is anything else you wish to have sent?'

'That will do for now.'

Coddington walked out of the room and called for one of his subordinates.

The bed had a polished brass frame. Quinn knuckle-tapped each of its legs in turn. The fourth had a more muffled, deader resonance than the other three. 'Inchball.'

That was all the command he needed to issue. Inchball tilted the bed back so that Quinn could examine the end of the leg in question. It was an open tube, stuffed with a roll of papers.

DCI Coddington returned just in time to see Quinn tease the papers out: letters, still in their envelopes.

'Lucky break,' said Inchball begrudgingly.

Coddington grinned as if he had just seen a stage magician pull off a particularly baffling trick. 'We looked under the bed, of course,' he said delightedly. 'We didn't think of looking in it!'

Quinn barely acknowledged his effusion with a non-committal grunt.

The Secret Letters

The letters unfurled slowly, flexing themselves out of the tight rolls they had been bent into. There seemed to be something almost animal to their uncoiling, as if they were awakening after a long hibernation.

There were six of them. On each envelope was written *Amélie* in a large, looping, slightly childish script.

'Cheap stationery,' remarked Quinn. 'Which means the letters are unlikely to be from the same person who gave her the furs.'

He extracted one of them from its envelope and straightened it out.

My Dearest Darlingest Darling,
I LOVE YOU!
Oh my dear, sweet darling, if you only knew what it means to me to be able to call you FRIEND! You are the dearest and sweetest and most loved of all friends. How could I not love you? How could anyone not love you? Everyone who sets eyes on you must fall instantly in love with you: INSTANTLY, I say!
And anyone who says they don't is a LIAR ... or a very big, stupid IDIOT.
Oh my dear Amélie, I know I am a very big

78

stupid idiot myself – a fool, a nobody, a nothing – and nobody should pay any attention to a word I say, but this is the truth and I will say it and I hope you will take this one thing I say seriously, though you may discount everything else I say as the nonsense of a flighty fool: *YOU SAVED MY LIFE!*

Yes, it's true. I am not exaggerating. Your friendship, *YOUR LOVE,* your kindness ... ~~SAVED MY LIFE~~.

When I first came to this place I was friendless. The moment I looked upon you I was smitten, though I never dreamt that we could be friends. You were so beautiful and perfect. How could someone like you ever be the friend of someone like me? The others said you were aloof. (But let us not worry about what the others say. They are unkind. Bitter, resentful, jealous – *FOOLS!* I pity them.) Suffice it to say, they were not encouraging. But I saw something in your eyes. I saw that you were lonely too; that you were friendless. And in my simplicity – for I am afraid that I am a very simple person – I dared to look into your dear, sweet, sad eyes and, with a silent look of hope, I reached out to you.

AND YOU RESPONDED! Your eyes met mine. Your silent gaze answered mine. I even saw a tiny flicker of a smile upon your dear, sweet lips. Or was I dreaming? If I was dreaming, it is a dream I never want to wake from.

And so, at first, our friendship was conducted in silence. In those small, timid glances, stolen while no one else was looking. Such small, fragile, fleeting things, like sunbeams hanging in the dusty air, gone

79

as soon as they are formed. How can such treasures be so insubstantial? They are nothing. They are everything. They were all we had.

Until one of us – was it you? Of course it was you! I should never have dared – ventured to give voice to the sentiments our eyes transmitted. How my heart fluttered to hear you speak to me at last! And to hear from you those words that saved my life: 'MA CHER AMIE.'

My dear friend – for you let me know straight away what your words meant. That was the first of our little 'French lessons'. You have been a wonderful teacher and I a hopeless pupil. But I hope that you noticed that, when I wrote 'amie', I remembered to add the e that makes it feminine, as you have taught me. How sweetly you scolded me the last time I made such a mistake! Yes, sweetly. For I confess that I would rather be scolded by you than smiled upon by anyone else. You are such a darling, lovable scold. How I wanted to kiss away the sweet frown that fell across your brow. Is it bad of me to want to make you cross so that I can kiss away that sweet frown? Is that the reason why I make so many mistakes when you are teaching me? I would like to say it is, but sadly it is because I am stupid and a poor student. I am afraid that I will never improve because I get so much pleasure from being wrong and being scolded by you! (I can see your frown now as you read this. Oh dear, sweet, darling Amélie! Please do not be too cross with me. Or if you must be cross, let me kiss away your frown.)

From that day on, from the day you called me friend, and allowed me to do the same, my life changed. No. It is more than that. My life began. I

80

came alive. You gave me life. You gave me reason to live. And, yes, it's true, I really mean it: YOU SAVED MY LIFE!
YOU ARE MY LIFE.
Your loving,
E.

Quinn handed the letter to Coddington, who read it with a devouring gaze.

'The others are in a similar vein,' said Quinn, handing them on. 'All signed by "E". And the stationery is the same in every case.'

'What do you make of it?' asked Coddington, handing the letter back. Quinn passed it on to Inchball.

'It's intensely passionate. There's a naïveté to the writing. Note the frequent capitalization of words and the almost childish phraseology in places. But there is an intelligence in evidence too. It's remarkably free from spelling mistakes and the other signs of poor literacy. One might almost begin to suspect that the naïveté is feigned. The writer has been educated to a respectable standard. Perhaps she comes from a good family...'

'She?' cried Inchball. 'What about all this *I love you* guff? It's a love letter, ain' it?'

'That doesn't mean it wasn't written by a girl.'

Inchball groaned.

'But I don't think it's a love letter in the sense you mean. It's the protestation of a deeply felt emotional bond – of love, yes ... but of the kind of love that is felt between two members of the

81

fairer sex. It puts me in mind of a schoolgirl crush.' Quinn turned to Coddington. 'The girl next door who's crying ... what did you say her name was, sir?'

'Albertine.'

'She's not French, though?'

'No.'

'So it's unlikely to be her real name.'

'You think she might be E?'

'The depth of her grief seems proportionate with the intensity of feeling expressed in these letters.'

'I'll talk to her,' said Inchball.

'Gently,' warned Quinn. 'For now, just find out what her real name is. Don't mention that we've seen the letters. And when you have done that, find the housekeeper and bring her to me.'

Inchball shot out of the room with a heavy, forward-leaning stomp.

Quinn met Coddington's questioning eye with a shrug. 'Despite what you say about Blackley not allowing admirers, someone must have bought her the furs and the other things. I suspect Miss Mortimer may know more than she has told you.'

'It's not *that* that I was wondering about.' Coddington cocked his head, listening to the ebb and flow of despair that sounded through the wall. They heard the door open and Inchball's heavy tread. The detective sergeant's muffled growl failed to stem the tide of weeping.

Quinn and Coddington watched each other

82

warily as they strained to hear what was transpiring in the next room. More footsteps, Inchball's judging by the weight and speed. Then a sound like a metallic groan: the bed springs straining under an additional weight, perhaps. The sobbing became somehow subdued – not calmer, but dampened, as though something large and soft had been placed over the mouth of the weeping girl.

Coddington made as if to dart from the room, but Quinn caught him by the arm and held him.

The timbre of anguish changed again. Desperate gasping for air. Then a sharp keening arose, a high, fierce spiral of sound. But it was immediately swallowed into the same smothering mass.

There was a low, indistinct rumble from Inchball.

The muted wail continued, before decaying into a jagged series of stifled sobs. The ferocity of the sobs gradually lessened at the same time as the interval between them increased.

Quinn rippled his brows questioningly as he faced Coddington; the other man's answering nod conceded whatever was implied by Quinn's expression.

Now there was only silence from the next room. For Quinn, it was a strangely thrilling silence, for it held in it the promise of a breakthrough. The girl had stopped crying. There was every possibility that she might speak.

At last it came. Her voice, a fragile tremor, little more than a throb in the air, but full of the heat of her tears. They strained to make out what she said but her words were barely articulate, a vocal wrenching rather than speech. Nevertheless, she had spoken.

'We couldn't get a word from her,' whispered Coddington.

'He is a father,' said Quinn, not bothering to lower his voice. 'He has a father's heart.'

'All the same, it is surprising.'

'That's what motivates him. It's why he does this job. Why I want him in my team.'

'And you, Inspector Quinn? What motivates you?'

Quinn looked down at the bed. 'I don't like to think of them getting away with it.'

Coddington smoothed out his moustache distractedly. 'It must be more than that.'

'Must it?' Quinn shook his head to deter a reply. He held up the letters as if to ward off further prying. 'Why did she hide these in the frame of her bed, do you think?'

'Embarrassment?'

'Then why not destroy them? No, she hid them in the way that we hide the things that are most precious to us. This is hidden treasure. She hid them from prying eyes. Perhaps from those who would coarsely mock the delicate feelings described in these letters. Or perhaps from one who might be jealous of this...' Quinn waved the letters gently. 'Love.'

'You think the letters are connected to her death?'

'Let's say they pique my interest. Do they not yours?' As an afterthought, almost insolently,

84

Quinn added: 'Sir?'

Coddington continued to fuss away at his moustache as if he was trying to work something out. 'Yes, of course.'

In the next room the bed springs sighed musically as a weight lifted from them. Inchball's terse footsteps clipped on the boards again. Quinn dashed for the door and intercepted him on the landing.

'Did you get a name?'

'Edna Corbett.'

Quinn nodded. It was as he had expected. 'Edna.'

'That's your "E", guv.'

'In all likelihood.'

'Shall I still fetch the housekeeper?'

'If you please.'

Quinn returned to Amélie's bedroom and passed on the name to Coddington.

'So, you were right. She is our letter-writer.'

Quinn made no comment.

Coddington's hand went back up to his moustache. 'I say, Inspector Quinn, here's a thought. You said that Amélie concealed the letters to hide them from someone who might be jealous.'

'I merely put it forward as a possibility. A theory.'

'Well, staying with that theory, what about this? Suppose this girl, Edna, or Albertine, or whatever you want to call her ... suppose she was the jealous one? Suppose she was jealous of Amélie's relationship with whoever gave her all these presents? It's possible, ain' it?

85

Couldn't that be a motive?'

Quinn looked down at the letters in his hand.

'All that passionate feeling,' Coddington continued. 'Love can turn to hate like that, you know.' He clicked his fingers.

'But have you seen her? There's hardly anything to her. She's a mite. Do you really think she's capable of strangling the life out of a healthy girl?'

Coddington parroted Quinn's own words. 'I merely put it forward as a possibility. A theory.'

Quinn screwed his face up in distaste.

'What's the matter, Quinn?' Coddington's tone was suddenly bullish. 'Is it because you didn't think of it yourself?'

The remark struck home. 'It's possible, of course. Sir. As yet, there are still many features of this case that we do not understand. We must try to bear all possibilities in mind. And not jump to any conclusions.'

'Of course, yes.'

'What you are suggesting is something along the lines of a *crime passionelle*, as the French have it. A crime of passion. And yet, the business with the lock rather militates against that. That smacks of premeditation, I think. And this girl, she may be capable of strangling her best friend, her beloved friend ... But is she also capable of contriving this feat of mystification?'

'Perhaps she had help?'

'You are proposing a conspiracy? A man to engineer the mechanical trickery? Then I am afraid it looks less and less like a *crime passionelle*, which therefore undermines the reason

why you suspected her in the first place.'
Quinn found himself stroking his own rather
insignificant moustache. He realized with
horror that he was unconsciously mimicking
DCI Coddington's trademark mannerism. His
hand flew away from his face. He glanced
quickly at the other man. Had he noticed?

Coddington's gaze was angled down towards
the bed. But the tail of a smile flickered across
his lips and vanished.

The Spare Room

Quinn turned his back on Coddington and crossed to the window, which looked out over a long, narrow garden at the back of the house. The sun was a soft flare high up to his right, just at the periphery of his vision. Sometimes, in the midst of a murder enquiry, it shocked him more to discover the sun still shining than to find a bloody handprint or a discarded garrotte. The garden itself had benefited from the recent downpours. It presented a lush, almost unruly abundance – predominantly green, but with other spring colours starting to come through. It was like something unleashed.

A vestigial path led away towards a high wooden screen at the bottom of the garden, fragments of paving stone peeping through the long grass of a loose-edged lawn. Long-established climbing plants – Virginia creeper, wisteria, ivy – covered the screen. Layers upon layers of concealment, everywhere he looked.

The structure of the house projected out on the right, with Amélie's room being set back in relation to it. Two other windows were set in the wall that came out, curtains drawn: more concealment. Quinn sighed. He made a half-hearted effort to lift the sash window.

'The window was fastened from the inside,' Coddington informed him. 'Besides which, as you can see, the woodwork is painted fast. It's immovable.'

'So whoever killed her did not get out this way?'

'It would appear not.'

The door opened. Quinn turned to see Inchball return. He stepped to one side, revealing Miss Mortimer behind him.

The housekeeper's face was set in an expression of impatient belligerence. 'What is it now? I have work to do, you know. The girls will be back soon, expecting their lunch.'

This revelation interested Quinn. 'They eat here? Isn't there a canteen for staff at the store?'

'Mr Blackley doesn't like the mannequins to mix with the other staff. Especially the men.'

'And no men were allowed inside the house, apart from Monsieur Hugo? Is that correct?'

'Yes.'

Was there a minute hesitation in her answer? And a telltale flickering of her eyes as she considered her lie. 'And you absolutely insist that Amélie had no male admirers?'

'What a question!'

Her answer was, of course, an evasion.

'Please.' Quinn gestured for her to follow him to the wardrobe. He took out the fur coat. 'Have you ever seen her wear this?'

'No.'

'Do you think a mannequin's wages run to such luxuries?'

'I really can't say. Staff receive a five per cent discount on purchases at the House of Blackley.'

'Five per cent! Even with five per cent off, I doubt she could afford to dress herself in mink. Or if she could, why hide it away in her wardrobe? You said yourself that you have never seen her wearing it.'

'Perhaps she got it as a reward for her work in the Costumes Salon. I know Monsieur Hugo thought very highly of her.'

'And this?' Quinn pulled out a black sequinned gown. 'Another reward? I did not realize Mr Blackley sanctioned such generosity. Her wardrobe is crammed with similar extravagances.' Quinn replaced the gown and waved briefly in the direction of the ornaments on Amélie's shelves. 'It seems she liked to treat herself. Are all the other mannequins' rooms similarly full of trinkets? I didn't notice any in Albertine's. Or should that be Edna's?'

'Oh? You've been prying in there, have you?'

'It is my job to look into these things. I take it you have keys to all the rooms?'

'Yes, of course. I am the housekeeper.' She produced a great fob of keys from her apron.

'Then you can show me round. I will want admittance to every room.'

'I told you, I have work to do!'

'And I am investigating a murder.'

Miss Mortimer's expression made clear her opinion on the relative importance of investigating a murder and preparing lunch for a group of fashion mannequins. 'If the girls are late back to the store there'll be hell to pay. You'll have to answer to Mr Blackley for it.'

Quinn caught Coddington's eye and shook his head in disbelief. He did not deign to answer Miss Mortimer's threat.

'What do you want *me* to do, guv?' asked Inchball.

'Perhaps DCI Coddington will be so good as to take you through the statements he has taken from the other mannequins. They will be home for lunch soon. It will be as well to do some prep before you have the pleasure of interviewing them.'

It soon became apparent that Amélie's was by far the largest of the mannequins' rooms. However, Quinn's investigation of the other girls' wardrobes – or 'snooping', as Miss Mortimer dubbed it – revealed that Amélie was not alone in possessing furs. 'Whose room is this?' he asked, as he pulled out a silver fox stole from one wardrobe.

'This?' Again the stalling reiteration. Why on earth should she be reluctant to answer his question? But there was no denying that she sounded despondent when she finally did: 'Marie-Claude.'

'Real name?'

'That's what I know her as. If she has any other name you'll have to get it out of her yourself.'

'Amélie has the largest room, does she not?'

'Monsieur Hugo's is larger, I would say. Not to mention the front parlour.'

'Very well. She has the largest room of the mannequins.'

'Someone has to.'

'That was all there was to it? It was not a sign of seniority perhaps?'

'Oh, no. Nothing to do with that. Marie-Claude is the eldest. She used to have Amélie's room but...' Miss Mortimer trailed off.

'What happened?'

'There was a vacancy in the mannequin house. Marie-Claude moved into the vacant room and Amélie was given her room.'

'But why? Why not simply put Amélie in the vacant room?'

'That was the way it was done.'

'So if the largest room is not a symbol of seniority, it is perhaps a symbol of favouritism. Marie-Claude fell out of favour?'

'I'm sure it wasn't that. Marie-Claude probably preferred this room because of its location. Or disposition. Or for some other reason. You know these girls. They will get all sorts of ideas in their heads. I can't keep up with them.'

Quinn continued to browse the girl's clothes. 'She does not have quite as impressive an array as Amélie.'

'That's no one's fault but her own.'

'What do you mean by that remark?'

'I'm sure I don't know what I mean. Only she ought to work harder ... then perhaps she would be better rewarded.' For the first time Miss Mortimer seemed almost flustered.

'So Amélie acquired her wardrobe solely through hard work?'

'She must have. I can think of no other way. As I said, she was very highly thought of. A true professional.'

'Were the other girls envious of her?'

'They had no right to be.'

'You liked her?'

'She gave me no trouble.'

Quinn replaced the fur stole and nodded. He had seen enough of that room.

Miss Mortimer followed him out on to the landing and locked Marie-Claude's door. 'Can I get back to work now? The girls will be home soon.'

'We haven't seen Monsieur Hugo's room yet.' Quinn pointed to a door at the end of the landing. 'Is it that one?'

'No, that's a spare room.'

'I'd like to see it.'

'Why? It's just a spare room. It doesn't belong to anyone.'

Quinn was even more determined to see it now that she had tried to deter him. 'Nevertheless.'

'It's been a long time since this room was opened.' Her tone was discouraging. She seemed to be suggesting that it would be a Herculean task to get the door open, given the aeons of unrecorded time during which it had remained closed.

He nodded once, not in encouragement but as a command. Even Miss Mortimer was not so obtuse as to ignore that, though of course she took her time finding the right key, shaking her head doubtfully all the time.

The room was disappointingly neutral, sparse in every sense, lacking any indications of personality; and certainly, at least at first sight, devoid of clues. A severely neat room. There was a single window in the far wall; next to it, a large mahogany wardrobe.

Quinn looked down at the bed, the sheets tightly drawn and tucked. It certainly did not look as though it had been slept in recently, if ever. He sniffed the air suspiciously. If what the housekeeper had said were true, he would have expected the stale, dusty itch of an unaired room; but he detected something else, a scent more animal, almost musk-like in its pungency. It was the scent of recent occupation.

'Why is the bed made?'

'*Why is the bed made?*' Miss Mortimer seemed outraged by the stupidity of the question. 'Why wouldn't it be made?'

'Because this is a spare room. No one sleeps here.'

'We must always have it ready. Just in case.'

'Just in case of what?'

'In case of guests.'

'What guests do you have? Are the mannequins allowed to entertain guests?'

'Mr Blackley might need to stay over.'

'Mr Blackley?'

'That's right. That's what I said. Sometimes his business keeps him late at the store. It is convenient for him to have a place to stay nearby. If he is exhausted he does not want to make the long journey back to Surbiton.'

'That's where he lives?'

94

'I should hope so. Otherwise, why else would he go there of an evening?'

'But he does not go home every evening? Sometimes he comes here.'

'Yes.'

'How often does he stay here?'

'It's difficult to say. It varies from week to week.'

'Let me make it easy for you. Did he stay here the night before last?'

The housekeeper hesitated. 'No.'

'You don't seem certain?'

'I did not see him.'

'And you would have seen him if he had been here?'

'Well, I would have known, I think. Though it is true to say that Mr Blackley has his own key. He lets himself in and out. Sometimes he works very late indeed. I believe I would have heard him come in – and I did not.'

'But you are a little deaf, are you not, Miss Mortimer? You find it hard to tell what people are saying unless you are looking at them?'

'Nonsense.' She shook her head vehemently. 'Besides, I would have had the bed to make. Even if he left without me seeing him in the morning.'

'But if he did not want you to know that he had been here? Might he not have made the bed himself?'

'Impossible!'

'Unlikely perhaps, Miss Mortimer. But not impossible.'

'Impossible!' insisted the housekeeper. 'Look

95

at it! A man did not fold that sheet!'

'From what I hear, Mr Blackley is a very clever man, capable of a great many things. Do you not think he is capable of making a bed?'

'No.'

'Miss Mortimer?'

She met his questioning tone with a shifty glance.

'When was the last time you were aware of Mr Blackley using this room?'

'Not for a long time. He rarely uses it.'

'But the impression you gave me a moment ago...'

'I can't be held responsible for any impressions.'

'You said the frequency of his stays varies from week to week. That rather implies that he stays here at least one night, most weeks, does it not? Is that not the case?'

'I told you, he hardly ever stays here.' She was becoming agitated, almost frantic, as if she was afraid that she had said too much already.

Quinn decided there was little to be gained from picking away at the inconsistencies of the woman's story. He walked round the bed to the wardrobe and tried the door. It was locked. 'Where's the key?'

Miss Mortimer shrugged. 'We never use that wardrobe. The key is missing, I think.'

Quinn frowned. It was not quite an answer to his question. 'You'll need to find the key for me. I will want to look in here.' He crossed to the window. He saw that it was actually set in a door that had been papered over. The frame, however, was clearly visible, and someone had cut through the paper all around the door, leaving the possibility that it could be opened. 'There is a door in this wall.'

'But it doesn't go anywhere,' objected the housekeeper.

Quinn peered through the window. 'It gives out on to the garden.'

'But there is no way to get down there. We are on the first storey. If you open that door and step out you will fall a good fifteen feet.'

'What's the point of it then?'

'There used to be steps up to it from the garden. But they rotted away and Mr Blackley had them removed. He saw no point in replacing them. The room was used as an upper drawing room by the house's previous owner. When Mr Blackley took it over, he converted as many rooms as possible to bedrooms.'

Quinn continued to peer through the window. A blur of movement in a cherry tree at the bottom of the garden caught his eye. At first he thought it was a grey squirrel, but the colour wasn't quite right; the movement and shape all wrong. Besides, there was something attached to the creature's head that looked suspiciously like a hat.

'Coddington!' he called out, running from the window. 'I've found your monkey!'

The Monkey in the Tree

Quinn picked up Coddington and Inchball on the landing and led them out to the garden. They were joined by a couple of the uniforms, whom Coddington directed to 'surround the cherry tree'. This seemed to confuse the policemen, who failed to grasp how two men could surround anything. Coddington's excitement only added to the confusion. His commands were practically incoherent.

The blossom was not yet out in the cherry tree, but it soon would be. Fine shoots laden with tight pink buds were already beginning to appear on the thick central boughs, groping towards spectacular fulfilment.

From the window the tree had seemed small, stunted almost. But this was deceptive. There was enough height to the topmost branches for the monkey to cower out of reach of the men. Not that any of them knew how to go about extricating a monkey from a tree. Coddington's nearly hysterical barking was not likely to help. Quinn kept his distance; Inchball even more so. 'Don't want to be anywhere near that thing if it starts throwing shit around,' the sergeant explained in a confiding snarl.

Miss Mortimer joined them in the garden, no

doubt drawn by the commotion. Quinn might have expected to see a look of detached irony on her face at the antics of the police. But her expression was cold and intense. She glowered at the monkey with something like hatred. Possibly fear.

Her habitual amusement returned when Coddington sent her back into the kitchen for a titbit to tempt the creature down. 'Do you have anything like a banana?' he asked.

'What is *like* a banana?' she wondered facetiously.

Coddington shared his thinking with Quinn. 'He must be hungry.'

Quinn said nothing. He preferred not to be implicated in Coddington's operation, which had the whiff of farce about it.

The monkey seemed to agree. It made a noise that was suspiciously close to laughter, and bared its teeth in an approximation of hilarity.

'It's mocking us,' said Coddington under his breath.

'What do you expect?' said Inchball.

The monkey ducked and shifted through the branches, a restless flurry of agitation. It kept its face hidden, only to peep out from time to time for a burst of manic cackling. There seemed to be something in what Coddington said. 'Now that you have seen the beast face-to-face what do you think, sir?' Quinn gestured up to the leering animal. 'Is that the face of a killer?'

Coddington frowned. 'I would not put anything past it.'

They were joined in the garden by Macadam, who had with him two men. Quinn recognized Blackley. The other was a large individual in an Inverness cape with a monocle lodged in one eye.

'What's going on?' demanded Blackley. At the sound of his voice the monkey gave vent to a scream of distress.

Blackley was clearly a man used to taking charge. Despite the brusqueness of his tone, he wore an easy smile that was no doubt intended to charm away any opposition to his commands. Perhaps that smile was a little too determined; it might even be described as fixed. But under the present circumstances that was understandable.

'We have found the monkey, sir,' said DCI Coddington – redundantly, it had to be said, as everyone was now looking up at the animal in question. The din of jabbering put an additional strain on Blackley's immovable smile.

Blackley and the man in the Inverness cape exchanged a look, the meaning of which was not clear to Quinn. The word 'conspiratorial' came to mind. 'Mr Blackley?' Quinn held out his hand. 'I am Detective Inspector Quinn of the Special Crimes Department, Scotland Yard.'

'I see. Very well ... The more the merrier, I suppose.'

Quinn turned to Blackley's companion. 'Who is this gentleman?'

'This is Mr Yeovil.'

'I'm afraid I don't quite understand,' said

Quinn. 'Why is he here?'

'He acts for me in a number of capacities, in particular as a legal adviser. He happened to be in the store so I asked him to accompany me.'

'It wasn't quite like that, sir,' put in Sergeant Macadam. 'Mr Blackley refused to come until he had tracked down the other gentleman.'

'As I said, I value his legal expertise. In addition, he has some experience as a private investigator. I commend his services to you. He can be Sherlock Holmes to your Inspector Lestrade.'

'There is more to being a detective than wearing outlandish clothes and affecting eccentric habits.' Quinn flashed a look towards Coddington to make sure the message was not lost on him either.

'That's true enough,' said Yeovil, his voice a booming rumble from deep within his great chest. 'One must understand the psychology of the criminal. To put it another way, one must think like a criminal. It helps if one has personal acquaintance with the darker side of human nature. Is that not so, Inspector?' He gave Quinn a knowing look, seeming to wink from behind his monocle.

Quinn had no time for the charlatan's antics. 'Besides, there is a conflict of interest in Mr Yeovil's involvement, surely. He is acting on your behalf. And yet, you may yourself be the murderer.'

'I? But that is an outrageous accusation!'

'It is slanderous,' advised Mr Yeovil.

'I am not yet in possession of enough

101

evidence to rule anything out. You have a reputation, Mr Blackley, for controlling every aspect of your employees' lives. Perhaps that now extends to their deaths too?'

'You go too far, sir,' said Mr Blackley's legal adviser. 'On what evidence do you base these evil suppositions?'

'Amélie Dupin worked as a mannequin in the Costumes Salon of your store, is that not so?'

'Of course.'

'And this is the house where the mannequins reside?'

'Yes.'

'The location of which is a closely guarded secret, is it not? Indeed, may we not go further to say that you are one of very few *men* who know the address?'

'I didn't kill her,' said Blackley bluntly, his northern vowels asserting themselves more noticeably than before. 'Why would I? Amélie was one of my best mannequins. No – *the* best,' Blackley corrected himself. 'It's the mannequins that sell the costumes, you know. My lady customers look at the mannequins and see themselves – perhaps as they dream of being, or perhaps as they once were. It was not in my interests to harm her – she was a valuable commercial asset. And another thing, this sort of affair is very bad for business, you know. A murder, and all the scandal associated with it ... It's the last thing I need.'

'Not necessarily. I'm sure you are familiar with the notion that there is no such thing as bad publicity. There was a major fire at your store a few years ago, I believe. If I remember correctly from my reading of newspaper accounts, afterwards you actually experienced an increase in sales. Customers were not dissuaded by the prospect of being burnt alive; rather they were drawn to Blackley's, whether out of sympathy for your misfortune or out of a ghoulish fascination, who can say?'

'Are you now suggesting that I set the fire myself? The cost of the damage was barely covered by any sales increase, not to mention the inconvenience.'

'And the loss of life?'

'Yes, that's what I said.' Though, in fact, he had not mentioned it.

At that moment, Miss Mortimer returned to the garden holding a banana in front of her between her thumb and forefinger, as if it were an object of some distaste to her. 'This is the nearest thing to a banana I could find.'

The sound of her voice provoked a similar response from the monkey as Blackley's had. A scream of rage.

Coddington took the banana and peeled it. He held the fruit up to the monkey. 'Come on, little chap. Doesn't that look tasty? A lovely banana. All yours. That's it.'

Coddington's plan seemed to be working. The monkey worked its way gingerly along the branch nearest the banana. As the creature approached, Coddington withdrew the prize a little, forcing the monkey to advance even further. The two uniforms closed in on either side, presumably in anticipation of snatching the animal as soon as it came within reach.

'That's it, my little friend. Come and get it,' murmured Coddington.

The noises from the monkey were calmer now. The prospect of a banana seemed to have had a soothing effect.

'He's quite tame, really,' Coddington said. But his smile of triumph proved to be premature. Until this point the monkey's movements had been slow and tentative, responding to the man's encouragements. It gave every impression of docility.

With a sudden dart it flashed out a hand and snapped off the top of the banana, scampering back into the deepest part of the tree, where it proceeded to gobble down its unexpected meal.

'Cheeky blighter!' cried Coddington. 'All right, PC Masterhouse. Get up there and get it.'

'Me, sir?' asked one of the uniforms disconsolately.

'Is there anyone else here called Masterhouse?'

'No, sir.'

'Well, then. Up you go.'

Masterhouse looked up uncertainly at the spreading branches and the monkey hiding within. One more unenthusiastic glance towards his governor told him that there would be no way out of this.

He removed his helmet and handed it to the other uniform to hold. Then spat on his palms and rubbed them together. Next he circled the tree repeatedly, as if he was looking for the stairs.

'Get on with it, man! We haven't got all day.'

Masterhouse swallowed unhappily. At last he grasped one of the boughs and attempted to pull himself up. The tree began to shake, prompting the monkey to screech. There was an alarming creak as if the branch would snap. Masterhouse let go. 'I don't think it will bear my weight, sir. Perhaps it would be better if I had a ladder.'

Coddington nodded impatiently. 'You, Miss Mortimer. Is there a ladder?'

'Is there a *ladder*? Good grief, what a question!'

'It seems a perfectly reasonable question to me,' objected Coddington.

'What would we be doing with a ladder?'

'You might have one for maintenance jobs.'

'The maintenance team from the store takes care of all that,' said Blackley. 'They have their own ladder. A very long one.'

'You will have to manage without a ladder then, Masterhouse,' said Coddington. 'Lappett, give him a leg up.'

The second uniform looked down at the helmet he was holding, his expression every bit as doleful as Masterhouse's had been when told to climb the tree.

Coddington was having none of it. He snatched the helmet out of Lappett's hands. 'Here, give me that. You men ... I don't know.'

Lappett stooped and cradled his hands for Masterhouse's boot. A strenuous lurch had the latter up in the tree, straddled over the apex of the trunk. His expression registered utter mystification at finding himself there.

'The monkey, Masterhouse! Get the monkey!' shouted Coddington.

But it was too late. The monkey scurried to the top of the tree, from where it leapt on to the high fence at the bottom of the garden. It perched there for a moment before disappearing over with a barrage of screeches.

The Mask Slips

If that was mockery, it was nothing compared to the sound that they heard next: the laughter that came from Miss Mortimer at the monkey's escape. An utterly startling sound, it drew the attention of every man in the garden. And now that she had unleashed it, it seemed that Miss Mortimer was powerless to stop it. It was wilder, stranger than mockery. It was unhinged. Hysteria.

'Shut up, you stupid woman!' The outburst came from Blackley, his face screwed up as tightly as a fist, beetroot red in his rage. His affable smile, for once, was nowhere to be seen. 'What in damnation are you laughing at? Someone has died. Do you understand? Have you any idea of the gravity of the situation? Well, have you? You, you, you ... *imbecile*?' He waited for an answer. But she was too shocked by the ferocity of his onslaught to say anything. 'Of course not. You have never understood a bloody thing throughout the whole of your useless life.'

Miss Mortimer's face was drained of colour. Her lips were compressed so tightly that they practically vanished.

Blackley shook his head in dismissal. His rage

had settled into something colder, more devastating: contempt. 'Get out of my sight.'

Miss Mortimer's head hung down. She walked away with the stiff, jerky movements of a scolded child.

Quinn was surprised to find that he felt sorry for her. He turned his attention to the man who had inflicted her misery. The choleric heat still showed in Blackley's complexion. It would take some moments for the blood to retreat. However, his irrepressible smile was back in place. If anything, bolder and brassier than before.

'Now then, gentlemen ... do you have any further questions or may I return to work? I hope you will not consider me rude if I remind you that I am a *very busy man*.' Blackley gave the last words a patronizing emphasis, almost avuncular, as if he were addressing young children.

'What's over that fence?' asked Quinn.

Another look passed between Blackley and Yeovil. A nod from the legal adviser released the answer from Blackley. 'I believe the garden backs on to our dispatch yard.' The smile quivered but came through.

'You mean the dispatch yard for the House of Blackley?'

'That's correct.'

'How does one get to it?'

'There is access on Abingdon Road.'

Quinn glanced at Coddington, who took the hint. 'Masterhouse, Lappett. Get round there.'

The constable in the tree dropped to the

ground, staggering upright as he landed. 'I think I've just sprained my ankle, sir.'

'Nonsense. Get after that monkey now, both of you.'

Masterhouse took his helmet back from Coddington with a wince of pain and limped away after Lappett.

'Shall I go with them, sir?' Macadam asked of Quinn. 'I have a chum who is a keeper at London Zoo.'

'What the bleedin' hell use is that?' cried Inchball.

Macadam was undeterred. 'I remember him once telling me about a technique he had for putting agitated monkeys at their ease. You mustn't look at them in the eye. The important thing, if I remember rightly...'

'There's no time for that, Macadam,' said Quinn. 'Just get round there and offer the constables your assistance.'

Macadam hurried away with a bow, while Inchball shook his head, muttering incredulously.

'Will that be all?' said Blackley, drawing himself up complacently.

'I have one more question for you, sir, if you don't mind,' said Quinn. 'Miss Mortimer tells me that you occasionally stay at the mannequin house. There is a spare room kept ready for you. Did you stay there the night before last?'

'Now hold on a minute,' interrupted Yeovil. 'Without knowing at all what Mr Blackley might say in answer to that question, I find I must intercede on his behalf. Come now,

Inspector. You know he cannot be expected to reveal information that might incriminate him. He is under no obligation to answer such an offensive question – one that is highly damaging to both his personal and commercial reputation. If you intend to arrest Mr Blackley, then by all means do so. But you should not forget that he has rights. And by Christ, you'd better be sure that you have evidence before taking such an egregious step!'

Blackley's smile gave the impression that he would love to answer Quinn's question if only he could; regrettably he was gagged by his legal adviser.

'It is a routine question. Naturally we're asking everyone about their whereabouts at the time of the murder.'

'So, you have established a time of death?' There was a glint of sunlight on Yeovil's monocle. It gave his face a mischievous twinkle.

'We don't yet have an officially confirmed time of death. But we are working on a theory that it was sometime on Tuesday night. Mr Blackley, where were you that night?'

'No,' insisted Yeovil firmly. 'I really can't allow it.'

'If he was in the house he might have heard, or seen, something significant. His refusal to cooperate can only be interpreted as a sign of guilt.'

'Under law, it can be interpreted in no such way. Besides, do you not think, wherever he stayed that night, if Mr Blackley had seen or heard anything significant, he would have already come forward?'

Blackley held up his hand to restrain his legal adviser. 'It's all right, Yeovil. I have nothing to hide. Naturally I want to get this business cleared up as soon as possible. I will therefore help the police in any way I can. I worked late that night, it's true. But I didn't stay at the mannequin house.'

'Where did you stay?'

'I worked through the night. At least that was my intention. I may have fallen asleep at my desk. It has been known to happen.'

'And is there anyone who can corroborate this?'

'Really!' protested Yeovil. 'You have Mr Blackley's word. Mr Blackley's word is his bond. He is known to be a businessman of absolute integrity. You may ask anyone about *that*!'

Quinn sighed.

'I'm afraid I don't think there is,' said Blackley. 'I was alone. I sent my secretary, Petherington, home at midnight. But by the same token, I vouch that you will not find anyone to testify that I left the store.'

Quinn decided that there was little to be gained from pushing Blackley, especially with Yeovil in attendance.

'The upshot is, Inspector, that Mr Blackley is unable to tell you anything about the happenings at the mannequin house on the night of the girl's death. I think you will have to agree that there is nothing to be gained from the further questioning of Mr Blackley.'

Quinn could not have continued the interview even if he'd wanted to. At that moment the garden was invaded by shrieks and giggles. A small riot of young women swept towards them, eyes gleaming with an almost predatory excitement. The mannequins, Quinn presumed.

Quinn acknowledged a complex mixture of emotions at the arrival of the mannequins. As a man he experienced a frisson of sexual interest, which in his case was both pathetic and absurd. None of these girls would have looked twice at him, except perhaps as an object of authority and therefore fear. And yet, given his own unhappy history with the fairer sex, it was he who was afraid of them, he had to admit.

A wild unpredictability animated the group. At first sight their mood seemed to be one of nervous hilarity. But Quinn realized there was more to it than that. They bubbled like a pot of boiling water with a dangerous energy. They were in a state of suppressed panic, he realized. Whatever their feelings towards the dead girl, they must have been afraid. A murderer had entered their abode and struck down one of their number. They took refuge in the heedless giddiness that was expected of them. But its tenor today was fierce and fey and empty. They seemed curiously heartless beings.

The unruly explosion of female youth was more wilful and uncontrollable than the monkey.

112

To the staid middle-aged men in the garden, it felt as though they were outnumbered. But once Quinn's emotional responses settled down, he was able to see that there were only four girls, though their excitability and restless mobility made it hard to count them. The men, in fact, outnumbered the girls. But were less vital presences.

Quinn instinctively glanced at Blackley to compare his own reactions to those of the great man. Far from being made uncomfortable by the arrival of the mannequins, Blackley was clearly in his element. He basked in their energy, as harsh and feral as it was. For the first time the smile on his face seemed genuinely one of pleasure. He positively beamed. Quinn was reminded of the expression on Mrs Ibbott's cat Mr Percy when he was being petted by Miss Ibbott. At the same time, Blackley almost seemed to increase in physical size. There was a sense that he was squaring up to the other men there, as if he was ready to face down any challenge to his dominance over the group of females. Of course, there was no one there who would have made such a challenge.

For their part, the mannequins were naturally drawn to Blackley. Their coquettish looks and giggles were, first and foremost, offerings for him. And he accepted them, expected them, as his right.

The sight struck Quinn as distasteful – grotesque almost, coming so soon after Amélie's death.

Quinn realized that he hated and envied the

man in equal measure: the same emotions he felt towards his landlady's cat.

What the mannequins' eyes were hunting for, it soon became apparent, was a glimpse of the monkey.

'Where is he?'

'Where's that monkey?'

'Monkey, monkey, monkey!'

'The monkey murderer!'

'Ooh-ooh-ah-ah-ah-ah!'

One girl in her exuberance even turned a perfect cartwheel.

They are little more than children, thought Quinn.

Did it require so little to distract them from the terror of death? Or had their dislike of Amélie been so great that they exulted in her demise?

A further possibility occurred to Quinn: that one or more of them had had something to do with her death.

He began to look more closely at the interactions between the girls. He noticed one whom all the others seemed to look up to; literally, because she was the tallest, but he also detected a subtle deference in their manner towards her. She was not a particularly attractive girl. Her face was too broad, her features almost coarse. And yet Quinn was fascinated by that face.

She was the only one who seemed in control of her emotions.

There was something going on between her and Blackley too, Quinn realized. Her glances in his direction were not the simple soliciting of approval that the other mannequins went in for. Her look transmitted first a question, then a warning. And something steelier than pleasure entered Blackley's smile in response. He admired her, that was clear; perhaps he feared her too.

Possibly, he wanted her.

'The monkey has gone.' Blackley was staring at the tall, broad-faced girl intently as he spoke. His words seemed to be charged with a meaning that only she would understand.

'Is it a big ape?' asked one of the other girls. 'It must be a big ape if it's the one what killed Amélie.'

''Course it's the one what killed Amélie,' said another girl. 'There wouldn't be another monkey on the loose, would there?'

'Oh, no, it's not big at all,' said Blackley. 'A tiny little fellow. I hardly think he could have been responsible for poor Amélie's death.'

'But that's what the papers are saying.'

'You shouldn't believe everything you read in the papers, should ya?' said the broad-faced girl, who kept her eyes on Blackley as she answered the other girl. It was the first time she had spoken. Her voice sounded remarkably mature – her tone, knowing – compared to the others.

'Marie-Claude is right,' said Blackley. 'Newspapers are not to be trusted.'

So, thought Quinn. *This is Marie-Claude. The other girl with a fur in her wardrobe.*

She must have detected his interest in her,

115

flashing a sly look in his direction. 'Aren't you going to introduce us to your friends, Mr Blackley, *sir*?' Her emphasis of the last word was almost sarcastic.

'Oh, these gentlemen aren't my friends!' laughed Blackley. 'They are policemen. Detectives.'

'I am Detective Inspector Quinn of the Special Crimes Department, and this is Detective Sergeant Inchball. We will wish to talk to all you girls individually, of course.'

'We've already spoken to the other feller,' said Marie-Claude, with a nod towards Coddington.

'Yes, but some new evidence has come to light. Besides, we are a separate department with specialist skills. We prefer to ask our own questions, in our own way.'

'New evidence?' The question came from Yeovil. 'You didn't mention anything about new evidence before.'

'I was not under the impression that I was obliged to.'

'What is this new evidence?'

'Naturally I cannot divulge that information.'

Yeovil stared fixedly into Quinn's eyes, angling his head down slightly. At the same time he held his right hand out to Quinn, as if inviting a handshake. But when Quinn reached out to grasp the hand, it was snatched away to execute a bewilderingly complicated movement in front of Quinn's face. At the same time, Yeovil leant forward to murmur something into Quinn's ear. The strange thing was that Quinn was aware of hearing what Yeovil said, but almost at the same moment had forgotten the words.

'Sergeant Inchball, take the young ladies inside and start going over their statements one by one.'

'I'll go over them, all right,' said Inchball with a leer.

The comment provoked a round of giggles from the mannequins.

Quinn drew his sergeant to one side. 'And you, a married man ... a father!'

'What's that got to do with the price of fish?'

Quinn glanced nervously at Coddington. 'You heard what Macadam said. The department is under scrutiny. We must comport ourselves with the utmost propriety at all times.'

'Well, yes. But with respect and all that, guv, that might be more to do with you always killing our suspects – more than with me having a cheeky larf with a bunch of pretty girls.' Inchball winked. 'You should try it yourself now and then, guv. You might bag yourself a lady friend. 'Course, not with this lot.'

'What do you mean, not with this lot?'

'Well, no offence, guv'nor, but you're old enough to be their father. You'll only make a fool of yourself.'

'And you won't?'

'I'm just trying to set them at their ease. A little bit of friendly banter never did no harm. They seem to like it so far.'

'Keep your mind on the job, Inchball. Is this

117

how you used to behave when you were in Vice?'

Inchball's tone became suddenly stern. 'That was different. These are good girls.'

'Do we know that, Inchball?'

Inchball narrowed his eyes as he assessed the mannequins.

Quinn attempted to bring the discussion back to the investigation. 'Did you discover anything useful from DCI Coddington's notes?'

'Shoddy work, sir.'

Quinn glanced in Coddington's direction. The DCI smiled back blandly. If he was curious as to what Quinn and Inchball were saying, he was too polite to show it.

'Even so, look out for inconsistencies with the accounts they've already given. And I am particularly interested in this mystery benefactor. I have a feeling Marie-Claude may know something about that, though I am not sure you will be able to get it out of her.'

'Leave it to me, guv.' Inchball nodded and immediately set about his commission with gusto. 'All right, you lovely ladies, who's going to be the first to bare all to Sergeant Inchball?' He rubbed his hands and winked at Blackley, whether to goad him or to acknowledge some kind of bond, Quinn did not know. If there was a kinship between men who were at their ease with women, he was excluded.

Obstructions

The garden was quiet again; the men in it suddenly bereft.

Quinn felt himself the centre of a circle of hostile attention, as if the others blamed him for sending the mannequins away.

'Well, if that will be all...' began Blackley with a disappointed air.

'Wait a moment, Mr Blackley, sir, if I may,' cut in Yeovil. He turned to Coddington. 'Detective Chief Inspector Coddington.' Yeovil spoke slowly, his voice a deliberate monotone. 'You need to go and help your men track down the monkey.' He nodded repeatedly as he spoke: small, obsessive movements that seemed intended to wear away all opposition in an onslaught of positivity.

'That's right,' agreed Coddington. 'The monkey. We must catch the monkey. Everything depends on that.' He stumbled off, half in a trance.

With Coddington out of the way, Yeovil repeated the strange hand gesture that he had executed in front of Quinn's face. 'Now then, Inspector Quinn, you were about to tell us about this new evidence you have found.'

Nearly, very nearly – his mouth was open,

and he had already drawn the breath to propel the words. But at the last moment Quinn realized that something was not quite right. 'No, I wasn't.'

'I'm sorry. A simple misunderstanding.'

'I don't know what you think you're up to with all this...' Quinn mimed Yeovil's peculiar hand movements. 'Nonsense. But it won't work with me, I can tell you that.'

'Yes, of course. I can see that. I apologize. It's true, I do have certain skills. A talent. But it only works on susceptible individuals.'

'You were attempting to hypnotize me? You have already hypnotized DCI Coddington – it's obvious. I suppose you put the idea of the monkey as the murderer into his head? For what reason? To divert suspicion away from your employer, Mr Blackley?'

'No, no. I assure you, DCI Coddington came up with that theory, all on his own. I may have reinforced the idea in his mind.'

'Why?'

'I was trying to help him clarify his thinking. But I did not seek to influence it. Inspector, there is no law against what I do. Indeed, you may find it a very valuable tool in your investigation. As Mr Blackley has already stated, I am at your service. I am willing to help you in any way possible.'

'Don't push your luck. Do you not realize how incriminating this is? You were seeking to exercise undue influence over a police officer. It is almost certainly an offence. No different from if you had attempted to bribe me.'

'No, no, no ... I'm sure that's not the case. I do have some legal background, you know. I was merely attempting to assist you. I have sensed that there is some resistance in your mind to the idea of my helping you. I clumsily endeavoured to bypass that resistance. I acted in your own best interests. In the interests of the case. If you withhold details of the case from me, how can I be expected to help you?'

'But you seem to overlook the fact that I have no desire for your help. I do not consider it help. I consider it the opposite of help. I consider it obstruction. Obstructing the police in the conduct of their duties most certainly is an offence. And it is one of which I take a very dim view indeed.' Quinn turned to Blackley. 'I advise you, Mr Blackley, to sever all connections with this man. He can only damage you.'

He turned and trudged back to the house. The long grass whipped around his ankles, spraying droplets of moisture as he kicked his feet through it. He had to dismiss the idea that it was Yeovil exerting some power over him. It was simply the garden holding him back.

There were two ways back into the house from the garden: a side door to the scullery, and French windows that led to a rear drawing room. Quinn chose the scullery. Truth be told, he hoped to find Miss Mortimer in the kitchen. He was keen to get a look at her after her roasting from Blackley.

Expecting Miss Mortimer, he was mildly surprised to see the maid, stooped over the

121

scullery sink, washing dishes. The girl had her back to the door, so wasn't aware of his entrance. Even from behind he could sense her unhappiness. She had the slumped, defeated posture of one who had so often been made to feel worthless that she had come to believe it. He stood for a moment watching her as she absent-mindedly splashed the pots with lather and swung them clumsily on to the draining board. She sang tunelessly to herself all the while. It was a mournful, vaguely Celtic sound, all the sadder for having an undertone of resignation to it.

He remembered that Coddington had described her as 'simple'.

'Kathleen, is it?'

The girl jumped and dropped a pan into the sink, splashing soapy water all over herself. 'Sweet Mary, mother of God!'

'I'm sorry. I didn't mean to startle you.'

'You frightened me!' She kept her back to him, cowering away from his sight.

'I am sorry. Please, there's nothing to be frightened of. I am a policeman. My name is Mr Quinn.' Quinn decided that there was little to be gained from giving his rank. It would only serve to intimidate her further.

'Policeman?'

'That's right. I'm here to try to find out what happened to Amélie.'

'Dead. Amélie's dead.'

'I know that. Did you like Amélie?'

'Yes. She went to church with me.'

'She was a Catholic? Of course. You went to

church together? The church on Kensington Road?'

She flinched at each of his questions but offered no answers.

'Our Lady of the Sacred Heart,' remembered Quinn.

Kathleen nodded stiffly. She had still not turned to face Quinn. 'Father Thomas.'

'You cleaned her room?'

'It was dirty. Horrible.'

'I understand. Did anyone tell you to clean it?'

'I did it for Amélie. She shouldna oughta have that monkey. If Mr Blackley finds out, she'll be in big trouble.'

'But you cleaned up the mess after Amélie was dead, did you not?'

Kathleen gave a jump, like a nervous mouse.

'You didn't want Mr Blackley to think badly of her? Was that it?'

Kathleen turned slowly towards him, her plump face creased and red with consternation. 'Mr Blackley is the Devil.'

'Why do you say that, Kathleen?'

'Father Thomas said so.'

'I see. Why did he say that, do you think?'

But Kathleen had clammed up. She returned to her task with an intensified vigour, scrubbing away at the bottom of a pan.

Quinn heard raised voices from the next room. He recognized one as Miss Mortimer's; the other was a male voice he had not heard before. Realizing that he was unlikely to get anything more out of Kathleen, he stepped

123

through into the kitchen to investigate.

A row seemed to be in progress between the housekeeper and a slender, immaculately turned-out man.

'I'm telling you, the girls must have their lunch now!'

'And I'm telling you, they'll get their lunch as soon as it's ready!'

'Mr Blackley will not be pleased.'

'I can't do anything about that. He will have to take it up with the police. It's the police's fault I am behind today.'

Quinn decided this would be a good point at which to make his presence known. 'Monsieur Hugo, is it?' Although he was confident in this identification, Quinn allowed a note of uncertainty to enter his voice.

'*Oui, je suis* Hugo. *Et vous?*'

'Ah yes, very good. French. I see. I get it. You're Monsieur Hugo and you speak French. Only I did just hear you speaking to Miss Mortimer. Your accent sounded more Balham than Boulogne.'

Monsieur Hugo considered his options for a moment, then demanded, without a hint of a French accent: 'Who are you when you're at home?'

'I am Detective Inspector Quinn, of the Special Crimes Department.'

'A copper.'

'That's right. Very good command of English vernacular you have there.'

'Aw righ', aw righ'. I'm not French, I admit it. Is it a crime?'

124

'That depends. Real name?'

'Hugh Leversage.'

'And you pretend to be French for what reason?'

'The ladies like it.'

'The ladies?'

'Customers. It's good for business. Besides, me ma's French, so it's not exactly a lie, is it?'

'I see. I need to talk to you about the events of Tuesday night. Perhaps we could go somewhere and leave Miss Mortimer to get on with her duties?'

Leversage gave Quinn a quick look of appraisal. 'We can talk in my room.'

Before accepting the invitation, Quinn paused to study Miss Mortimer. She met his enquiring glance with a look of impassive calm. One eyebrow rippled, perhaps quizzically, perhaps ironically. Her recent brush with the rough edge of Blackley's tongue had left her curiously unperturbed. He could only deduce that she was used to it.

It was clear that Leversage took pride in his room. As he held open the door for Quinn there was the hint of a challenge in his gaze. He seemed to be defying Quinn to criticize what he was about to see.

Leversage's taste was what was commonly described as 'artistic'. Indeed, it was almost confrontationally so. The fabrics that hung on his walls were in garish colours, like the abstract paintings that might be found in a modernist art exhibition. His furniture was upholstered in a similarly bold style, so that when Quinn sat down on a gaudy ottoman he half expected to hear the crack of a splintering picture frame.

A poster for the Ballets Russes and sketches of dancers' costumes declared a theatrical bent.

Leversage raised an eyebrow, inviting comment, but Quinn kept his counsel. 'Your position here in the mannequin house is rather interesting, isn't it?'

'What do you mean by that?'

'You are the only man.'

Leversage gave a small moue of inconsequentiality, as if the observation had never occurred to him before now.

'I have heard it said that Mr Blackley does not like men to come to the house. Apart from you. And himself, of course.'

'Mr Blackley has the girls' best interests at heart. He is like a father to them.'

'And you?'

'I beg your pardon?'

'How would you describe your relationship to the mannequins?'

'I'm more like a brother. A big brother.'

'Tell me about Amélie.'

Leversage fanned the emotion away from his face. His eyelids fluttered as if he was struggling with tears. 'That poor girl.'

'You were fond of her?'

'I loved her,' insisted Leversage. 'Like a brother,' he added quickly.

Quinn thought for a moment how best to respond to that. 'I ... yes ... I believe you. But

126

the other girls...'

'Oh.' Leversage shook his head dismissively. 'The other girls were jealous of her. It goes without saying. Only natural, you understand. She was so ... good. So perfect. So much better than them. But they din' mean nothin' by it. They're good girls really. Honest, they are.'

'So you don't think one of them could have been responsible?'

'One o' my girls do that? Are you crazy?'

'Are you aware that Amélie had a fur coat and fur stole in her wardrobe? And many other expensive items in her room.'

'I never saw her wearing anything like that.'

'But it doesn't surprise you?'

'I din' say that. I find it very surprising, if you must know.'

'Have you any idea how she came by them?'

'No idea at all.'

'She didn't receive them from you, as a reward for her work at the store?'

'She most certainly did not.'

'Could she have stolen them?'

'Amélie would never...!'

'Then the only possible explanation is that someone gave them to her. A man, for instance.'

'I don't know anything about that.'

'But you knew Amélie. You can help me guess who might have given them to her. It must have been someone wealthy, must it not?'

'I'm sorry, I can't help you.'

'Did you see Mr Blackley in the mannequin house on the night of Tuesday the thirty-first of

March?'

'Mr Blackley?' There was an unmistakable note of panic in Leversage's stalling.

'Yes, Mr Blackley. You know ... Mr Blackley who owns the House of Blackley department store. Your employer?'

'Oh, that Mr Blackley.'

'Yes. That Mr Blackley. Is there another?'

Leversage ignored that question to answer Quinn's original one. 'No. I didn't see him.'

'Did you notice anything unusual that night? Did you see anyone at all who should not have been here? Were there any callers to the house?'

A splinter of hesitation before 'No.' Leversage's eyes oscillated wildly as he made the denial.

Conversations with Mannequins

Quinn caught up with Inchball in the hall. 'How are you getting on?'

'No one's giving anything away. Tight-lipped little bitches. They all claim to be the dead girl's dearest friend, of course. Don' believe a word of it.'

'They weren't behaving like there was any love lost earlier.'

'Exactly. Managed to turn on the waterworks when I spoke to them, though. Very convenient. How did you get on, guv?'

'I spoke to Monsieur Hugo – or Hugh Leversage, to give him his real name. I can tell he's hiding something but I don't know what yet.'

'Shifty blighter, is he?'

'Something like that.'

'Never trust a man who pretends to be a Frog.'

'I shall try to remember that advice. I also met the maid. Kathleen. She told me a few interesting snippets. I think we may be able to get more out of her, but we'll have to go carefully. Have you spoken to all the mannequins now?'

'One more to do. Marie-Claude. I was saving the best till last. She's in her room. Want to come with me?'

Quinn nodded.

Marie-Claude stood by the open window, smoking. From time to time she wafted the smoke away from her, encouraging it to float outside. She had a room at the front, a view over the street. She looked out warily, keeping herself as far as possible out of sight of anyone below. 'I could get fined if any of his spies see me smokin'. 'Ere, you ain' gonna tell on me, are you?'

Quinn shook his head.

She seemed satisfied with this. 'I ain' gonna pretend. I din' like her. What's the point of pretendin'?'

'No point,' said Quinn. 'It's much better if you tell us the truth.'

'Of course. I know that. I ain' stupid.'

'I can tell that. In fact, I would say you're very smart. Your real name isn't Marie-Claude, is it?'

'Do I sound like I'm bleedin' French?' A gurgle of laughter sounded in her throat, expelling smoke. She became suddenly serious. 'An' you ain' gonna tell him I swore either?'

'We're not interested in that.'

'That's sixpence fine. Diabolical liberty, it is. Diabolical bleedin' liberty.'

'You don't like working for Mr Blackley?'

The girl's expression narrowed suspiciously.

'I like it well enough.'

Quinn nodded, signalling that he would not pursue that line. 'So what should we call you?'

'Daisy. My name's Daisy.'

'Surname?'

'Popplewell.'

''Ere, guv, that bleedin' fool Coddington din' even get their real names,' confided Inchball in an aside.

'So you didn't like Amélie. Any particular reason?'

Daisy shrugged. 'I wun' say there was, no. Just her and me. Chalk and cheese.'

'It wasn't anything to do with her being given your room?'

'Do me a favour. Wha'cha think I am? Twelve years ol'? I couldn' care less about *tha*'.'

'It wasn't your choice to give up your room, though?'

'We do what we're told 'ere.'

'And who told you to do it?'

'Who do you think? Who always tells us what to do?'

'Mr Blackley?'

A minimal movement of the head. Smoke blown out through a tautly drawn mouth. Quinn took it that his guess was correct.

'So what was it between you and Amélie? There must have been something?'

'She thought she was better than the rest of us.'

'Monsieur Hugo – as he's known – says she was.'

'What would he know?'

131

'She had furs in her wardrobe.'

'Oh, yeah?'

'Any idea how she might have come by them? Not on a mannequin's wages, I dare say.'

'I don' know nothing about that.'

'Has anyone ever given you furs?'

'You been snoopin' in 'ere already?'

'A girl like you – I expect you've not been short of gentlemen admirers.'

'Mr Blackley don' allow it.'

'So I hear. That doesn't mean he can do anything to stop it. Or perhaps he is the admirer?'

'I don' know wha'cher talking abahh.' The force of her protestation played havoc with her vowels and consonants.

'Of course not.'

'You won' find anyone to say anythin' bad about Blackley.'

'That doesn't mean there isn't anything bad to say?'

'Not me. Not anyone.'

'You're very loyal.'

'I know what side my bread's buttered on.'

'Perhaps Amélie did not?'

'She thought she was better than the rest of us. That's all I'm saying.'

'Thank you. We'll leave you to smoke the rest of your cigarette in peace.'

But at that moment a gong sounded for lunch.

'No such luck,' said Daisy, squeezing the cigarette out and returning the extinguished butt to its tin.

★ ★ ★

'What do you make of that, guv?'

'Her honesty is refreshing. So far as it goes. Of course, she wasn't telling us everything she knows. Perhaps one can't expect someone who didn't like Amélie to care that much about finding her murderer. But does it not strike you as strange, Inchball, that none of these girls seem frightened for themselves? They are curiously energized by what has happened, but not particularly afraid. It is as if they know who killed Amélie and know that they themselves are safe from further attack. Why should that be?'

'They haven't the wit to be afraid, if you ask me,' said Inchball forcefully. 'I have to say, guv, apart from that Daisy or Marie-Claude or whatever you call her, I have never met such an empty-headed bunch of tarts.'

'What about the other one? Albertine ... Edna ... How did she strike you?'

Inchball's demeanour softened. 'Genuine,' he declared decisively.

Edna was curled up on the bed, knees tucked against her chest, her head craned downwards. She had stopped weeping now. Indeed, she hardly seemed to be breathing. A sprawl of hair covered her face like a veil of mourning, sealing out the world and sealing in her grief. Quinn could not tell if her eyes were open or closed behind it.

A shadow of moisture on her pillow marked where her tears had been absorbed. The align-

133

ment of her body gave the impression that her misery was far from spent.

She looked as frail and fine – and somehow alien – as a dead petal.

There had been no answer to Quinn's gentle knock. And so he had eased open the door, suddenly fearing the worst. It was not unheard of for someone to take their own life in such circumstances. And in the instant before he saw her, it even seemed possible that she might have simply expired under the unbearable weight of her grief; from a broken heart, in other words.

An infinitesimally small movement reassured him – the regular expansion and contraction of her chest, the dead petal stirred by the lightest of breezes.

Quinn prompted Inchball with a nod.

'Edna, love. It's me. Remember? Sergeant Inchball. Inchie, my pals call me.' Inchball flashed an abashed glance towards Quinn. But Quinn nodded encouragement. 'You can call me Inchie, if you like. I mean, we're pals, ain' we? You and me. Inchie and Edna. Pals. That's right, ain' it?'

The only sign of acknowledgement from the bed was the absolute cessation of movement. She was holding her breath, waiting for him to go on.

'I've brought another pal with me. My guv'nor. Why don't you say hello? He won't bite.'

The curve of her body tightened as she pulled herself further away from the world.

Inchball winced in disappointment.

'Hello, Edna. I'm Silas. I'd like to be your friend too. Can we be friends?'

A convulsion passed through the body on the bed. The convulsion decayed into an exhausted quaking.

The manifestation of raw unhappiness repelled Quinn. But Inchball went towards it, perching himself on the edge of her bed, laying a hand on her shoulder. His touch was a lightning rod to her grief, which seemed to pass out of her. She sat up and held on to him, hugging him tightly.

Quinn watched, his fascination tinged with envy.

The touch of another human being unleashed a further bout of sobs. Her grief, it seemed, was greater than her exhaustion.

At last she fell still, surrendering to the fold of Inchball's massive arms. Quinn discovered that the tenderness of a brutal man is especially touching. His patience miraculous.

Inchball eased her back on to the bed. She shook the damp hair out of her face and stared up with enormous, terrified eyes.

Inchball nodded consolingly. 'It's all right, Edna, dear. It's all right.'

For a moment, her face was almost blank. But then the memory of her loss contorted it into a mask of anguish. 'She's gone.' Her voice was barely more than a gasp.

'I know ... I know, love.'

'She's gone!'

'You liked her, din'ya?'

135

'I loved her.'

'I know.'

'I've ... got ... no one now! No one! I am all alone.'

'No, no, no ... No, no, Edna. That's not true. You got me, ain' ya? You got me and Silas.'

'She was the only friend I ever had.'

'Wha'? No. No, I don' believe you.'

Edna nodded insistently. 'The only true friend.'

'What about the other girls? You must have some friends there?'

'They hate me!'

'Nah! Nah, I'm sure they don't.'

'They do. They hate me, just like they hated Amélie.'

'Edna?' cut in Quinn. 'Do you have any idea who might have killed Amélie? Was there anyone who might have wanted her dead?'

'They all hated her.'

'You think one of the other girls might have done it?'

Edna's features crumpled as the tears came again. 'I don't know.'

'I'm sorry to have to ask you all these questions, Edna, at such a difficult time. But if we are to have any chance of catching the person who did this to Amélie we must act quickly. You want us to catch her killer, don't you?'

Edna nodded jerkily, her movements barely under control.

'You and Amélie were very good friends, weren't you?'

'Yes.'

'I expect you told each other everything. If she needed to confide in anyone, it would be you. Is that not so?'

More nods.

'She kept your letters, you know. She kept them hidden. That shows she treasured them.'

Edna looked up, an eager hope enlivening her eyes. 'My letters? You found my letters?'

'We have.'

'May I have them?'

'Not just yet, Edna. We need to keep them for the time being, to help us with the investigation. You do understand, don't you?' But it was hard to be sure that Edna understood anything at the moment. 'Edna, dear, did Amélie ever write letters to you?'

She shook her head with an earnest, over-determined motion. 'She didn't need to. She ... she ... it was enough just to hear her voice. She was everything to me.' Her eyes widened with awe. 'She was a goddess.'

'Did she ever tell you about a gentleman friend? A gentleman friend who might have given her gifts?'

Edna shook her head.

'Are you saying there was no one? She had no ... male admirers?'

There was neither a nod nor headshake at this. She averted her eyes, as if she was shying away from having to consider the question.

'Edna, love,' encouraged Inchball. 'Answer Silas's question, dearie.'

Edna closed her eyes. Her breath came in sharp snatches as she swallowed back tears.

'There was one.'

'Go on,' said Quinn. His voice had none of the gentleness or patience of Inchball's.

'He came here.'

'To the house?'

'Yes. He called on her. Miss Mortimer wasn't going to let him in, but Amélie said it was all right.'

'Who was he?'

'I've seen him at the store.'

'He works at the House of Blackley?'

'Yes.'

'In what capacity, do you know?'

'Sales...'

'A salesman?'

She nodded.

'In what department?'

'Near the Costumes Salon. Locks and clocks and things.'

'Locks and clocks? How very interesting. I thought Mr Blackley kept the location of the mannequin house a secret from the men at the store. How did he know where she lived?'

'He must have followed her,' said Edna.

'Or she told him,' suggested Inchball.

'What happened when he came round?' asked Quinn.

'Sh-sh-she agreed ... to take tea with him. In the drawing room.'

'Miss Mortimer allowed that?'

'She didn't like it. Was all for telling Mr Blackley, but Amélie pleaded with her.'

'I see. And what happened?'

Edna gave a great sigh, which seemed to rally

138

her strength. She was able to sit up and speak with some fluency, although her words had a slightly detached quality. 'It did not end well. He made a scene and stormed off. I believe she rejected his advances. Amélie told Miss Mortimer never to admit him again.'

'Do you know his name?'

Edna sank back on to the bed, her head quivering in a spasm of negation.

'Can you describe him?'

'Lean, angry, selfish face.'

She closed her eyes. Her breathing settled into a regular pattern. Sleep was her escape; sleep, or something more profound: the oblivion of complete physical collapse.

Locks, Clocks and Mechanical Contrivances

Inchball hurtled down the stairs, the soles of his boots hammering out an eager tattoo. Quinn followed more tentatively, but he too sensed the promise of a breakthrough. If he resisted going towards it, it was only because his instincts drew him in a different direction. He was not convinced that a young salesman would be able to afford furs any more than a mannequin could.

Inchball ran into a crestfallen Macadam at the foot of the stairs. 'What's the matter with you? You've got a face like a smacked arse.'

'It got away.'

'What did?'

'The monkey.'

'Your pal's little technique din' work then?'

'It was all DCI Coddington's fault. I would have had it if he hadn't turned up and scared away the little fellow.'

Quinn joined them in the hallway. 'Where is it now, do you know?'

'It got into the warehouse and disappeared behind the packing cases. I nearly had it too.'

'Never mind,' said Quinn. 'I'm not sure we

will get any more out of the monkey than we have already.'

His two sergeants exchanged frowns of deep bemusement.

'We have a lead,' Quinn informed Macadam. 'Not much of one, but still: a lead, all the same. The first.'

'Missy had an admirer at Blackley's,' said Inchball. 'They had a barney an' all. I reckon she broke it off with him.'

'We don't know that,' said Quinn. 'But we're going round to the store to talk to him.'

'I'd better come with you,' said Macadam.

It was Quinn's turn to frown. Macadam's tone suggested a lack of trust. 'Are you afraid that I will do something unfortunate?'

Macadam's answer didn't come quickly enough to convince. 'Not at all, sir. He may try to make a run for it. The more of us there are, the less chance he has of getting away.'

The three policemen entered the store through the goods entrance on Abingdon Road. A horse-drawn delivery van, immaculately paint-ed in bottle green and black, pulled in at the same time. They were obliged to dash out of the way as it thundered past. A heedless, unstoppable force, the symbol perhaps of Blackley's commercial rise. For indeed THE HOUSE OF BLACKLEY was spelled out in a grandiose arch of letters on the side of the vehicle, with the legend *A World of Provision* beneath.

A sullen-looking warehouseman wielding a

broom came out, drawn by the clatter of hooves and the rattle of the wagon over cobbles. He greeted Macadam with a terse nod of recognition. A small curl of sarcasm twitched on his lips, around the tail end of a cigarette. He was no doubt remembering Macadam's earlier efforts at monkey-catching.

'Any sightings of the beast?' asked Macadam.

The warehouseman shook his head as he blew out smoke. He took a moment to contemplate the burning tip of his cigarette.

The driver jumped down from his wagon, whistling cheerily.

'Look lively there, Kaminski. I ain' got all day.'

The warehouseman threw the still-glowing stub of his cigarette casually over his shoulder and dropped the brush. It bounced with a lithe and resonant twang, lying haphazardly where it fell.

The man's carelessness drew Quinn's attention; he slowed his step to eavesdrop on the exchange between the two workmen. Inchball and Macadam hung back to wait for him.

'Mr Blackley'll fine you if 'e sees that,' warned the driver, a sudden wariness stifling his chipper demeanour.

'Blackley ain' 'ere,' growled the warehouseman. His accent was heavy: Eastern European corrupted by Cockney.

The driver smiled uneasily, aware of the lurking presence of three strangers.

'Don' vurry 'bou' dem. Dey go' bigger feesh to fry. Or should I say, monkeys.'

'I ain' got the faintest idea what you're on about. As usual. All I know is we'd better get the ol' van loaded PDQ so I can be on my way again. Wha'cha got for me?'

Losing interest, Quinn led his men on through the loading bay into the cavernous interior of the warehouse. He sniffed the itchy scent of sawdust and cardboard. A dim light from high, grimy windows gave the place a semi-mysterious air. Stacks of boxes loomed, mountains of promise and potential. Who knew what treasures their bland exteriors concealed?

Macadam directed them to a swing door at the far end of the warehouse. They stepped through into a realm where those mountains of promise and potential were fulfilled.

It was evident that the news of Amélie's murder had done nothing to dent the public's enthusiasm for Blackley's great emporium. The shop floor was bustling. 'Is it normally like this?' Quinn asked incredulously.

'Well, I've never been here on a Thursday morning before,' said Macadam. 'But it's easily as busy as any Saturday afternoon I've seen, on the times I've been here with Mrs Macadam.'

Quinn detected the same fierce, almost hysterical excitement in the eyes of the jostling shoppers as he had seen in the mannequins when they had burst on to the garden. They were thrilled to be there. They seemed to be on the lookout not for bargains, but for dead bodies. 'Strange,' he observed. 'The effect that murder has on people. They seem ... enlivened

143

by it.'

Inchball grunted noncommittally. Macadam's expression was anxious.

Quinn continued to observe the streaming crowds. He felt he understood the primitive urge that had brought them there, the need to place one's self close to catastrophe, in order to face up to it. And was there an element, too, of warding off its return? A superstitious belief in the principle that lightning never strikes twice? 'They're after souvenirs,' he realized.

'They ain' gonna make our job any easier,' grumbled Inchball.

'Do you know your way around this place, Macadam?' demanded Quinn.

'The Costumes Salon is through there. Mrs Macadam always will insist on visiting that place.'

'We're looking for locks and clocks.'

'You mean Locks, Clocks and Mechanical Contrivances? Straight ahead. Next to the Menagerie.'

'The Menagerie? That's interesting,' said Quinn.

'It was there that Mr Blackley came to pick up Mr Yeovil, sir.'

'Yeovil was in the Menagerie?'

'That's right, sir. Right there, next to the parakeet cage.'

'What was he doing there?'

'He appeared to be watching the neighbouring counter.'

'Locks, Clocks and whatever?'

'That's right, sir.'

'Watching it? What do you mean?'

'It was almost like he had it under surveillance. I would not say he was hiding, exactly. A big man like that would find it hard to hide anywhere. But he was standing in such a way that he could not be easily seen by the gentleman on Locks, Clocks and Mechanical Contrivances. And when we approached him, he fair jumped out of his skin, sir.'

'I bet he did,' said Inchball. 'The sight of you is enough to give anyone a fright.'

'I got the distinct impression that he was engaged in some kind of clandestine activity.'

'And that was the gentleman he was watching?' Quinn pointed to the man behind the Locks, Clocks and Mechanical Contrivances counter.

The man appeared to be about sixty years old, his bald head framed by stiff, unruly tufts of white hair. A once rangy figure, now starting to stoop with age, he peered out myopically through a bent and battered pince-nez. In truth, he looked an unlikely candidate for Amélie's suitor. At present, as far as Quinn could see, there was no one else behind the Locks, Clocks and Mechanical Contrivances counter.

The elderly salesman's expression was somewhat harassed, his nerves evidently in a precarious state. He was clearly struggling to keep up with the unwonted demands for service from the impatient customers crowding his counter. Some even resorted to pilfering goods, and under his very nose too; a practice that

145

quickly spread when it was seen that these endeavours were met with impunity. It was ironic that a department devoted, at least in part, to security was the object of widespread casual larceny.

Inchball had no patience for such illegality. 'Oi, oi, oi, oi! Put that back! Yeah, I saw you!'

'What's it go' 'a do wiv you?'

'What's it got to do with me? I'll tell you what it's got to do with me, missus. I'm a policeman, that's what it's got to do with me. And so's he. And so's he. So if you fancy a little trip down the nick, then carry on. Otherwise, hop it.'

The counter cleared.

'Thank you so much,' said the salesman, dabbing away perspiration from his forehead and temples.

'S'all righ'. Just doing my job.'

'I've never seen them like this. It's as if they are possessed. Something ugly has got into them.'

'You on your own here today, mate?'

'Yes. Spiggott hasn't turned up.'

'Spiggott?'

'He's my assistant.'

'Young feller, is he?'

'Yes, that's right.'

'Don't you have anyone else to help you, Mr...?'

'Anderson. No. It's just me and Spiggott.'

'And Spiggott ain' here?'

'No.'

'What's he like, this Spiggott?'

Anderson pulled a face.

'A waste of space?' volunteered Inchball.

Anderson contented himself with: 'Well, he isn't here, is he?'

'Lazy.'

'He's filled his head with too many...' Mr Anderson removed his pince-nez from his nose, as if this would help him find the word he was groping for. 'Ideas.'

'What sort of ideas?' asked Quinn.

'Ideas above his station. If he would only concentrate on what he's supposed to be doing. On his job ... And forget all these other...' Anderson waved his pince-nez around, again hunting for the *mot juste*. It turned out to be the same one. 'Ideas.'

'He's ambitious, is he?' said Quinn.

'Oh, ambitious doesn't come into it.'

'Ambitious but lazy,' said Macadam. 'Not a good combination.'

'So the lazy bleeder din' turn up for work this morning,' summarized Inchball.

'In point of fact, he went missing yesterday. He turned up for work in the morning as usual, but when the news of that poor girl's death became known he grew exceedingly distracted.'

''E did, did 'e?' said Inchball suspiciously. He gave a terse nod to Quinn, as if he believed this detail settled the matter conclusively.

'Oh, we all did. It was terrible. The whole world went mad. And then they started coming.' Anderson held his pince-nez up to his eyes and peered fearfully through the lenses towards the surging throng around them. 'Rather

147

macabre, if you ask me.'

'And Spiggott was affected too, was he?' asked Quinn, his voice eager.

'Yes, but it was different with him.' The pince-nez was back in place.

'In what way?'

'Oh, I don't know. It's hard to say.' Anderson's hand went back up to the pince-nez. He hesitated, torn between taking it off again and leaving it where it was. 'Well, he was angry. Everyone else was infected with a kind of...' The pince-nez was back in his hand. 'Well, glee. It's the only word for it. But Spiggott was angry. Then again, Spiggott is always angry.'

'So what happened?'

'I don't really know. I mean, I was very busy myself, you understand. I had a lot on my plate. But I was aware of his not being here quite as much as he might be. It was a source of frustration to me, as you can imagine. I had determined to speak to him about it. But by the middle of the afternoon he was nowhere to be seen. After closing time I went to look for him in the usual places. To give him a piece of my mind, you understand. I made enquiries among his associates but no one knew where he was. This morning it was the same. Mr Davies, who has the bed next to him in his dorm, informed me that he did not sleep there last night. So I'm afraid I had no choice but to report his absence. He's going to be in a lot of trouble when he comes back, I can tell you that.'

Quinn nodded, almost absent-mindedly. His

148

attention was caught by a large clockwork automaton of a Columbine, fashioned from burnished brass. It was about a third life-size. The toy, if toy it could be called, was performing incessant, identical pirouettes. He found himself wondering if Miss Latterly would like it.

Anderson noticed his interest. 'A very fine piece. Are you a connoisseur of automata?'

'Not exactly. How much is this piece?'

'That? Oh, that is seven guineas.'

'To be honest, I was looking for something a little smaller,' said Quinn quickly. 'A music box, for instance.'

'Our musical boxes are over here. They are considerably smaller, as you can see. And cheaper.'

'Do you have anything with a dancing ballerina? Perhaps one that plays the theme to *Swan Lake*?'

'Why, yes, indeed! And very popular it is too.'

Mr Anderson opened the back of a glass display cabinet and pulled out an identical musical box to the one which Quinn had found in Amélie's room.

Quinn took it and examined it as if he were considering it for a gift. 'It's very nice. And how much is it?'

'Two and six.'

'Yes, that's more what I had in mind.' Quinn nevertheless handed the box back. 'Did Mr Spiggott ever purchase such a music box, do you know? There is a discount scheme for staff, I believe.'

'Spiggott?'

'Is he a connoisseur of such things?'

'Not that I know of.'

'What is his area of expertise then? Locks perhaps? Or clocks?'

'I am not sure that he can be said to have an area of expertise. Though, of course, like all young men, he considered himself to be an expert on everything. You could not tell him anything.'

'I know exactly what you mean. Well, Mr Anderson, we are very desirous to speak to Mr Spiggott. Do you have any idea where he might have gone? Back into the bosom of his family, for example?'

'Spiggott and I never talked of such things. Ours was a professional relationship.'

'You mentioned a Mr Davies. Where will we find him?'

'Davies? He's upstairs in Soft Furnishings.'

The sea of customers surged around them. A new wave crashed into the Locks, Clocks and Mechanical Contrivances department. They moved like all crowds do, driven by an unconscious, collective will, dividing around obstacles, filling whatever spaces were available to them. Seizing with spontaneous delight upon whatever was presented to them.

Quinn, Macadam and Inchball found themselves prised away from the counter. A look of panic flashed across Anderson's face as they left them to it, King Canute against an importunate tide.

'So,' said Macadam. 'He's done a bunk.

Reckon he's our man, sir?'

'Why else would he run off?' demanded Inchball belligerently.

'There may be all sorts of reasons,' said Quinn. 'It doesn't necessarily mean that he's guilty.'

'He works with locks,' pointed out Macadam reasonably. 'Perhaps he had the know-how to rig the room up so that it appeared to be locked from the inside.'

Quinn considered this briefly. 'I got the impression, from what Anderson said, that Spiggott would lack the skill. He's just a salesman. You don't need to understand how locks work to sell them.'

'Maybe he just wanted Anderson to think that?' speculated Macadam.

'Spiggott hides his light under a bushel?' wondered Quinn.

'Yes. Or maybe, like many men of the older generation, Anderson is in the habit of belittling his junior colleague. It's possible he underestimates Spiggott's qualities, either through ignorant prejudice or deliberately, because he feels threatened by the young man's ambition and talent.'

'Possibly.' Quinn noticed that Macadam was staring pointedly at Inchball. The difference in the sergeants' ages could only have been a few years, perhaps as little as eighteen months. He was not even sure who was the senior and who the junior; but it seemed that Macadam was very conscious of a disparity.

'And there is the music box to take into

account,' said Quinn. 'I found one in Amélie's room identical to the one Anderson showed me. Although Anderson was not aware of Spiggott buying one, he may have taken it at some time while Anderson was away from the counter.'

'Do you fancy Spiggott for the killer then?' Inchball pressed.

Quinn looked around cautiously. He remembered how an inadvertent word from Coddington had disseminated the story of the monkey-murderer. It was not inconceivable that there were journalists mingling with the crowds at Blackley's today. 'I'm certainly anxious to speak to Mr Spiggott, so that we can rule him out from our investigation.'

'He done it!' cried Inchball. 'Why else would he do a runner?'

'I'm not so sure,' said Quinn, lowering his voice in the hope that it would encourage Inchball to do the same. 'According to Anderson, Spiggott disappeared after the news of Amélie's murder became widely known. If he was the murderer and he wished to flee, wouldn't he be more likely to do so at the time of the actual murder? That is to say, the night before Amélie's death came to light?'

Inchball shrugged. 'I dunno. Maybe he panicked. Thought he could bluff it out, but when it came down to it, when he started to feel the heat, he couldn't handle it. Everybody talkin' about it. Maybe somebody remembered he'd been round to the mannequin house. So he scarpered to avoid answering any awkward questions.'

'At any rate, we need to find him,' said Quinn. 'In order to put those awkward questions to him.'

'They should have his family details in the personnel office,' said Macadam. 'Perhaps there's an address. A next of kin. The offices are in the basement, I believe. Would you like me to go down and take a look, sir?'

'Thank you, Macadam.'

That was all the command that Sergeant Macadam required.

'Inchball, I want you to go upstairs to the Soft Furnishings department and see if you can get anything out of this Davies fellow. Find out if he can vouch for Spiggott's whereabouts on Tuesday night. I would also like to know more about these *ideas* of Spiggott's. And of course, any information about his possible whereabouts now would be most welcome.'

Inchball grimaced. 'With respect an' all that, guv, today ain' the best day to talk to any o' these shop people. I mean, look at it.'

'On the contrary, the pressures they face may prompt them to be less than guarded. Davies may let something important slip without even realizing it.'

'And what will you be doin', guv, if you don' mind me askin'?'

Quinn glanced towards the Menagerie. 'I need to see a man about a monkey.'

The African Grey

Quinn didn't like the way the parrot was eyeing him up. It was looking askance at him, there was no other way of putting it. Getting the measure of him with a nasty sidelong stare.

The parrot is the most ill-mannered of birds. A feathered lout. This one squawked and wolf-whistled before showing Quinn its arse and squirting out a calculated insult.

It had to be said that Quinn didn't like anything about the parrot. He didn't like its stilted sideways shuffle along the perch, or its vicious hooked beak, or the self-righteous way it fluffed up its dirty grey neck feathers. Clearly it considered itself to be better than Quinn.

But the thing he liked least about it was its eye. Quinn felt an instinctual revulsion towards small eyes and the creatures that possessed them. It might be called a prejudice, except that he only realized he possessed this aversion now, staring into the glassy surface of one of the parrot's abhorrently diminutive eyes. It was too primitive an organ to be comprehended by a complex large-eyed being such as himself. The antipathy he felt was therefore quite natural.

It wasn't an eye; it was a tiny black lacquered

stud. Everything evil in the world was concentrated into it.

He experienced his hatred as an overriding impulse to wring the creature's neck.

'May I help you?'

It was a relief to turn and gaze into the eyes of a human being, to see there a gentle despondency, the intimation of fellow feeling, of suffering, and therefore sympathy. The sales assistant was aged somewhere in his forties, with a leanness of figure that hinted at an active life. The animals kept him on his toes, it seemed. But there was a sense, too, that the spring had gone from his step in recent years.

However, his expression lacked the harassed fatigue of his colleague in Locks, Clocks and Mechanical Contrivances. Although there was a constant trickle of shoppers going through the Menagerie – an offshoot of the main torrent that flooded the store – the department seemed to be one of the least crowded. Perhaps this was because all the goods it sold – the animals, in other words – were locked away in cages. It was a less attractive prospect to would-be shoplifters.

The inconvenience of a living souvenir also probably contributed to the area's relative unpopularity. It was one thing walking off with a pilfered trinket from the store where a famous murdered mannequin had worked. It was another thing entirely taking home a terrapin, or some other creature that would either have to be cared for and fed for years to come; or allowed to die and put out with the rubbish.

'I see you are admiring our African grey.'

'No,' said Quinn hastily.

The salesman ignored the denial. 'Appropriately enough, as she's called Miranda.' He smiled at his own wit, a momentary lifting of the sadness that seemed to possess him. 'She's a very clever mimic, you know.'

Not quite managing to prove the point, a grotesque, empty parody of human speech came back at them: *Mick! Mick! Clever Mick!*

'I'm looking for something a little quieter. Perhaps a monkey. A macaque, for instance.' Quinn could not say why he chose to initiate his inquiries in this way. He knew this about himself: when left to his own devices he often resorted to subterfuge, even when there was nothing obvious to be gained. It was second nature, part of his defensive armoury, by which he sought to conceal the uncomfortable truths that shaped his psyche, even from himself. Deceit was his emotional carapace.

That's not to say the question was an out and out lie. He still had it in mind to buy a gift for Miss Latterly. An idle, absurd fantasy flickered into life in the picture palace of his imagination: the image of him presenting her with a monkey in a cage. Would this be all it took to win her over?

He mistrusted the fantasy profoundly, because in it she smiled at him.

'A macaque? Is this because of what happened to that young girl?' The sad-faced salesman regarded Quinn suspiciously, as if to decide whether he was a genuine macaque fancier, or

156

just a ghoulish sensation seeker drawn there by the news of the murder. 'The papers said that a monkey was involved somehow. And that the police suspect the monkey of her murder. Preposterous. A macaque could never strangle a human. The police are clearly idiots.'

Quinn was surprised to find himself defending Coddington. 'I think they may have been misrepresented in the press. But, tell me, do you have any? Macaques, that is.'

'We only have one in store at the moment.' The remark was made discouragingly, the inference being that one macaque could not possibly be enough to satisfy Quinn's need for monkeys.

'May I see him?' Quinn sensed the salesman's reluctance. 'I am looking for a gift. For a lady friend.'

This seemed to win the other man's confidence. 'In that case, Shizaru will do very well.'

'Shizaru?'

'Shizaru, yes. That's what we call him ... Little Shizaru. Though of course, if you purchase him, you may call him whatever you like.' This was added in a resigned but far from encouraging tone.

'*Shit! Little shit!*' suggested the parrot.

'No, Shizaru will do very well.'

The salesman cast a look of mild rebuke towards Miranda. 'He is in fact a very amiable and lively chap. And very dapper, in his little fez! I am sure your lady friend will adore him. Would you like to see him?'

'Yes, I would like to see him very much.'

157

'He's just here.' The salesman gestured to a hutch nearby, the largest in a wall of hutches and cages. The smell of urea-dampened saw-dust and dung was overpowering. Rodents huddled in the corners of their cages, turning their backs on the blandishments of potential owners.

The salesman peered through the wires of the monkey's hutch, which at first sight seemed to be empty. 'That's unusual.'

'What is?'

'Well, he seems to be hiding. He's not norm-ally so shy.' He opened the front of the hutch, exposing the creature's sleeping quarters. Empty. The Menagerie salesman cried out in alarm. 'No!'

'Problem?'

'Shizaru ... has gone!'

A second sales assistant, a ginger-haired youth of about fifteen years, came hurrying up. 'What's wrong?'

'Have you sold him?'

The youth shook his head. 'No, I have not, Mr Kenning.'

'Then where is he, Mr Eccles?'

The youthful Mr Eccles made a deliberate show of looking into the empty hutch, as if he might be able to see what his elder colleague could not. 'He's not there.'

'No. He's not.'

The boy looked at Quinn, as if he suspected him of having something to do with the mon-key's disappearance.

'When did either of you gentlemen last see

him?' said Quinn.

'It was a few days ago now,' said Eccles, his voice cracking with fear.

'A few days ago! You're supposed to feed him every day. It's your *duty* to feed Shizaru.'

'But Mr Kenning, I was told that *you* would be taking over the feeding of Shizaru.'

'You were told what? By whom?'

The youth's brows creased in consternation. 'I can't remember who told me, but it was somebody.'

'But it wasn't me, you fool!'

'*You fool!*' squawked the African grey.

'Mr Kenning, please. Not in front of Miranda.'

'You have been neglecting Shizaru and look what has happened! He has been stolen!'

'He may have escaped?' suggested Quinn.

'Impossible!' said Kenning. 'Shizaru was quite happy here. He has never shown the slightest inclination to escape.' Kenning looked disconsolately into the empty hutch. 'Besides, even if he was able to get out of the hutch – if, say, someone had carelessly left it open...' This was said with an accusatory glare at Eccles. 'Is it likely that he would be able to close it up behind him?'

'I didn't leave it open!' protested Eccles. 'I swear I didn't!'

'Even so, it was still your responsibility to check on him every day.'

'I swear, I received instructions that you would be taking over Shizaru's care.'

'When it comes to the care of the animals,

159

you take your instructions from me, Mr Eccles. Not from anyone else.'

'I understand. I'm sorry.'

'I'm sorry! I'm sorry!' The parrot's unfeeling repetition mocked the young man's apology.

'Mr Blackley will have to be told. The cost will no doubt come out of your salary.'

Young Eccles hung his head in shame.

'And as for poor Shizaru...'

'Shit! Shit!'

'You don't think he could be the monkey that...?' began Eccles.

'No! That couldn't be. Not Shizaru.'

'You did say he wore a hat?' said Quinn, picking up on Eccles's speculation.

'What of it?' said Kenning.

'I believe the monkey that was in the mannequin's room was seen with a hat on.'

'Shit! Shit!'

Quinn saw a tear trickle down from Kenning's eye. The older man was staring into the empty hutch, seemingly willing the monkey to reappear.

Eccles must have noticed the tear too. His face flushed, until it was almost as deep a red as his hair. 'There, there, Mr Kenning. Shizaru'll turn up. You'll see. He's a clever monkey.'

'He was part of our original stock, with us in the old Menagerie. One of the few animals who survived the fire.'

'Fire!'

'Ah, yes, the fire,' said Quinn. 'That must have been terrible for you. A tragedy. To lose so many of the animals in your care.'

'Yes, it was,' said Kenning simply.

'There were rumours that the fire was started deliberately.'

'Oh, it was arson, all right.'

'*Arse!*'

'But the arsonist was never caught?' said Quinn.

'*Arse!*'

'That's right.'

'And there were no more fires. Almost as if the loss of life shocked even the arsonist.'

'*Arse!*'

Quinn frowned. The parrot's interventions were becoming really quite trying. 'Perhaps he only intended to hurt Blackley where he would feel it the most – financially, I mean. Perhaps he never intended to kill anyone.'

'Well, he should have thought of that before he went around setting fires.'

'*Fire! Fire!*'

'But he cannot have imagined it would result in such wholesale destruction – so rapidly. I remember the newspaper accounts at the time. They reported that the place burnt to the ground like that.' Quinn snapped his fingers. 'It was said that Mr Blackley had ignored fire regulations in arranging the interior of the store and that that contributed to the speed at which the fire spread.'

'*Fire! Fire!*'

'I don't know anything about that.'

'And that he has chosen to ignore the same regulations in his reconstruction. Perhaps he has saved money in other ways that could prove to be dangerous. The electrical wiring, for instance. Ah, but at least he moved the Menagerie closer to an exit. That will facilitate getting the animals out in the event of another fire. Strange, isn't it, how there was a greater public outcry about the deaths of the animals than there was for any of the fire's human victims.'

'Fire! Fire!'

It was only now that Quinn noticed a change in the mood of the shoppers flocking through the House of Blackley. He no longer had that sense of a lurid hunger for sensation, the desire to snatch hold of a moment charged with significance. When he had first taken an emotional reading of the crowds around him, he had sensed a certain detachment in their bearing, a belief in their own invulnerability. Their eagerness to be there was only possible because of a confidence that the thing they sought proximity to – death, in other words – could no longer harm them. These were cautious, cowardly people, engaged in a fundamentally vicarious activity; they would not be there if they had thought there was any risk.

Death had already struck, sensationally. And moved on. It was safe now to come and wonder at its wake.

But now, that complacency was gone. Something went through the crowd like an electrical current. It was the sudden realization that death is indiscriminate. That one day it would find them too, and strike them down. And that

162

perhaps that day was today.

Someone had picked up Miranda's imbecilic cry of *'Fire!'* and had invested it with an authority it did not merit by repeating it. To hear the word cried out by a human voice, in a building notorious for conflagration, was indeed a chilling experience. Even for Quinn, who knew the source of the panic. For a split second he heard it and believed it to be a genuine alarm.

'No, no! It's just the parrot!' he cried, when he at last understood what was happening.

But his lone voice could not compete with the roaring chorus of catastrophe around him. He heard the cry carry through the crowd, passed from department to department. And then he heard it echo back to them from distant quarters. Departments out of sight of the Menagerie, where there was no inkling of the existence of an evil-eyed parrot, were infected with the terror that that cry inspired.

Formerly the movement of the crowds had been an impatient crush inwards, towards the centre of the store, wherever that might be believed to be. But now the tide turned, and with a vengeance. Impatience became urgency. Crush became stampede. They were running for the exits.

The new Menagerie, of course, was positioned near the Abingdon Road exit. And so it was a conduit for escape. Quinn and the two salesmen were pushed out of the way. Cages toppled and sprang open. Birds flew out. Huddled rodents jumped to life and joined the

163

fleeing tide.

That wasn't the worst of it.

Quinn was pinned against Miranda's cage, unable to move by the constant press of bodies that now filled the Menagerie aisles. He could see the door that everyone was making for; and could see, too, that it was blocked by people still trying to get in. In their frustration, and fear, those trying to get out began to physically assault the ones blocking their way. Fists were swung, insults hurled. Umbrella tips jabbed viciously at eyes. Cries of panic were mixed with those of incomprehension.

Then, a scream of an altogether different calibre was heard. It was as if all the fear and panic and hysteria spiralling wildly around that building had suddenly organized itself to form one representative sound. A refractive focusing of terror. High, sharp, piercing.

For a moment, all other sounds were stilled, even the beat of Quinn's heart. So that the heavy thud that followed it, the thud of something falling from a great height, was clearly audible. And equally so in every corner of the building, he imagined.

More screams – splinters of the original as it shattered in the unseen fall – rose and reverberated. Quinn imagined a vast kettle drum filled with human distress. *Hell must be something like this*, he thought.

The battle at the door intensified. He saw weaker members of the crowd – the old and the infant – pushed to the ground. A baby's perambulator was prised away from the mother –

what was she thinking, to bring her baby *here*, today? Quinn watched as the perambulator toppled over. He could not see what happened to the baby. Not directly. But he saw its fate mirrored in the horrific transformations of the mother's face.

Lessons Learnt

'Three dead,' said Sir Edward. His face was hidden from Quinn by a copy of the *Evening Standard*. 'And seventeen treated for injuries. One in a critical condition.'

A spasm convulsed Quinn's mouth but he said nothing. His gaze settled on the green leather of Sir Edward's desk. He was grateful for its blankness. He had already seen too much that day.

'One woman threw herself off the third-floor balcony of the Grand Dome. An elderly gentleman suffered a heart attack.' Sir Edward at last looked up over the top of the paper. 'And a baby was trampled.'

Still Quinn was unable to speak.

'Do you have nothing to say, Inspector?'

Quinn curled his hand into a fist and placed it over his mouth. He shook his head.

'You were there, were you not?'

Images of the melee and its aftermath came back to Quinn. When the crowds eventually eased and the realization struck home that there was no fire, no danger other than the self-generated danger of mass panic, the mood of those remaining turned truly nasty. It was almost as if they felt cheated; that they had expended so much terror for no good reason. They naturally looked for someone to blame and turned on the store. The sly pilfering that had been in evidence earlier turned into open, angry looting. And what couldn't be taken away easily was vandalized, or so it seemed.

When this second wave of madness was spent, the store was left looking like a hurricane had passed through it. In the midst of the devastation, a mother clasped a tiny, bloody bundle.

'I was there, yes.'

'There was no fire?'

'No. Of course not.'

'What? Eh? What do you mean, *of course not*? Something made these people believe in the idea of a fire.'

'It was ... it was a parrot.'

Sir Edward let the paper drop. The rise and fall of his eyebrows was more than eloquent; it was devastating. 'A parrot?'

'I believe so.'

'What has led you to this belief?'

'I was in the Menagerie, questioning a potential witness...'

Sir Edward frowned. 'What witness?'

'The salesman there. I was trying to find out about the monkey in the victim's room. I believe it came from the Menagerie at the House of Blackley. It was seen heading back into the store. It may have been trying to find its way back to the Menagerie, which it considers to be its home. A macaque has gone missing from the Menagerie, under unusual – one might

167

even say suspicious – circumstances. The description of the missing macaque matches that of the monkey seen at the mannequin house.'

'What?' demanded Sir Edward incredulously.

'I said...'

'Three dead,' repeated Sir Edward, cutting Quinn off sharply. 'And you talk to me of parrots and monkeys!'

Quinn decided that the wisest course was to keep silent until Sir Edward's rage was spent.

'This was the first day of your investigation and we have...' Sir Edward picked up the paper, only to throw it across the desk at Quinn. It fell short, which only seemed to add to Sir Edward's fury. 'Three dead!'

Quinn flinched. 'The crowd ... the crowd was possessed, sir. Like the swine. In the Bible, sir.'

'I take it that by that you are referring to Luke, chapter eight, verse thirty-three. "Then went the devils out of the man, and entered into the swine: and the herd ran violently down a steep place into the lake, and were choked." '

'Yes. That's the passage I was thinking of.'

'So that's your explanation? The crowd was demonically possessed?'

'Not literally, sir. Obviously. But something took hold of them. If you remember, sir, there was a fire at Blackley's once before. In which several people, and animals, lost their lives. I imagine that memories of that fuelled the panic. In all honesty, sir, having seen the behaviour of the crowd, I am surprised that the number of dead is so low. It was horrific in there. I have never seen anything like it.'

Sir Edward rubbed his palms against his face wearily. 'Where do we go from here, Quinn?'

Quinn frowned, unsure what was expected of him. 'With all respect, what happened has no bearing on the case, sir. The investigation must continue.'

'Yes, of course. That's not at issue. What is at issue is your role in the investigation.'

'I am making progress. I have made *good* progress today.'

'You think this has been ... a *good* day? A day on which you can use the word *good* in any context? In any sense?'

'As far as the case is concerned...'

'You are quite something, Quinn.' Sir Edward winced, as if at a stab of sharp physical pain.

'Your wound troubling you, sir?'

'Never you mind about that.'

The two men were silent for some moments, one simmering in rage, the other in a sense of injustice. 'I cannot be blamed for this,' said Quinn at last, quietly. He paused before continuing: 'I have always believed you to be a fair man, Sir Edward. I remember how you spoke on behalf of your assailant.'

'There's no need to bring that up again.'

'You were able to look with sympathy upon a man who tried to kill you. It's undeniable that Alfred Bowes was guilty. And yet, here am I, not guilty of anything, at least in respect of these tragic deaths. Not even charged with them. On no evidence whatsoever, purely on the basis that I was there, you have decided that this terrible disaster is my fault. You have already judged me. What happened to *Judge not, that ye be not judged?*'

Heat came to Sir Edward's cheeks. He was evidently embarrassed by the reminder of the biblical quote.

'You forget, I was there,' continued Quinn. 'I saw the baby separated from its mother. I saw the perambulator tip up. I saw the mother's face as the crowd surged over the spot where her mite had fallen. If I thought for one moment that I was in any way responsible for that, if I believed that any act of mine had led to that child's death, do you not think that I would take my revolver and blow out my brains? Straight away. Do you think I would be able to live with myself?'

'I am quite aware of your morbid inclinations, Quinn. And have often thought that your antics can be explained by a desire to draw the angel of death towards yourself. You rather mope after death, like ... well, like an un-requited lover. So, yes, I do believe you. It would take far less provocation than this to have you ... do something regrettable.' Sir Edward shook his head impatiently. 'It is just so confoundedly inconvenient, Quinn.'

'You don't need to tell me that, sir.'

'I am thankful to you for reminding me of the verse.'

Quinn bowed his head. He could risk a gesture of meekness and surrender now; he had the sense that the crisis had passed.

He was wrong.

'Unfortunately there are those above us both who do not seem capable of following that lesson. It has again been suggested to me, Quinn, that you should be removed from your command. There is no logic to it, of course. But we both know that the powers that be are not always guided by logic. I myself accept that you cannot be blamed for this terrible tragedy. My masters are keen to blame someone. And I am afraid that your previous behaviour has not done you any favours here. Your handling of the last case in particular is being held against you.'

'Sir Michael Esslyn is behind this, is he not?'

'What? Eh? Let's leave the Home Office out of this, shall we? I'm afraid the general feeling is that you can no longer be trusted to run the department. However, I have managed to persuade them that you should be kept on the case, for the time being at least.'

'Thank you, Sir Edward.'

Sir Edward waved a hand in demurral. 'However, you will conduct the case under supervision from now on.'

'I see. Who, sir?'

'Who?'

'Who will you be placing over me?'

'I need to think about that, Quinn. You shall know my decision in the morning.'

'Very well, sir. Will that be all?'

'The important thing now is that you solve the case. As quickly as possible, and without further mishap. Is that understood?'

'Yes.'

'You will share everything, all your discoveries, and any theories you have been pursuing, with the officer I appoint to oversee the case – whoever that may be. And you will follow his direction in terms of the future conduct of the case.'

Sir Edward pursed his lips and gave a terse nod to dismiss Quinn. But he had one more thing to say. 'What lesson have we learnt from all this, Quinn?'

'Lesson?' Quinn's voice betrayed his apprehension that Sir Edward was about to subject him to another biblical homily.

'Events, Quinn. We are all the victims of events.'

For once, he did not want her to look at him. He knew she was there, at her desk. He could hear the clatter of her typewriter. He recognized her angry energy in the rapid tap-tap-tap. More than that, he could sense her awareness of him.

He did not flatter himself. Her interest was wholly hostile.

What he wanted most from a human being now was a sympathetic glance. An encouraging word, even. But these were things he knew he could not expect from her. She hated him; it was as simple as that.

No, he did not want her to look at him. And he would not be so weak as to look at her.

Except, how could he prevent himself?

He stood over Miss Latterly's desk until she stopped typing and looked up at him. 'Yes?'

Her voice was charged with its usual antagonism.

A stab of disappointment twisted itself into Quinn's misery. He shook his head and moved on.

'I heard what happened,' she called after him.

He stopped and half-turned back. Something in her voice, not quite softness, but a relenting, delayed him.

'At the House of Blackley.'

Quinn waited for the words of bitterness and accusation that would inevitably follow.

They did not come. Only: 'You were there, weren't you?'

'Yes.'

'It must have been terrible.'

Quinn nodded acknowledgement of her concern.

'I heard a baby died.' Her voice was suddenly very fragile and then, in almost the same moment, broken. Her face all at once tear-soaked. Quinn was shocked by the convulsive force rippling in her throat, shaking out bawling sobs of pain.

He rushed to her, knelt and put a comforting arm around her shoulder. He pulled her hot face into his chest.

She pulled away from him abruptly with a stifled cry of repugnance. Quinn backed away too, averting his eyes from her distress, allowing her to compose herself.

He thought he sensed her usual stiffness return, as she struggled to regain control of her emotions. 'I am sorry.'

173

His nervous glance caught her dabbing at her eyes. Her face was flushed with colour. He was taken aback by the sudden realization of her beauty.

'I don't know how you bear it,' she continued. 'You must have to confront so much tragedy.'

'We all have our own ways of dealing with it,' said Quinn automatically.

'And what is yours?'

Quinn hesitated, forced to consider the pat formula he had uttered without thought. He was not sure he knew the answer to her question. 'In truth, I have never had to deal with anything like this before. I would say, usually, I deal with ... tragedy ... with death, violent death ... I deal with it by setting myself against those responsible, and not resting until I have brought them to book. In this case, however, it is impossible to say who was responsible. There is no one for me to set myself against. I cannot round up everyone who was in the House of Blackley today.'

'It was an accident, a terrible accident.'

'Was it? Something took over the crowd – something malevolent, unruly, evil. It was almost as if those who died were sacrificed to it. And the spirit that possessed them seemed to exult.'

'You're frightening me.'

'I'm sorry. Forgive me. I didn't mean it. They were just people. People panicking.'

'But people can do these things. People can do such horrible things.'

'And it is my job – the job of men like me – to stop them.' Quinn smiled and nodded reassuringly. 'Are you all right?'

'Yes. Thank you.' Miss Latterly smiled bravely. 'And here was I, trying to...' She broke off and dipped her head shyly.

'I beg your pardon?'

'I was trying to ... I hoped I might...' Miss Latterly looked up, her eyes wide and unblinking as she stared into his. 'I could see your unhappiness. How miserable you were. How upset you really were by this. I thought it might help you if you were able to talk about it. But I can't ... I'm not strong enough ... I don't want to know about these things.'

'There's no reason why you should.'

'But it's cruel of me. I realize that I have been cruel to you.'

'No.'

'Oh, yes. And the worst of it is I can't help it. I can't be any other way. I can't help you.'

'You have helped me.'

'I want you to know the pain, the horror, the suffering ... *And I want you to keep it a long way away from me!*' It was almost a command. Her words were steeled with a forbidding despair.

Quinn rose to his feet and bowed. He had glimpsed the depth of feeling of which she was capable, only to have it snatched away from him.

Miss Latterly pushed out both hands, as if he was still in front of her and she was driving him away. 'I can't ever, *ever* love you!'

175

What was most extraordinary – and most devastating – about this statement was the acknowledgement that she had considered the possibility.

The Eyes of Miss Dillard

The sun was setting as Quinn darted out of New Scotland Yard. He had his head down, scanning the pavement of Victoria Embankment as if for scraps of comfort, shunning the mindless beauty of the evening. As he came out he had carelessly caught a glimpse of it: the sky igniting in streaks of copper fire. It stirred him to revulsion. *Mindless*, yes, that was the word for it. Mindless and heartless and mocking. An empty spectacle. Gaudy and in poor taste. If this was Sir Edward's God attempting to make amends for the horror of the afternoon, then Quinn rejected Him with contempt.

He could not be bought off, like a child with a treat.

He fled north towards Piccadilly, half in a trance, numbed by the day's events.

A different contempt drove him to avoid the faces of the pedestrians who crossed his path. They were the guilty ones. And their God, who had allowed it, was complicit.

But there was something unacknowledged at the heart of his misery. Oh, it was true enough – as he had avowed to Sir Edward – that he could not be held responsible for what had happened. But there was more to it than that. There was something he had to confront. And

177

it was harder to face than the easy glory above his head.

Quinn passed the newspaper vendor outside Piccadilly Circus tube station without buying a paper. The placard the man was wearing put him off: THREE MORE DEAD AT BLACK-LEY'S.

He entered the booking hall. The tube was not his preferred mode of transport. Normally he liked to sit on the open deck of an omnibus, looking down on the streets it was his duty to protect. Occasionally he would extend his journey, taking circuitous routes so that he could take in more of the city. He'd even do so in the rain, exulting in the privilege of isolation while other passengers huddled inside. On such days it was possible to believe that the city belonged to him alone.

This evening some instinct drove him underground. He had had all privileges revoked, he felt. Even that of sitting on the upper deck of an omnibus.

Was he mad? To go into the bowels of the underground railway system, into a crowded and confined place, after what he had experienced at Blackley's?

Or was he simply punishing himself? It couldn't be discounted.

He showed his warrant card to the guard at the ticket barrier.

The stairs descended in a dizzying spiral. With each step he felt himself coming closer to the confrontation he dreaded. The weight of an unacknowledged guilt pulled him down. If this turned out to be the stairway to hell he would not have complained.

He had shared their excitement. He had understood their glee. If he had not been there to investigate Amélie's murder, he could well have gone out of the same ghoulish curiosity as everyone else; out of the same primitive urge to place himself close to death, in order to prove himself stronger than it.

And if he had been there as a member of the crowd it was perfectly conceivable, when the mood had changed and panic had taken hold, that he could have been the one who trampled the baby.

There but for the grace of God...

Was that the point of God, then? As a recipient of our pathetic gratitude for having once again escaped the fate of some other pitiable wretch?

And if we choose not to give thanks? If we choose instead to rage against the humiliation of it all, to wrest back some power to ourselves; to declare that it is not through God's grace but through our own bloody-mindedness that we survive: where does that leave us?

Quinn articulated the conclusion to which he had been led: *it leaves us in a place where we have no one to answer to but ourselves.*

He came out on to the westbound platform of the Great Northern, Piccadilly and Brompton Railway. The platform was crowded but Quinn had never felt more alone. The isolation that had once seemed a privilege was suddenly a curse.

Quinn inserted his front door key with a frown. He had no memory of making the short walk from Brompton Road tube station to his lodging house, and he was so wrapped up in his thoughts that he made no effort to suppress the creak of the front door as he opened it.

The door to the dining room opened almost immediately and his landlady, Mrs Ibbott, bounded out. Her eyes looked upon him with solicitude; her gentle smile beamed a good-hearted welcome. It seemed almost as if she was about to throw open her arms and pull him into her spreading bosom.

At that moment it struck him that the sun setting over the Thames was not nearly as beautiful as this kindly, middle-aged woman.

'Ah, Mr Quinn, it is *you*! This is fortuitous. We are just about to serve dinner. Would you care to join us? I know you normally prefer to eat in your room, but after what happened today we thought it would be nice if we all sat down together.'

'How do you mean? What happened?'

'The disaster at Blackley's. Did you not hear about it?'

'Oh, yes. I do beg your pardon. I thought you were perhaps referring to something else. Something to do with you, or Miss Ibbott, perhaps.'

'I think it is at times like this that we must come together and...' Mrs Ibbott broke off while she sought the right word. '*Appreciate* what we have.'

'What we have?'

'One another, I mean.'

Quinn was astonished. It had never occurred to him to think of his relationship to the other occupants of the house in such a way. 'We have one another?'

Mrs Ibbott missed the interrogative tone in Quinn's words. 'Very well put, Mr Quinn. We have one another.'

Quinn stared at her in amazement.

'So you will join us?'

'I must take off my hat.' Quinn put this forward as if it represented an insurmountable hurdle.

'And after that, you will join us.' Mrs Ibbott returned to the dining room. As far as she was concerned, the matter was settled.

Whether it was Quinn's unwonted presence or some other influence, the mood in the dining room was muted. Invariably the voluble banter of the two youngest male residents of the house, Messrs Appleby and Timberley, could be heard through the wall. The braying sound was usually enough to send Quinn tiptoeing upstairs; the only reason he might welcome it was because it distracted attention from his entrance.

Appleby and Timberley both worked in some capacity at the Natural History Museum. The two men shared a room on the first floor of the house. They took delight in baiting some of the other lodgers, especially the older ones. In this, they were vying for the appreciation of Miss

Mary Ibbott.

Miss Ibbott pretended to a degree of daintiness and even elegance in her demeanour, which the two young wags constantly set themselves to undo. The weapon they used against her was her own frivolity, the true nature of which had a touch of coarseness to it. If they could provoke her to fits of uncontrollable guffawing, they considered their work well done. An unladylike snort was their most sought-after prize or, failing that, a mock expostulation such as 'You're wicked!' (When they all knew that Miss Ibbott was the wicked one, a willing accomplice in their mischief and her own downfall.)

But it was all done in the most good-natured way. And the high spirits of 'the young people' were tolerated, and even enjoyed, by those who sensed themselves to be the butt of the jocularity but had the wisdom not to be offended by it, even when they did not understand it.

Tonight, however, Messrs Appleby and Timberley were subdued, as was their audience, Miss Ibbott.

As Quinn entered the room all eyes turned towards him; he sensed a kind of desperation in the eagerness of this communal glance – not for his presence in particular, but for any kind of relief from the tedium of their own company. In that moment he thought he understood the forced exuberance of the two young men. It was to hide from them all the emptiness of their existences.

It was not quite true to say that all eyes had

turned towards him. One pair remained stead-fastly averted. A pair of eyes that he had only recently looked into. And although these eyes were hidden from him now, the memory of their colour – the unexpected richness of those pewter-grey discs – still startled him.

The eyes of Miss Dillard.

It had to be said that her eyes were the only impressive thing about Miss Dillard. And because most people never took the trouble to look into them, they never saw the strength and the humanity that resided there. To the other residents, she was a pitiable figure. *Poor Miss Dillard*, were words that often went together. A woman of a certain age. Her looks, never much to speak of, now on the verge of collapse. Her clothes, long out of fashion and visibly repair-ed, hung loosely with a wan, threadbare shape-lessness. Her breath, stale and possibly sickly – and these days too often tinged with a whiff of sherry.

The smell of alcohol and the looseness of her clothes were connected. The small annuity that had come to her after her parents' deaths did not always allow her to do all that she wished to do. Once the rent was paid and other ex-penses taken care of, it was sometimes a choice between regular meals and the occasional consolation of fortified wine.

It was small wonder that no one looked into her eyes. Doubtless they were afraid of what they might see there.

But Quinn had once dared to. At that mo-ment, he had ceased to pity her; he had begun

183

to understand her. For her part, it seemed her gaze was not one of simple neediness, as he might have expected. He saw compassion there, compassion that was directed towards him. It was strangely humbling.

The only spare place at the table was the one next to Miss Dillard. At one time, the prospect of sitting next to her would have filled him with dread. Not so long ago there had been a rumour circulating that she had set her cap for him, after she had been disappointed in love by one of the other male lodgers, since departed.

Despite the fact that she had not turned to look at him, in fact, perhaps because of that reticence on her part, Quinn felt that she was the only friend he had in the room. A part of him still feared the awakening of her emotional interest in him. He knew from that glimpse of her eyes the depth of feeling of which she was capable. It was simply not something that he could afford to encourage.

And yet, as he took his seat, he found he craved a glance from her. He sensed her nervous fidgeting and sought to ease it with a reassuring smile. Her cheeks seemed to have slackened perceptibly in the few days since he had last looked closely at her face. Her mouth sagged weakly. But her eyes shone with that same lustrous colour that he remembered, an almost mercurial luminosity.

Mrs Ibbott ladled mock turtle soup from a tureen. It was white china, decorated with the same blue pattern that was on the bowls and plates. 'This dinner service came from Blackley's,' she was saying. 'As did the table we're eating off ... And the chairs you're sitting on...' With each bowl of soup she handed out, she enumerated another item bought from Blackley's. 'The rug in the front parlour ... The wallpaper in the hall ... The armchairs in the back parlour...'

'The antimacassars?' enquired Mr Appleby as he took his bowl.

Miss Ibbott stifled a snigger.

Mr Timberley gave a warning shake of his head, in all likelihood as satirical as Appleby's original question had been.

Mrs Ibbott paused to give the question the serious consideration she believed it merited. 'Yes, I do believe so. The antimacassars. And all our doilies ... I always get my doilies from Blackley's.' She continued ladling. 'And the curtains ... Most of the lampshades in the house are Blackley's.' Her tone became almost indignant here, as if she believed that this alone should have acted as a restraint on the crowds. 'Really, I don't know what the world is coming to!'

This provoked an outburst from a retired army colonel called Berwick. 'Where were the police? They should have come down on them like a ton of bricks. Round up the ringleaders and hang them. Thrash the rest. That's how we dealt with riots in my day. Country's gone to the dogs.' But it was not clear that Colonel Berwick knew which country he was in.

Quinn sensed a meek flicker of concern from Miss Dillard. For a long time he had believed

185

that no one in the house knew what he did for a living. He certainly had never told anyone. But recently he had realized that his occupation was an open secret. Miss Dillard's sensitivity on his behalf suggested that she was in on it.

'I blame Blackley and his ilk,' said Mr Finch, a lean and rather austere school teacher with a copious beard and socialist leanings. 'He's spent his whole life whipping up a frenzy of consumerism. He can hardly complain if he now falls victim to it. He has created a Frankenstein's monster.'

'Has he really?' said Mr Timberley. 'I would very much like one of those. Which department is it sold in, I wonder? Freakish Experimental Creatures? Or Allegories of Human Arrogance?'

It was Mr Appleby's turn to shake his head. He added something in Latin – or at least Quinn presumed that was the language. The two young men had a habit of communicating asides to one another in Latin.

The other diners concentrated on their soup, the furious clink of spoons registering their irritation. There was silence as the bowls were taken away by Betsy, the maid.

'If you had been there, you wouldn't make jokes about it.' Quinn looked at no one as he made the remark, his voice a barely audible murmur. He saw Miss Dillard's hand dart out towards his arm, only to be retracted at the last moment.

Betsy began to bring out the main course,

liver and bacon with mashed potatoes.

'Were you there, Mr Quinn? You speak as if you were,' said Mrs Ibbott.

'Are you investigating the murder?' wondered Mr Timberley.

'That poor girl!' cried Miss Dillard.

'An extremely interesting case, Quinn,' continued Timberley. 'I envy you.'

'I have not said that I am on the case.' He had not said that he was a policeman. The mashed potato was both watery and lumpy in his mouth.

'Oh, but you don't need to. One only has to look at you. Ashen-faced.' Timberley waved a fork in Quinn's direction. 'Shock, that is. That's the face of a man who's just seen his murder investigation turn into a public catastrophe. What do you think, Mr Quinn? Would I make a consulting detective? Perhaps you would like to make use of my services?'

'Perhaps Mr Quinn has had some bad news of his own – of a personal nature,' suggested Miss Dillard. 'Into which it is not our business to enquire,' she added quickly.

Quinn remembered Miss Latterly's last words to him. *I can't ever, ever love you!* He chewed a piece of liver. The texture was dry. It became almost impossible to swallow.

'Of course, my expertise is not in simian behaviour,' continued Timberley. 'I have no experience in that area other than a long acquaintance with Mr Appleby. However, in all modesty I would venture to suggest that a scientifically trained mind such as my own could be of use to the police.'

Quinn gulped down the liver with a mouthful of water. A rubbery sinew had lodged in the gap between an upper canine and incisor. 'Are you serious?'

'I believe I am,' said Timberley, his eyes popping slightly as if this realization came as a surprise to him. He gave a high nervous laugh that struck Quinn as feverish.

'And what of Mr Appleby? Will he be your partner in crime-solving? The Doctor Watson, perhaps, to your Sherlock Holmes?' Quinn felt a stab of shame, remembering that Blackley had made almost precisely the same joke at his expense.

'I'm more the Moriarty of the piece,' said Appleby, twirling a non-existent moustache.

Timberley's hilarity in reaction to his friend's quip was strangely overdone. A fit of silent sniggers shook his body. Tears began to trickle from his eyes. His face flushed an unhealthy purple. A sudden explosion of noise from him seemed to leave him gasping for life more than laughing. He slumped in his seat, banging the table so hard that all their plates jumped, provoking the mildest of reprimands from Mrs Ibbott. 'Mr Timberley!'

'Timberley, you idiot,' said Appleby, but his smirk betrayed his pleasure.

'It wasn't that funny,' remarked Miss Ibbott, who at times could be the severest of critics.

But Timberley had gone past the point of registering amusement. His emotions seemed genuinely beyond his control. The tears of laughter were now simply tears. His chair toppled over as he rushed from the room.

'What's the matter with him?' asked Mr Finch bluntly.

'Highly strung,' said Colonel Berwick.

Quinn didn't question the instinct that made him turn to his right, towards Miss Dillard. He wanted to see her eyes, to understand through them what she had made of the scene. And therefore, what he ought to make of it himself.

'Poor boy,' she said, and her eyes reinforced the sincerity of her compassion. He knew immediately from her reaction that there was something difficult and serious going on with Timberley. He remembered a time recently when he had crossed the young man on the stairs and thought he had been crying. He had put it down to a decline in his fortunes with Miss Ibbott, or a quarrel with his friend, Appleby. He now saw – or rather Miss Dillard enabled him to see – that there was more to it than that. Whatever had disturbed Mr Timberley was more savage and more destructive than simple unhappiness.

It was only afterwards that it struck him as odd: that she was the one he turned to. And that the act of turning had felt as natural as that of breathing.

That night, he dreamt of the House of Blackley. To be more accurate, he dreamt of Mr Blackley. At first he didn't recognize the great man of commerce, who was dressed in the red and white costume of Father Christmas, com plete with a large white false beard. He was dispensing gifts to children. The children waited their turn in a long queue with unnatural patience. They were disturbingly impassive, faces without any expression of excitement or joy, bodies listless and enervated.

Although he was not a child, Quinn found himself standing in line waiting for his gift.

The line moved forward with infinite slowness. Quinn saw that the Father Christmas figure, as yet unrecognized, was handing out tiny automata in the shape of animals. The toys were extremely lifelike in their rendering and the movement of their parts. In fact, they did not seem like toys at all, but miniature versions of living creatures. He realized too that the animals were limited to the larger species of pachyderms – that is to say, elephants, rhinoceroses, hippopotamuses. Every now and then – presumably for a child who had been especially good – Father Christmas would produce a tiny woolly mammoth from his sack.

Quinn began to feel extremely anxious that Father Christmas would run out of pachyderm dolls before he reached the front of the line. There were children behind him now, waiting just as patiently, and silently, as those ahead of him. Quinn was the only one showing signs of agitation, which were exacerbated by the growing awareness that he needed to urinate. What if he had to rush off to the lavatory and by the time he came back Father Christmas had finished giving out the toys?

His sense of urgency rapidly grew into panic.

190

He felt a kind of repugnance at the mute impassivity of the children. He realized, with a sudden dawning horror, that they were dead. He was terrified of looking down at himself, in case he saw that he, too, was a child. If that were the case, he would have to accept that he was dead also.

For some reason, his dreaming mind decided that the only way out of this situation was for him to shout: 'The animals are escaping!'

The dead children began to scream and run about. Quinn knew that he was secretly pleased by their new-found liveliness. He felt that it justified his cry of false alarm. He had brought them back to life. Surely that entitled him to move to the front of the queue?

It was only now that he recognized the man in the Father Christmas costume as Benjamin Blackley. Now, too, that he saw the pool of red liquid at Blackley's feet, and realized that the red colour of Blackley's costume was due to it being drenched in blood.

Blackley's hand reached into the writhing sack of automata. His eyes were fixed on Quinn's. It was at this precise moment that Quinn became aware that he was in a dream, a dream from which he desperately wanted to wake. But at the same time his fascination at what Blackley would produce from the sack held him. He had the premonition of an even greater horror than any that the dream had presented to him so far.

Blackley's hand came up slowly. Until the moment it emerged from the sack, Quinn had no idea what it would be holding, though somehow he knew it would not be a miniature pachyderm.

All horror fell away. Quinn felt a wave of joy wash over him. He felt at peace, redeemed.

There, balanced on Blackley's blood-soaked forearm, its head nestled into the crook of his elbow, was a perfect living baby, kicking its legs and clenching for life with its tiny fists.

Quinn was weeping as he woke from the dream.

A New Broom

Inchball and Macadam looked up apprehensively from their desks. Relief swept over their faces at the sight of Quinn. He was not sure who they were expecting. Situated in a cramped attic in a forgotten part of New Scotland Yard, the Special Crimes Department received few casual visitors and no passing trade.

Then it struck Quinn. The last time he had seen his two sergeants was after the debacle at Blackley's but before his meeting with Sir Edward. They had fully expected him to be suspended from duty.

Quinn shook the rain off his herringbone Ulster and hung it on the coat stand just inside the door, placing his bowler on the longer hook above. He negotiated his way along the highest part of the room, the only area where he was able to stand upright, to approach the one full-length wall. It was blank now. The photographs from their last case had been pulled down and filed away. But some haunting vestige of their presence remained; a projection of his memory. Unlike the monochrome images that had in reality been fixed there, his mind supplied the colours of the crimes, the blood, the naked flesh and what lay beneath that flesh, the glistening secrets of the dissecting table.

The only way he could block these images out was to begin to cover the wall with new evidence. Old crimes obliterated with new. 'So, what do we have?'

'Are we carrying on with the case?' asked Macadam.

'Of course. What happened at Blackley's store had nothing to do with our investigation.'

'It was on our watch,' said Inchball flatly. 'That's how it works. Don't matter if it ain' your fault; if it happens on your watch, you carry the can.'

'Sir Edward doesn't operate like that.'

'So that's it? We're in the clear?'

'Not quite. He's bringing in another officer.'

'Over us?'

'Over me. So, yes, therefore over all of us.'

'A new Head of Special Crimes?' said Macadam. His voice trembled. 'Who?'

'I don't know. We'll find out this morning.'

'But if he accepts you ain' done nothin' wrong, why shaft you like this?' wondered Inchball.

'I hardly think of it as being shafted,' said Quinn. 'In fact, I'm grateful. Ever since this department was set up I have been lobbying Sir Edward for more men. Today, finally, I have my wish.'

Inchball eyed him sceptically.

'In the meantime, I suggest we carry on as normal. That is to say, we review the evidence we have discovered so far. Inchball, how did you get on with Spiggott's friend, Davies?'

But before Inchball could answer, they heard the approach of steel-capped footsteps. The door opened to reveal a familiar figure in a herringbone Ulster, his mouth hidden by a drooping moustache.

'DCI Coddington?' said Quinn. 'What are you doing here?'

'I ... well ... the truth is, Quinn...' Coddington had the decency to appear abashed, but only for a moment. He drew himself up and met Quinn's incredulity with a defiant gaze. 'I'm your new commanding officer.'

'You? But...' Quinn cast his mind back to Sir Edward's first briefing on the case. The commissioner had been frankly derisive of the local CID's conduct so far. Was it really possible that he had now placed the man responsible for that farce over him?

There could only be one explanation. The choice of Coddington for the job was Sir Edward's way of ensuring that Quinn would retain effective control of the department. Quinn tried to suppress a smile.

Coddington took a few strides forward, possessing the room. The cramped attic could barely accommodate three men at the best of times, but with this new addition, Quinn felt the walls closing in on him. The swoop of the angled ceiling was like a guillotine blade. He almost ducked away from it.

'Sir Edward called me himself this morning and told me to make my way directly over here.' Coddington's tone was complacent, as if all this was perfectly natural. 'I have just come

195

from his office now. He asked me to give you this.'

The envelope bore Quinn's name. The letter inside was typewritten. So, *she* had seen his humiliation, had played her part in drafting it.

He scanned the lines, hunting for confirmation of his theory about Coddington's appointment. He found some comfort. 'I see that it is to be a temporary secondment. For the duration of the case.'

Coddington waved this aside. 'What happens to the department afterwards will be reviewed at a later date.' It seemed that as far as he was concerned, this allowed the possibility of his command being made permanent. Quinn could find nothing to corroborate that in Sir Edward's letter. 'It all depends on how the case turns out,' continued Coddington. 'If we are successful in bringing the killer to justice, then all well and good.'

'And if we're not?' demanded Inchball.

'This morning, in his meeting with me, Sir Edward raised the possibility of closing the department down.'

'He can't do that!' cried Inchball.

'Oh, *you* men needn't worry,' said Coddington to the two sergeants. 'You will be absorbed back into the Met – the regular Met, I mean. You'll be found posts at some station or other.'

'What about Inspector Quinn?' Macadam bridled defensively.

'Sir Edward didn't go into all the details.' Coddington's answer was ominously vague; he avoided looking at Quinn when he gave it.

'None of that matters now. And none of it should be allowed to distract us from the task in hand, which is to track down Amélie's murderer. That is our first priority.'

Quinn was not sure he liked the new tone of authority that Coddington was adopting. He seemed to have no awareness that he had been brought in as a straw man. Or, at the very worst, that he was being used as a stick to beat Quinn, in punishment for past misdemeanours.

'Of course,' continued Coddington, 'Sir Edward was also explicit in his instructions to me that for the case to be considered successfully resolved we must ensure that no one else dies. And that includes whoever we finally apprehend for the crime. We must endeavour to bring him in alive. This time.'

'And what if the killer strikes again?' asked Quinn.

'What makes you think he will?'

'It has been known to happen. In my last case...'

'If I were you, Inspector Quinn,' DCI Coddington cut in sharply. There was a new steeliness to his tone; the esteem, or rather fawning admiration, that he had displayed towards Quinn the previous day was gone entirely. 'I wouldn't be so quick to bring up your last case. Sir Edward held it up to me as precisely the kind of disaster we must avoid.' Coddington even allowed himself a vindictive smirk, or at least that's what Quinn assumed the strange writhing of his moustache to be.

So that's how it is, thought Quinn.

'Clearly it is vital that we apprehend the killer before he has a chance to strike again.' Coddington took off his Ulster and hung it over Quinn's almost identical garment, before finding a hook for his own bowler.

He settled himself behind Quinn's desk, leafing idly through the papers that were lying there. 'So, what have you discovered?'

The two sergeants looked to Quinn, signalling that they would take their lead from him. Quinn nodded calmly. The one thing he must not do was to let his true feelings show.

It was a question now of biding his time. He would let the situation play out and take his punishment like a man. Nothing had really changed. Coddington was still a fool, he was convinced of that. And that was the essential fact he had to hold on to. In all honesty, it was easier to deal with his out-and-out antagonism than his false admiration.

In the meantime, as Coddington had pointed out, the priority was to crack the case. On that they could agree. 'We learnt from Edna Corbett, also known as Albertine, that the dead girl had an admirer. We believe this to be a young man who works at the House of Blackley in the Locks, Clocks and Mechanical Contrivances department – a certain Mr Spiggott. However, Mr Spiggott seems to have done a bunk, his disappearance coinciding with the news of Amélie's death. Macadam, did you manage to get anywhere with the personnel department at Blackley's?'

198

'They had an address for his next of kin. His father, Alf Spiggott.' Macadam consulted his notebook. 'Seventy-three, Cornwall Street, North Lambeth. I presume you would like me to get round there, sir?'

Quinn began to answer but Coddington cut him off. 'I'll decide that, Macadam.'

They waited for his decision.

'Yes, of course. Get round there. Talk to the father; see if he's seen his son. The son may even be hiding out there. Arrest him. Bring him in. Get a confession.'

'Unlikely,' said Inchball.

Coddington's moustache twitched uneasily. 'What?'

'Before it all kicked off yesterday, I had a chat with this feller, Davies, see. Spiggott's chum. Well, nearest thing he has to a chum, I reckon. Davies said that Spiggott hates his old man. A complete wastrel, by the sounds of it. He might even have form. Petty thieving, fraud, that sort of thing. We ought to check with the local nick. Spiggott couldn't wait to get out of the family home. His ma died some years ago, see. And Spiggott blamed his father.'

'I see,' said Coddington. 'So it is unlikely that Spiggott would go to his father's ... There will be no need for you to follow up that lead, then, Sergeant Macadam.'

'Although,' began Quinn, 'whatever a young man might say about his relations with his father, when he finds himself in a fix, blood is always thicker than water, is it not?'

'So Macadam should go round there?'

'On the face of it, that might be a good idea.'

'Right,' said Coddington decisively.

'However,' continued Quinn, 'if the father is sheltering the son, he is hardly likely to give anything away to the police.'

'We can get a warrant? Search the place.'

'We don't need a warrant, sir, given the extraordinary licence under which Special Crimes was instituted. That is to say, we have a de facto permanent open warrant, approved by the Home Secretary. Did Sir Edward not explain that to you?'

'Now that you mention it, yes, I'm sure that he did. So we should get round there straight away?'

'But I hardly think it likely that Spiggott will be holed up at his father's house, do you, sir? Surely they'll have found somewhere else to hide him?'

'Well, what do you suggest, Quinn?'

'One possibility is to ask the local CID to keep an eye on Spiggott's father's house. If Spiggott is hiding there, they may see something – perhaps a figure in the window when the old man is out. If Spiggott's holed up somewhere else, someone – perhaps his father, or a sibling – will be supplying him with food and water.'

'Very good. That's what we'll do.'

'It's probably a waste of time, though. Given what this Davies says, Spiggott is unlikely to go anywhere near his father.'

Coddington's face crumpled into an expression of pain and confusion. 'But ... you ...

what? You said...'

'I agree with you, sir, that it's important to act decisively. However, we mustn't rush into fruitless action that will only serve to waste time and resources, simply out of a desire to be seen to be doing something. The chances are that Spiggott has nothing whatsoever to do with Amélie's death. The evidence against him is extremely circumstantial and hardly compelling.'

A look of sudden comprehension came over Coddington. 'Oh, I know your little game. Trying to make a fool of me, ain' ya? Well, don't push it, Quinn. That's all I've got to say to you. Don't push it. One word from me and you could be drummed out of the force. I'm surprised at you. Playing games like this when there's a killer on the loose.'

'I'm not playing games, sir. This is essential work, I assure you. And it's how we approach every case. First we explore the possibilities in here.' Quinn tapped the side of his head. 'Then we gather the evidence out there.' Quinn gestured vaguely to the window. 'It saves time in the long run, trust me.'

Coddington's eyes narrowed suspiciously. 'Very well. Go on.'

'With your permission, sir, I am interested to know if Sergeant Inchball learnt anything else from his conversation with Davies.'

'Yes. Inchball?'

'Wha'?'

'Did you learn anything else from your conversation with Davies?'

'Well, funny you should ask that,' said Inchball, with a wink for Quinn. 'He did confirm that Spiggott held a candle for Amélie. And that something had happened that had sent him into a decline. I asked him if they'd had a bust-up. He laughed and said...' Inchball read from his notebook. *'If you have a bust-up you've got to have an understanding in the first place.'*

'What did he mean by that?' asked Coddington.

'I take it that he meant that it was all on one side. Spiggott held a candle for Amélie, but she din' want anything to do with him. That's what upset him.'

'And provided him with a motive for murder!' cried Coddington. 'He works in Locks, Clocks and Mechanical Contrivances, does he not? It's possible that he has the skill to engineer the mystery of the locked room.'

'He's a salesman, not a locksmith,' objected Inchball, with a shake of his head.

'However, he did know where Amélie lived,' said Quinn. 'We can't rule out the possibility that he has the knowledge to rig the lock. And if he's capable of that, it's possible that he could have picked the lock to get in when everyone was asleep. Could Mr Davies provide Spiggott with an alibi for Tuesday night, by any chance?'

Inchball consulted his notepad. 'He said that he, Davies, went to bed early that night because of a headache. He cannot say with any certainty what time Spiggott entered the men's dorm, if he indeed did.'

'Spiggott is our man,' said Coddington conclusively. 'Now all we have to do is find him.'

'There was one other thing,' said Inchball.

'Yes?' Quinn and Coddington fired the word at him simultaneously.

'I got the impression that Davies was holding something back. There was something about Spiggott that he wasn't telling me.'

'Do you know,' said Macadam, 'I had the same impression when I was talking to the clerk in personnel. Tight-lipped don't come into it. He knew who Mr Spiggott was all right. Bit of a trouble-maker, our Mr Spiggott is, I'd say.'

'In that case,' said Coddington, with some relief, 'it's decided. Sergeant Macadam, get over to his father's house and see what you can find out. At the same time, I shall request assistance from the local CID. We could do with having someone watch the place.'

Macadam seemed relieved too, glad to have something definite to do. He grabbed his hat and mackintosh from the coat stand.

On his way out he passed the post boy bringing the morning mail. 'Officer in Charge, Special Crimes Department?'

Quinn avoided Inchball's eyes.

'That's me,' said Coddington.

The post boy held out a large brown envelope. As Coddington took it, his moustache tilted upwards on one side, riding a smirk.

The Medical Examiner's Report

A sudden shower lashed the roof. Peas thrown against a drum.

Quinn was inside the drum. Extremes of weather always made him uneasy in that attic room. He felt both exposed and trapped, intimidated by the proximity of the elements. Too hot in the summer, frigid in the winter, in amongst the thunder when it stormed.

Quinn glanced bitterly at the coat stand. This question of the identical herringbone Ulsters would have to be resolved. But he was damned if he was going to be the one forced to change his style of overcoat.

Coddington flashed Quinn a strange, almost exhilarated glance as he laid down the document he had been reading and turned his attention to the photographs of the dead girl that had been enclosed with it.

Quinn knew a medical examiner's report when he saw one. 'May I, sir?'

Coddington grunted acquiescence.

Office of the West Middlesex Coroner
Medical Examiner's Report
Post-mortem examination performed 2nd April,

1914, 8.00 a.m., by Dr James Prendergast, Chief Medical Examiner for the Royal Borough of Kensington.

SUMMARY REPORT

Name: DUPIN, Amélie Yvette
Date of Birth: 6th July, 1893
Age: 20 years
Sex: Female
Occupation: Mannequin
Date of death: 31st March, 1914
Body identified by: Alice Mortimer, Housekeeper

POSITION OF BODY

1. The body was found barefooted but otherwise fully clothed (undergarments in place and intact) on the middle of the bed, lying flat on back. Deceased was dressed in a fashionable satin gown of a pale gold colour, as if for an evening out. Items of jewellery were present on deceased: pearl ear studs, pearl necklace, gold charm bracelet. Head was facing forwards, eyes open. A red silk scarf was found around the neck, knotted in such a way as to form a loop. The loop was sufficiently loose around the neck for a hand to be comfortably placed between the scarf and the neck. The knot was tightly tied and positioned to the anterior of the neck.

EXTERNAL EXAMINATION

2. The body measured 5'6", a normal stature for an adult female. Weight was 7st 2lbs, which is significantly below average for the normal population. Lividity fixed in face and distal parts of the body. Eyes open with petechial haemorrhaging present in the conjuctival surfaces, consistent with death by asphyxiation. Upon removal of the silk scarf, no traumatic lesions were evident. This need not

205

preclude homicide by strangulation, but suggests that the minimum force necessary was employed. (My own as yet unpublished paper on strangulation posits that a force of 7lbs 1oz is sufficient to occlude the airways, whilst a force of 4lbs 6 1/2oz is sufficient to occlude the venous system with fatal consequences. Given the malnourished state of the deceased at the time of death – see below – it is possible to conjecture that an even lesser force would be sufficient to achieve death.)

3. A faint but distinct (and distinctive) elongated contusion was visible at the jaw line below right ear.

4. A degree of muscular atrophy was observed on the arms, which were bare. When the body was undressed, its appearance was found to be highly emaciated, with breasts shrunken and ribs showing through, consistent with low body weight. Areas of dry skin were observed passim. Deceased was found to be wearing a wig. Her own hair was brittle and thinning; scalp flaky. Incipient lanugo on back and arms. Nail missing from fifth toe on left foot. Widespread dental caries. Upper right molar missing. Angular stomatitis evident at labial commissures. Infected lesions also evident on distal section of index finger of right hand, close to nail.

5. The genitalia are of normal development for an adult female; contusion of vaginal labia consistent with recent forced penetration of vagina. Contusions on both inner thighs, again consistent with the use of force. Otherwise, no evidence of defence injuries. Signs of historic contusions passim.

INTERNAL EXAMINATION

6. Hyoid bone and laryngeal cartilages found to be intact; presence of edema in larynx; fracture of the right superior thyroid horn with ecchymosis. This is consistent with the application of minimal force necessary to cause death.

7. Petechial haemorrhaging present in the mucosa of the lips and the interior of the mouth. Otherwise, mucosa intact. No injuries to the lips, teeth or gums.

8. Acute pulmonary oedema; post-mortem blood fluidity.

9. Female genital system structures are within normal limits. Examination of the pelvic area indicates the deceased had not given birth and was not pregnant at the time of death. There is evidence of recent sexual activity; indications that the sexual contact was forcible.

10. Stomach severely distended; gastric walls swollen. Bezoars of undigested food present in gastric contents. Negative presence of alcohol and other identifiable toxicants. Blood tests negative for identifiable toxicants.

CAUSE OF DEATH

11. Anoxic anoxia (asphyxia) caused by ligature strangulation.

FURTHER OBSERVATIONS

12. Microscopic silk fibres were found on the neck of the deceased, identical to fibres from the scarf placed around her neck. It is therefore highly probable that the scarf was the ligature used to inflict death, despite the looseness of the scarf around the neck.

13. There is evidence that the deceased unsuccessfully fought against an act of rape. There is no similar evidence that she fought against her death. The question will quite reasonably be asked by investigators, given the circumstances of the body's

discovery, whether it is possible for the deceased to have self-administered the fatal constriction of her own airways. The investigators will be well aware that self-strangulation (as distinct from hanging) is conventionally held to be impossible. It is certainly inconceivable without some kind of mechanical intervention (e.g., a tourniquet) to override the victim's natural instinct for self-preservation, which would otherwise interrupt any attempt at self-strangulation. A tourniquet or some other device would also be required to maintain the necessary force once the victim has passed out: experimentation shows that one may attempt to strangle one's self to the point of becoming unconscious, but at that point one must necessarily release one's grip unless, as stated above, a mechanical contrivance preventing this was involved. Given the evidence as so far discovered, self-strangulation must be considered impracticable if not impossible. As for that other question an investigator may reasonably put – whether death may have occurred accidentally, that is to say by misadventure – this certainly is not beyond the bounds of possibility. It may, for example, be counted death by misadventure if some animal of sufficient body mass (i.e., > 7lbs 1oz) were to be imagined hanging on the back of the knotted scarf, pulling it tight for a sufficient length of time to fatally occlude the airways; that is to say for 2–3 minutes, or less given the presumably weakened state of the deceased. However likely or unlikely such an accident may be considered in other respects, from a medical point of view at least it is possible. From the medical evidence alone (leaving aside the anomalous circumstances of the scene of crime), *by far the most likely explanation for this fatality is homicidal strangulation. The evidence of rape would argue persuasively for homicide, as it is well known that sexual attack and murder are frequently associated.*

14. As for the time relationship between the sex attack and death, the contusions sustained during rape are such as to indicate it took place shortly before death, certainly on the same evening.

15. The various indications detailed in paragraph 3 above are consistent with malnutrition, whether due to self-induced inanition, deriving from the condition anorexia nervosa as identified by Gull, or to insufficient dietary provisions at the house where she resided. Arguing in favour of the former is the presence of angular stomatitis already noted; according to Lasègue, these small lesions at the corners of the mouth occur in some cases of anorexia nervosa and are thought to be caused by the habit of self-induced vomiting. One possible cause of the infected lesions on the index finger of the right hand is repeated forcing of the finger down the throat to induce vomiting. The widespread presence of contusions does not necessarily indicate a history of violent abuse; vitamin deficiencies due to malnutrition may render the skin prone to bruising. There was no evidence of physiological causation for inanition, e.g. convolvulus of oesophagus.

As an addendum, Dr Prendergast had listed the weights of the deceased's various internal organs.

'So, what do you make of that, Quinn?' said Coddington. His tone was chipper, almost bullish.

Quinn was non-committal. 'Interesting.' He handed the report to Inchball, who had risen from his desk in his eagerness to see it.

'Is that all you have to say?' Coddington's moustache became frantically animated. 'Does it not rather vindicate my original theory concerning the monkey?'

Quinn took the photographs from Coddington without answering. The first showed Amélie fully clothed in a shot of her head and upper torso. It was hard to believe in the beauty she must have possessed in life. Even in the black and white image, the bloated purpling of her face was manifest. Her hair appeared almost luminously blonde in comparison. One might have mistaken it for a sign of health. But Quinn knew from Dr Prendergast's report that it was a wig.

The next photograph was full length. In it she was naked – more than naked, it seemed, because the wig had been removed too. The contrast with the previous image was shocking. Her ribcage was visible and her pelvic bone jutted out sharply below a sunken abdomen. Quinn had never been more aware of the skeleton beneath the skin. Thin wisps of dark hair were plastered to her scalp.

Various close-up photographs were also included. One of her throat, presumably to show the absence of a ligature mark. Another showed her mouth, with the angular lines of cracked skin at the corners that had indicated a habit of self-induced vomiting to the doctor. The associated cracks on her index finger were also represented. Somehow Quinn found these the most disturbing of all the photographs. The bruises on her thighs, shadows of a male brutality, affected him too, of course. But the emotion they stirred served a purpose: it provoked the familiar rage that would enable him to hunt down the perpetrator.

In the face of the damage that she had done to herself, he felt strangely powerless.

Quinn handed the photograph of her thighs back to Coddington. 'Did the monkey do that?'

'No, of course not. That's not the point. We're not investigating a rape. We're investigating a death. The doctor's report leaves the door open to the possibility that she was accidentally killed by the monkey. I don't know what a macaque weighs, but having had sight of that particular beast, I would say it is more than seven pounds.'

'We were not investigating a rape because we did not know that a rape had been committed. Now we do.'

Inchball took the photographs and flinched at the bruises. 'Nasty.'

'According to witnesses,' continued Quinn, 'the only male present in the mannequin house on Tuesday night was Monsieur Hugo – or Hugh Leversage, to give him his real name. And somehow I don't see him as a rapist, do you? We need to explore the possibility that another man had secreted himself in the house that night. And the two most likely candidates are Spiggott and Blackley.'

'Mr Blackley?' Coddington was alarmed. 'Steady on, Quinn. You must be careful before you go accusing a prominent gentleman such as Mr Blackley of ... *this*!'

'You're right. It will do no good to accuse him directly. We must get at him through his creature. Monsieur Hugo knows more than he is letting on, I'm sure. We need to lean on him. Get him away from Blackley and he will crack.'

'Would you like me to do the leaning, guv?' asked Inchball, one eyebrow whipping up sharply.

Quinn deferred to Coddington. The senior officer floundered. 'I am not sure what you hope to achieve by this. If we examine the logic of the medical examiner's report, the girl *must* have died as a result of a freakish accident, with the monkey hanging from her scarf. There is simply no other explanation. The internally locked door and sealed window force us to conclude that no one could have escaped from that room. That she killed herself is also out of the question. The doctor made that clear. Remember *The Sign of the Four*, Quinn. "Eliminate the impossible, and whatever remains, however improbable, is the truth." What remains, in this case, is death caused by the accidental agency of the monkey.'

'But what of the rape?'

'The rape is not our concern here. The poor girl is in no position to make a complaint, alas, so there is little to be gained in pursuing an investigation. We can never know who raped

212

her, because she is no longer alive to tell us. There are no witnesses to the act. We may enter the fact in the case notes, of course. But beyond that, I honestly don't see what we can do.'

'But if we can prove that Blackley was in the house that night...'

'Blackley? This fixation with Mr Blackley does you no credit, Quinn! And do you not think that if that were the case we would have discovered it already?'

'Not if everyone is afraid of saying so. Besides, it need not be Blackley. It could have been Spiggott.'

But Coddington did not even wish to countenance the possibility of Spiggott as the rapist. 'Even if we do discover evidence to support such a proposition, it can only ever be described as circumstantial. No jury would convict. In the meantime we will have caused irreparable – and unjustifiable – damage to a gentleman's reputation. For no good purpose, Quinn. Are we even certain that she *was* raped? Doesn't Doctor Prendergast say something about mineral deficiencies and bruising? Perhaps it was just a bit of rough play that got out of hand. A bit of slap and tickle that left a mark. The bruises in themselves prove nothing. She was certainly no virgin, whatever Miss Mortimer might say about her being a *good girl*!'

'But Prendergast was clear that on the medical evidence alone, the most likely cause of death is homicide. Homicide linked to rape.'

'Then it falls to you to explain how the murderer contrived to escape from the room and leave an internally locked door behind him.'

'Yes, of course. I am aware of that.'

'Have you an explanation?'

Quinn faltered slightly before claiming, somewhat unconvincingly: 'I have several, naturally. But whether any of them are the correct explanation, I am not yet in a position to say.'

'Several?'

'Yes.'

'Pray share them with us.'

'I am not ready to.'

'Ah! Yes, of course. A classic ploy. Sherlock Holmes would be proud of you. Well, I must say, I have always rather sympathized with Doctor Watson when it comes to Holmes's irritating habit of mystification. I am not Doctor Watson. So I am afraid to say that if you cannot offer up an explanation, we will be forced to proceed on the basis that it is simply impossible. Which means that we must accept the doctor's suggestion – the *doctor*'s suggestion, I repeat, not mine – that the hapless monkey was responsible for poor Amélie's death. I shall make my report to Sir Edward.'

'But you cannot simply dismiss the fact that Prendergast offers three possible explanations. Self-strangulation. Accidental death caused by the monkey swinging on the scarf. And homicide. Yes, he discusses in a theoretical way the relative merits of each explanation, reaching the conclusion, I think, that none is entirely satisfactory. Knowing Sir Edward as I do, his first question will be to inquire what practical steps you have taken to prove your preference for one unlikely theory over two marginally more unlikely ones. Where is your evidence, in other words?'

'That's where you come in, Quinn. You have to prove it for me.'

'Prove that the monkey killed Amélie?'

'Yes.'

'And how would I do that?'

'Find the monkey. And weigh it. If it's over seven pounds, we have a likely suspect.'

'And if it weighs less than seven pounds? What then?'

'You could always feed it bananas.'

The downpour had passed. Sunlight flared at the window, filling the attic with a fatuous mockery of optimism. Only Coddington seemed to fall for it. He sighed with satisfaction as he stretched back in Quinn's chair. 'Well, what are you waiting for? Go on, find the monkey!'

A Chip off the Old Block

'I'd like to wring his bleedin' neck,' said Inchball as he and Quinn emerged on Victoria Embankment.

Quinn seemed to give the suggestion serious consideration, before deciding: 'There's nothing to be gained from doing that.' He looked up at the sky. The day was far from settled. The brief show of sunlight was behind them now. Massing clouds threatened another burst of rain. But Quinn had left his Ulster upstairs. He seemed to be losing his enthusiasm for it. 'Besides, we have to face the fact that he may, after all, be right. The monkey may have caused the mannequin's death.'

'You seem bleedin' calm about it all, I must say,' observed Inchball.

Quinn looked both ways up and down the Embankment. With Macadam away in Clapton, they would have to take a taxi. There were none to be seen. The recent rainfall had no doubt increased demand. 'It's necessary to stay focused, despite these distractions.'

''Ere, have you really worked it out? More than one way an' all?'

But before Quinn could answer, a taxi came into view.

Given the havoc that had been wrought the day before, Quinn was surprised to see Benjamin Blackley in place outside the entrance to his department store, ready to greet customers with his habitual smile firmly in place. Today, however, there were few customers for him to greet.

'Inspector Quinn, good to see you again.'

Quinn glanced sceptically over Blackley's shoulder into the interior of the store. 'You're open?'

'Of course.'

'But I saw what it was like yesterday.'

'That's behind us now. My staff worked through the night – in shifts, of course. I'm not a slave driver, no matter what you might read in the gutter press. We managed to have the store open by eleven. It's business as usual for us.'

'I witnessed wholesale looting – and worse.'

'And you did nothing to stop it? You, a police officer!' Blackley made the complaint cheerfully, with a wink for Inchball to secure his complicity in the tease.

Blackley's apparent levity was chilling. But there was something persuasive about it too. Quinn began to doubt whether the disaster of the previous day had really happened; or rather, a small part of him considered grasping the fantasy that Blackley, with his remorseless business-as-usual attitude, seemed to be offering. The image of the baby's perambulator falling over came back unbidden. But so too did the dream-image of Blackley, with the baby restored to life, balanced on his forearm.

'Does it really not concern you? The destruction? The dead? Would it really be too much for you to close shop for a day out of respect?'

Blackley took a moment to consider this, but only – Quinn suspected – from a business perspective. 'Life must go on, Inspector. And commerce ... is life. I have, of course, instituted a fund for the child's family, to cover funeral costs and other expenses. The old man who had a heart attack? Well, these things happen. And as for the woman who threw herself off the balcony ... I believe, if you look into it, that you will find she had a history of madness. Mr Yeovil has already discovered that she had spent time in Colney Hatch. So as you see...'

'Colney Hatch?'

'The lunatic asylum there. Are you not familiar with the place?'

In fact, it was not because he was unfamiliar with the term 'Colney Hatch' that Quinn had questioned it. Quite the contrary. He had spent some weeks confined in a ward in the north London asylum during his breakdown many years ago. 'I have heard of it,' he said darkly.

'Well then, as you see,' resumed Blackley, 'I have given consideration to these things. And upon reflection, I find that it is important that we show the world our mettle, if you will. Opening today makes a statement, Inspector. And that statement is – *Victory!* We have shown the forces of lawlessness that we will not be cowed by them. You as a policeman should understand that. We owe it to those who gave their lives to open our doors as soon as possible.'

Quinn was not strictly sure that he understood the logic of this. In what sense, he wondered, could the dead baby be said to have given its life, which implied some kind of willing sacrifice for the good of a cause?

But Blackley left him no time to formulate an objection. 'Are you looking for something in particular? A gift perhaps ... for a *lady friend*?' Blackley's expression was heightened with knowing significance. So, the Menagerie salesman had reported back to him.

Quinn knew very well what he was looking for. But he did not want to give Blackley any inkling of it. 'Have there been any further sightings of the monkey?'

'I'm not aware of any.'

'You don't mind if we ask around?'

'Are you really here to hunt down that poor unfortunate animal?'

'Those are my orders, Mr Blackley. I think I will start in the Costumes Salon. Any idea where I might find that, sir?'

The crowds that had been in evidence the previous day were nowhere to be seen. Perhaps shame kept them away. There was certainly a chastened atmosphere to the deserted store. In the cold light of the morning after, anyone who had indulged in such excesses would surely want to do their best to forget them. Under any other circumstances, the men and women (*mostly* women, it had to be said) Quinn had witnessed running amok would have appeared perfectly law-abiding, if not respectable citizens. Some had even struck him as well-off.

There were no obvious marks of criminality about them, unless criminality is defined as a kind of hunger. He had detected something akin to hunger in their eyes, or perhaps more accurately, the sating of a wild and previously unacknowledged appetite.

They found Hugh Leversage, in his Monsieur Hugo persona, overseeing a costume display in the centre of the department. Taking his directions was a young man with a pale face and a fragile expression. Things were not going well. The young man was slow to respond, evidently clumsy and incapable of doing as he was told. Such was the impression given by Monsieur Hugo's bad-tempered commands.

'*Non! Non! Pas comme ci! Imbécile. Sot!*'

The young man was not so much arranging as doing battle with an army of headless padded dummies. The more Monsieur Hugo shouted at him, the more flustered he became. At one point he tripped up over a fallen enemy torso, knocking over the few dummies that he had so far managed to wrestle into position.

'*Mon Dieu! Incroyable!*' Monsieur Hugo issued a stream of French oaths with impressive fluency.

The young man cowered on the floor. 'Sorry, Monsieur Hugo. Most terribly sorry, sir. I don' know wha' came over me, sir. I confess I am a little tired, sir. Sorry, sir.'

Monsieur Hugo seemed to relent. Or perhaps it was Hugh Leversage who did so, for the French language was abandoned. 'For God's sake, Arbuthnot! Don't let Mr Blackley see you like that! You'd be out that door faster than you could say pinafore dress with a sailor collar.'

Leversage held out his hand and helped Arbuthnot to his feet. 'It'll be lunchtime soon. You can get forty winks then.' Leversage frowned suspiciously and sniffed the air in front of Arbuthnot's face. ''Ere, 'ave you been drinkin'?'

'No, sir. You know me. Never touch a drop. On account of what happened to my old man.'

Leversage seemed unconvinced but said nothing, catching sight at that moment of Quinn and Inchball. He reverted to French: '*Reprens-tu à travailler! Vite, vite!*'

To Quinn he said, in English: 'You again.'

Quinn pointed to Arbuthnot. 'Am I to take it that this is the gentleman who, along with Miss Mortimer, found Amélie?'

The young man's face flashed apprehension.

'I would like a word with him, if that's possible, Monsieur Hugo. I shall not keep him long. And after that I would like to ask you a few more questions, so please don't go far.'

Monsieur Hugo moved away, muttering and waving his hands in what he no doubt judged to be a Gallic manner. '*Moi? Je ne peux pas du tout sortir de cet Salon! Pas du tout! Vous comprenez? Il faut travailler. Toujours travailler!*'

Quinn turned to Arbuthnot. 'There's nothing

221

to be afraid of. I just want to check your account next to Miss Mortimer's.'

Arbuthnot gave a shudder. 'Funny woman. Very odd. Don't you think?'

'Why do you say that?'

'She didn't seem all there to me.'

'Indeed.'

'Take that business with the picture.'

'You are talking about the picture in the hallway? The one which you broke?'

'*She* broke it. *She* moved the chair, not me. I didn't ask her to move the chair. There was no reason to move the chair. We could have got round it perfectly easily. I swear I had nothing to do with it. What business does she have telling you I broke it?'

Quinn nodded with satisfaction, as if he had learnt something he particularly wished to know. 'Did you notice anything unusual about the key when you got into the room?'

'I didn't really think about the key. I was more bothered about Amélie.'

'Of course. Mr Blackley had sent you round there to see what had become of her, is that correct?'

'Well, yes. He gave me a message for her.'

'I see. What was the message?'

'It was for her ears only. He made me promise not to tell another soul. I could lose my job.'

'You will be in far bigger trouble than losing your position if you do not tell me. You will be charged with obstructing a police officer in the conduct of his duty. It is a custodial offence.'

Arbuthnot shook his head. 'I gave my word.'

222

'You have been drinking, I think. What is the punishment for drinking during shop hours?'

Arbuthnot didn't answer, although the fresh misery of his expression was eloquent enough.

'If you tell me what he said, he need never know. However, if you don't tell me, I shall see to it that he is informed of your inebriation. That is a promise.'

'Oh, you're a devilish hard-hearted individual and that's the truth!' Arbuthnot squeezed his eyes closed in distress, shaking his head violently. A sheen of perspiration slicked his forehead. 'I was to tell her that he was sorry. That he begged her forgiveness.'

'For what?'

'He didn't say.' Arbuthnot opened his eyes again, releasing a flash of genuine fear. 'Listen, you promise you won't tell Mr Blackley that I told you?'

'I shall certainly be discreet concerning your drinking. That is what I promised, I believe.'

'You said he need never know.'

'That was before I discovered the significance of the message. *He need never know* does not constitute an undertaking. It is, rather, a conditional statement – conditional upon factors unknown at the time.'

'I'm done for.'

'Mr Blackley need not know that I heard about it from you.'

'Who else would you have heard about it from?'

'I'm sorry. I can't help that. But I assure you that you have nothing to worry about. The law

223

will protect you. You cannot be fired for assist-ing the police in their enquiries. Now, if you don't mind, would you please tell Monsieur Hugo that I wish to see him?'

Arbuthnot fixed Quinn with a look bereft of hope. He went away, shaking his head and muttering, 'That's a hard, hard-hearted man.'

After a moment Leversage reappeared, snif-fing the air disdainfully. Quinn decided there was no time for pleasantries. 'According to the medical examiner's report, Amélie was raped before she died. Do you know anything about that?'

The shock that registered on Leversage's face was clearly unfeigned. 'Oh, that poor girl.'

'You must understand, as the only male resident of the mannequin house, suspicion naturally falls on you.'

'But ... but I loved Amélie ... as a *sister*. I would never do anything like that. *It's not in my nature!*' Leversage's eyes implored Quinn to understand the full meaning of his emphatic denial.

'Very well. Let us accept that you did not. But some other man did. Do you still maintain that Mr Blackley was not in the mannequin house that night?'

'Mr Blackley?' Again that strange, hesitant stalling that Quinn had noticed the last time he had asked Leversage about Blackley's presence in the house.

'He was there, wasn't he? Come on, admit it, man! It's either that or be charged with the rape yourself.'

'But that's...' Leversage's look of outrage crumpled quickly into one of defeat. He was suddenly bereft of all illusions and hope. 'Mr Blackley wasn't there. That is to say, Mr Benjamin Blackley, the owner and founder of the House of Blackley, wasn't. His son, Benjamin Blackley Junior, the young Mr Blackley, he was in the house that night. He spent the night in my room.'

Even Quinn had not seen this coming. 'Good God.'

'You're bleedin' jokin', ain' ya?' said Inchball.

'It was not anything like that, not what you are thinking. If you are thinking what I think you are thinking. There is nothing between young Mr Blackley and myself – except a certain antipathy. However, I agreed to help him because ... well, because he had acquired certain information regarding my past which he was threatening to make known to his father – which, if he had, could have made things extremely difficult for me here.'

'Criminal convictions?' guessed Quinn.

Leversage closed his eyes and nodded once.

'So you helped him. To do what, exactly?'

'To spy on his father.'

'His father was there, then?'

'No. Young Mr Blackley wanted to discover if his father was having an affair with one of the mannequins. Mr Blackley had announced his intention to his wife to work late at the store that night. Young Mr Blackley suspected that this signalled Mr Blackley Senior's intention to visit the mannequin house. You know that

225

people call it his harem, don't you? And so young Mr Blackley spent all night listening at my door. Well, in truth, all I can say for certain is that he was listening at the door when I fell asleep. When I woke up in the morning he was gone.'

'Where will we find young Mr Blackley now?'

'He will be downstairs. In the basement. He keeps an office down there, next to his father's.'

'Thank you. Oh, one other thing. You haven't seen that damned monkey around, have you?'

But Quinn did not wait to see Leversage's confused frown at the unexpected bathos of this parting question.

Quinn led Inchball past a sign that read MEMBERS OF STAFF ONLY to descend a grubby staircase. Unlike in the store itself, the electric lights here were of low wattage. They gave off a gloomy, parsimonious glow. One or two bulbs flickered, the evidence perhaps of faulty wiring. Below stairs, evidently, no effort was made to match the impression of opulence and welcome of the store itself.

They passed a row of booths like rabbit hutches, where the back-room workers were busy at their tasks: accounts clerks examining their ledger books, fabric buyers feeling sample books, tea tasters slurping from deep tasting spoons.

At the end of a dim corridor they reached two doors: one marked MR BLACKLEY, the other MR BLACKLEY JR. A male secretary at a desk outside served as sentinel to both. He

226

looked up at them enquiringly, leaping to his feet in protest as Quinn rushed past and opened the door to Mr Blackley Jr's office.

There was no mistaking whose son was the young man seated behind the large oak desk. True, he lacked the distinctive mutton-chop whiskers, and instead of an affable smile he wore a look of pinched resentment; but here was the image of Benjamin Blackley, though thirty or so years his junior. To look at him at least, he was a chip off the old block.

'May I help you gentlemen?'

'You are Benjamin Blackley Junior?'

'Yes ... I ... What's this about?'

The secretary was at Quinn's back, remonstrating. 'You can't go in there. Begging your pardon, Mr Blackley.'

'We are police officers,' said Quinn. 'May we come in?'

Young Mr Blackley nodded. 'It's all right, Petherington. You may go back to work.'

Quinn closed the door on the secretary. 'I am Detective Inspector Quinn and this is Detective Sergeant Macadam. We're investigating the death of Amélie Dupin.'

'Ah, yes. Of course. A terrible business.'

'Why have you not come forward before now, sir?'

'Come forward?'

'You were in the mannequin house on the night of Amélie's death. Therefore, we naturally want to speak to you as a witness.'

'I was there ... it's true. But I saw nothing.'

'You were there to spy on your father, is that

right?'

Young Blackley hesitated, momentarily abashed. 'Yes.'

'You suspected him of having an affair with one of the mannequins?'

'One of them? Everyone knows he takes his pick from them all!'

'If everyone knows it, why was it necessary to spy on him?'

'There had been this fellow ... making trouble.'

'Spiggott?'

Young Blackley gave a slight frown of surprise. 'Yes. He'd been round to the house. Upsetting Mama.'

'He was trying to blackmail your father?'

'Oh, it wasn't that! If it was just that we would have bought him off.'

'What was it then?'

'He claimed ... he claimed that the old man was *his* father! Claimed that he'd seduced his mother when she worked here as a shop girl years ago. That he had even promised to marry her. And that Father's rejection of this slut had led to her subsequent alcoholism and death. He was threatening to go public with this whole sordid story. He was demanding a share of the company. Equal shares with me and my brother and sister, for God's sake! With Daddy's real children.'

'Why did this make it necessary for you to spy on your father?'

'Mama was at the end of her tether. She's put up with a lot over the years, you know. We had

228

just begun to hope that the old man was over all that. Of course, this was ancient history, but it reopened an old wound. We had a family meeting. Father promised that it was all in the past.'

'But you didn't believe him?'

'Mama deserved to know the truth.'

'She asked you to spy on your father?'

'Good God, no! I did it on my own initiative. Mama knows nothing about it.'

'And what did you discover? Did your father make an appearance in the mannequin house that night?'

Young Blackley's brow furrowed in momentary consternation. 'No.'

'You may wish to reconsider that answer, sir. We have evidence that Amélie was raped before she died. If your father wasn't responsible then you become our most likely suspect.'

'Raped? No. That's not possible.'

'Was your father there, Mr Blackley?'

'No. I swear on my mother's life that he wasn't.'

'Then you place us in a difficult position. We may be forced to charge you with the rape of Amélie Dupin.'

'Do you really think I would rape a girl my father had slept with? What kind of a monster do you think I am?'

'I don't think you're a monster at all. I think you may well be the son of a monster. Which creates within you ... divided loyalties, shall we say? A confliction of emotions. You love your father. At the same time, you hate him for what

229

he has done to your mother. And for what his past misdemeanours threaten to do to you. You must be worried that the arrival of this illegitimate son on the scene will diminish your inheritance. God knows how many other bastards there might be waiting to come out of the woodwork. How many more could he still create if he carries on with this behaviour? You want to rein him in, but you don't want to destroy him. You're prepared to confront him with evidence of his peccadilloes in the hope of controlling him. But it's another thing to expose him to public scandal. Be careful, Mr Blackley. One can understand your reluctance to destroy him. When all's said and done, he is your father. The danger is, if you're not careful, he may well end up destroying you.'

Quinn took out a business card and handed it across the desk. He smiled encouragingly as Blackley Jr accepted the card. 'Perhaps you have forgotten quite what you saw or overheard at the mannequin house on Tuesday night. Perhaps you need some time to go over it again in your mind. If anything comes back to you, please do not hesitate to get in touch.'

At the door, Quinn turned back to Blackley Jr, shaking his head in gentle remonstration. 'Your *mother's* life? Really, Mr Blackley? Your mother's life is worth less than your father's preservation?'

The young man dipped his head.

Sanctuary

The very first time Quinn had glimpsed the arched opening on Kensington Road he had felt drawn towards it. A breach in the facade of Blackley's dominion, it seemed to promise revelations and discoveries. There had been something personal, too, in the fascination it held for him. As if what he would discover when he ventured through it would have significance for him outside of the case he was investigating.

As he approached it now on foot, he felt that it held the promise of benign mystery. After the pressures of his last case, together with the catastrophe of the previous day, there was something more than inviting about the entrance. It exercised a powerful, attractive force.

'A church?' said Inchball; there was a note of disappointment, almost disgust, in his voice.

They stepped through into a paved courtyard. A single mature lime tree towered over a park bench, its abundant foliage more than enough to fill the space with leafy calm. At some deep level of his being, Quinn felt an impulse to linger. Although the courtyard was narrow, there was comfort in the seclusion it offered. More than that: hope of some kind of

231

restitution, or at the very least of refuge.

'This case has just taken a turn for the darker, Sergeant. And in truth, it was dark enough already.'

'What d'you mean?'

'Think of the young man, Spiggott. He was in love with Amélie. Imagine the impact on his psychic and emotional stability on discovering that she has been sleeping with his natural father – or the man he believed to be his father. Furthermore, we cannot rule out the possibility that Amélie had slept with both Blackley and Spiggott. Or that one of them had forced his attentions on her. And in that case, imagine the impact of that on *her* once she discovered the connection between the two men!'

'What you sayin'? You think she could have topped herself, after all?'

'Doctor Prendergast raised it as a possibility.'

'I thought he said it warn' possible?'

'Well, yes, granted. On the evidence we have so far, it is impossible. There may be something we have overlooked.'

'And you think we'll find it here?'

'Amélie was a Catholic. According to the Irish maid, Kathleen, she attended Mass here. If there was something troubling her – something of this magnitude – it's reasonable to speculate that she might confide in her priest, is it not?'

Inchball gave a noisy dismissive sniff. ''Ere, what about this bleedin' monkey though? Ain' we supposed to be looking for that?'

'Ah, yes. Shizaru. It would be rather nice to

find him for DCI Coddington. Where would you go if you were a frightened fugitive, Sergeant?'

Inchball shrugged and looked up at the ecclesiastic facade ahead of them. 'A church?'

'It can't do any harm to look, can it?'

'But I ain' a monkey!'

'The reality is he may have gone anywhere. Which surely gives us licence to conduct our search anywhere, does it not? And if, while we look for him, we ask the people we meet questions regarding other matters that are of interest to us, no one can object to that, can they?'

Inchball gave a small smirk of appreciation and nodded for Quinn to lead on.

The door closed with an echoing boom, which was quickly swallowed into the prevailing hush.

The scale of the church's interior was the first revelation: surprisingly grand, given its narrow frontage. Quinn thought in passing how it must have rankled with Blackley to have had this prime commercial plot withheld from him. In truth, the impression of scale came mainly from the building's height. Stone arches drew the gaze up to a vast space beneath the vaulted ceiling. Quinn didn't know much about church architecture, but he recognized that the building was not as old as it aspired to be. It was done in an ancient style, but the fabric of the structure, as revealed in the bare stone walls, was suspiciously pristine. An example, he imagined, of Victorian Gothic revival.

Christened in the Church of England, Quinn

had been brought up notionally as a church-goer; that is to say, he was dragged along now and then, mainly during his early years, and in a desultory fashion. Neither of his parents had been particularly religious: his father, not enough to prevent him from taking his own life; his mother, not enough for her to receive any consolation for that dire event. As far as Quinn knew, she never set foot in a church again after her husband's funeral.

At the time of crisis in his own life Quinn had tried to make sense of the world by the exercise of extreme rationality. He was a medical student and considered himself a scientist. He had not sought solace. He had not turned to prayer. He had simply tried to get to the bottom of the mystery of his father's death. And the attempt had almost driven him mad.

His illness had cut short his studies. But it had also awoken in him what might be called the detecting instinct.

He had failed to solve the mystery of his father's death – failed, because the only solution acceptable to him was that his father had not taken his own life. That was a solution that the available facts refused to allow. His way out of this impasse was to believe that there were circumstances as yet undiscovered which would provide the solution he craved. He could not see that this was an act of faith, every bit as irrational as the belief in God that he had come to reject.

He had come to trust in the idea and act of detection, that there were solutions to mysteries, and that they were discoverable, given time and patience. It had felt like a vocation. He had entered the police.

Of course, this church was subtly different to the one he had been taken to as a boy. But as soon as he was attuned to the difference, the signs of its Roman denomination leapt out at him. The abundant flash of gold, the flickering of candles. Rich hanging drapes and ornate crucifixes. The quiet, but inescapable opulence everywhere.

The walls were crowded with paintings, not just of Christ but of obscure saints with gold leaf haloes. Mary, too, was much in evidence, both in paintings and statuary. The most prominent piece was a painted statue of her holding an infant Christ. Quinn felt an inexplicable knot of emotion at his throat as he considered it.

The altar was like a massive elaborate sideboard, a priest's magic box, both ridiculous and impressive. The glinting candelabra seemed like levers waiting to be pulled to operate the machinery of faith.

From somewhere the parish priest had appeared, dressed in the cassock favoured by Roman Catholic clerics. Quinn was surprised by the man's unassuming appearance. His mildly enquiring face, myopic eyes blinking behind wire-framed glasses, was the sort that was easily forgotten, if it was noticed in the first place. If Quinn's reaction was anything to go by, the tendency was to look at the robe rather than the face, to be impressed by the office not the man. He was short too, which added to a general sense of physical negligibility. In point of fact, he was a little on the plump side.

'May I help you?' He was softly spoken but not timid. His smile was gently encouraging, eyes unafraid as they stared searchingly into Quinn's. In that steady gaze Quinn glimpsed a surprising strength. He wondered whether there was more to the offer of help than he had first assumed. He felt that the strange little priest could see the trouble in his heart. He experienced an unfathomable urge to reach out and hold on to the man as if his life depended on it.

'We are police officers. This is Detective Sergeant Inchball and I am Detective Inspector Quinn of the Special Crimes Department. We're investigating the death of Amélie Dupin. I believe she was a parishioner of yours?'

The priest nodded. 'I wondered how long it would take you to get here.'

'You were expecting us?' said Quinn.

'Yes, of course. He's in the sacristy. I've spoken to him. Prepared him. He's ready to talk to you.'

'Who is?' For one absurd moment, Quinn thought the priest was talking about Shizaru.

'Peter.'

'Peter who?'

'Peter Spiggott. I presume that's who you're here to see?'

'Spiggott is here?'

'Yes.' The priest caught the preparatory bristling in Inchball's stance. 'Don't worry, he won't go anywhere.' He glanced towards a doorway in the side of the church, towards the rear. 'He can't get away without coming through here. I've locked the other door.'

'Is he a *Catholic*?' Quinn was not quite sure why he felt the need to ask this question, or why it came out in such an incredulous, almost angry tone. It seemed as appropriate a way to express his amazement as any other.

'No. Not yet. I'm working on it, of course. What he is, is a hater of Mr Blackley. That we have in common. It's not the only thing that has drawn us together. We both loved Amélie. I, as her priest and confessor. He ... well, his relationship with her was problematic, shall we say?'

'Guv,' Inchball cut in. 'Shouldn't we...?' He angled his head towards the sacristy door, the movement tense and minimal.

Quinn nodded.

Slowly, silently, with infinite care, Inchball withdrew a revolver from inside his jacket.

'No!' cried the priest.

Quinn gestured for Inchball to put the gun away. At a further signal from Quinn, the two policemen swept, with the stealth and suddenness of spiders, towards the sacristy door and threw it open.

The door on the other side of the room was open inwards, giving a glimpse of brick wall outside. An empty camp bed, the blanket discarded untidily on the floor, was the only sign of Spiggott that they found.

Sergeant Inchball jerked his head towards the

237

open door. 'I suppose you want me to...' But before he could give chase, the little priest darted across the room and outside.

A Question of Conscience

A moment later, two men returned. The priest and a young man with a lean, unhappy expression.

'I managed to prevail on Peter to come back. I told him you would listen to his side of the story and not prejudge him.'

'I didn't kill Amélie,' Spiggott insisted.

'Did you rape her?' asked Quinn.

'Rape her?' Spiggott's face was already drained of colour. It turned from white to grey. His whole being seemed to shrink in on itself. 'She was raped?'

'Sweet Mary, mother of Jesus, as if that poor girl hadn't suffered enough...'

'Wait till I get my hands on that monster.' A grim intensity sharpened Spiggott's stare.

'Who do you mean, *monster*?'

'Blackley, of course. That's who did it. Blackley raped her. I'd swear on it. And he killed her. He must have.'

'Benjamin Blackley? Benjamin Blackley Senior, just to be clear?'

'Yes.'

'Those are very serious accusations, Mr Spiggott. If you have information concerning Mr Blackley and Amélie, why did you not come

239

forward before now?'

'Because I knew you wouldn't believe me.'

'But why run away?'

'To get away from Blackley. You don't know what he's capable of. I was afraid. I needed time to think. As soon as I heard about Amélie's death I knew he was responsible. But I couldn't go to the police. Blackley would just deny it and I had no evidence. Somehow he'd turn the tables on me. I needed to think things through. To come up with a plan. I knew this was the one place that Blackley would never come. I knew that Father Thomas would be sympathetic.'

'You were afraid, you say? Of your own father?'

'You know about that? Who told you?'

'It doesn't matter. You've been making trouble about it. There are plenty of people who have heard you.'

'He *is* my father. All I have been doing is stating the truth.'

'But he doesn't acknowledge you?'

'Of course not! He has his *reputation* to maintain. I first came to him five years ago. After my mother died. She told me on her death bed what my true heritage was. Of course, Blackley denied it then. But he tried to buy me off all the same. He gave me that pathetic job to shut me up. Why would he have done that unless he felt guilty?'

'Perhaps he felt sorry for you. That doesn't prove you were his son. I imagine a wealthy man like Blackley has all sorts of individuals making claims on him.'

'But my claim is valid!'

'That was five years ago, you say?'

'More or less.'

'And you kept quiet about it until recently? Kept your head down, got on with the job? Is that so?'

'Yes.'

'Why the change?'

'That day when I first went to him he refused to acknowledge me, of course. He was angry. He swore. He threatened me. Then, when he saw I wouldn't be browbeaten, that I was determined – he changed his tune. Oh, he still wouldn't admit it, though he did admit that he remembered my mother. He seemed quite upset by the news of her death. And then he offered me the position. I thought, I allowed myself to hope, that one day he might acknowledge what he could not then. I felt as if I was on probation – to see if I would pass muster as his son. "We'll see," he had said. "Come and work for me and we'll see." Those were his final words of that first interview. No doubt he wanted me in the store so he could keep an eye on me. I do believe I was being spied on. There was a man. A curious man with a monocle. But I didn't mind. I had invested all my hopes in the half-promise of that "We'll see". But I came to realize that he had no intention of acknowledging me, ever, no matter what I did. "We'll see" was just to keep me in line. To make sure I behaved myself.'

'And then you met Amélie?'

241

'Yes. I dared to hope...' Spiggott corrected himself: '*We* dared to hope ... that we might one day marry. If that was to be, I realized that I needed to improve my prospects. So I went back to Blackley and restated my claim. His position hadn't changed. I'd done everything he'd asked, but he still wouldn't acknowledge me.'

'Why did you run away just now?'

'I didn't run away. I went outside for a breath of fresh air. I was only in the passageway.'

'But Father Thomas had locked the door.'

'Yes, and he left the key in it.' Spiggott swung the door to, revealing the key still in place on the inside.

'Well, that explains *that* little mystery!' said Father Thomas cheerily.

'I didn't realize I was a prisoner.' Spiggott glared resentfully at the priest.

'It was for your own good, Peter. I was worried about you. Some of the things you said last night ... I was worried what you might do.'

'You hate Blackley as much as I do. You called him the devil incarnate.'

'Yes, and I am sure that he will be judged and receive his punishment in the next world.'

'I don't believe in the next world. I want him punished now.'

Quinn intervened. 'What exactly were you worried about, Father?'

The look Father Thomas directed at Spiggott was unexpectedly stern. 'Peter said some rash things last night. I had a duty to take them seriously.'

'Please be more specific.'

'There's no need to be.' The priest spoke with quiet authority. 'The crisis has passed, I am confident.'

'He threatened to kill Blackley? Is that it?' said Quinn.

'It doesn't matter. I took precautions to ensure it didn't happen. Mr Blackley is still alive, I presume?'

'Though evidently you *didn't* take precautions,' Quinn pointed out. 'You left the key in the door. Perhaps secretly you hoped he would go through with his threat. Your subconscious mind sabotaged the conscious act.'

'Is that psychology?' asked Father Thomas. His air of innocence seemed intended to mask a hostile sarcasm.

'You mentioned before that you were Amélie's confessor?'

'Yes. However, you'll understand that I'm not at liberty to disclose what has been revealed to me in the sanctity of the confessional.'

'I'm afraid that English law no longer recognizes the priest-penitent privilege, Father.'

'Ah, but it's a question of conscience, isn't it, Inspector? I'm sure you wouldn't want to force me to do anything that goes against my conscience.'

'And *I'm* sure that won't be necessary. You've talked these matters through with Mr Spiggott?'

'To some extent, yes.'

'But not in the confessional box?'

'No.'

'So you can have no compunction about revealing what has been discussed between the two of you?'

'That's ... true, I suppose,' Father Thomas conceded reluctantly.

'Very well. What was the nature of the relationship between Amélie and Mr Blackley Senior?'

'A complex one. That of an employer and employee. Of a master and servant, you might say – or more accurately, slave. Of a powerful bully of a man and a meek, lonely, submissive girl.'

'Was she his mistress?'

'Mistress? What a word is that for what goes on between a man like Blackley and a girl like Amélie!'

'He bought her things, I believe. Expensive gifts.'

'Are you saying she was his whore?'

'Oi, language. An' you a man of God,' said Inchball, with deadpan and deliberate irony.

'You cannot serve God fully unless you are well versed in the workings of the Devil.'

'But their relationship was of a sexual nature, was it not? And had been going on for some time?'

'For long enough, I suppose.'

'And you, Mr Spiggott – you were in love with Amélie, were you not?'

Spiggott clenched into a knot of misery. 'You have no idea how painful this is for me.'

'Were your feelings for her requited?'

'I believe so, yes. I had reason to hope.

Until...'

'Until Amélie found out about your relationship to Blackley? That you were his son, or believed yourself to be. That was the day you went round to the mannequin house and were witnessed arguing with her, was it not?'

'Yes. I ... had no idea about ... well, about her and Blackley. I decided to tell her that I was Blackley's son because ... well, because it's true ... but also because I thought it might change her view of what my prospects were. As Blackley's son, I have a right to expect a quarter share of the company when he dies. He has three other children with his wife.'

'Yes. I have met his eldest son, Benjamin Blackley Junior.'

'No! I am older than Ben Blackley! I am Blackley's first child!'

'What was Amélie's reaction when you broke this news to her?'

'It was not what I had hoped for. She became very upset. She said it could never be. I couldn't understand. And then she told me.'

'About Blackley?'

'Yes.'

'And your reaction to that?'

'I don't know. I was numb. I knew that I hated him even more.'

'So it was over between you and Amélie?'

'Was it? I hoped she would finish with Blackley. I believe that's what she intended to do.'

'Why do you believe that?'

Spiggott cast a sly but revealing glance towards Father Thomas.

'Oh, I see,' said Quinn. 'It is acceptable to reveal the secrets of the confessional to this young man, but not to an officer of the law?'

'No,' said Father Thomas. 'You're wrong. It was not like that. But I did offer Peter guidance. He came to me as a troubled soul. My assistance was of the most general kind.'

'But informed by what you had heard in the confessional?'

'I knew that Amélie was determined to break off with Blackley. If necessary, to leave the House of Blackley altogether. I encouraged her in this. A conversation that was begun in the confessional was continued outside it.'

'Do you have any idea when Amélie was intending to break with him?'

'We talked about it last Sunday. The situation had reached a crisis. She was desperately unhappy. We speak of a girl being ruined. But she was, in a very real sense, a ruin of the beautiful person she had once been. The girl she was when I first met her.'

'When was that?'

'Not so long ago. A year at the most. That's all the time it's taken for Blackley to destroy her.'

'You are convinced that Blackley is to blame for this?'

Father Thomas's gaze was unwavering. 'Absolutely.'

Quinn turned to Spiggott. 'Where were you on the night of Tuesday, March the thirty-first?'

'You're not serious?'

'I must ask the question. I would be failing in my duty if I do not.'

'I was in the men's dorm at Blackley's.'

'Can anyone vouch for you?'

'I suppose someone must have seen me. Davies? He's the fellow who has the bed next to mine.'

'Mr Davies went to bed early with a headache that night. He has no recollection of seeing you in the dorm.'

'I don't know. I suppose I must have spoken to someone. I don't have many friends at Blackley's. I keep myself to myself. I'm not sure anyone would have noticed if I was there or not.' Spiggott must have detected the scepticism that his answer provoked. He switched tack. 'Tuesday night, you say? I remember now, I did go out. I just walked the streets. Trying to get my thoughts in order. It was late when I got back to Blackley's. Past the curfew. But that doesn't matter. There's a window in the staff quarters. The fastening doesn't work properly on it. You can get it open if you know how.'

'And you know how, working in Locks, Clocks and Mechanical Contrivances?'

'It's nothing to do with that. All the chaps can do it. Some of the women too.'

'It would have been better if you had not gone out that night,' said Quinn. 'We could have eliminated you from our enquiries. As it stands...'

'I didn't kill her! I loved her.'

'But what if you couldn't have her? What if she decided to finish with both you *and* Black-

247

ley? She could hardly be blamed if the thought of sexual relations with both father and son was repulsive to her. Had she denied *you* what she gave willingly to *Blackley*? She gave herself to him in return for furs and jewellery that you could never afford. Because, let's face it, Blackley is never going to acknowledge you. All your talk of inheriting a quarter of the House of Blackley was just a dream. Did she point that out to you? Did she mock you? Did she make you feel worthless because she had chosen the man you hated most in the world over you? She had chosen to grant your enemy the privilege that you most desired! That you truly deserved! How you must have hated to think of *him* and *her* together.' Quinn's mouth contorted itself around his words, which were shot through with a personal bitterness. He was thinking of another *him* and *her*, from a distant, unhappy time in his own life. 'There could be no way out of it, could there? Other than to kill ... someone ... her ... him ... it doesn't matter. Both would be preferable.'

'Inspector, are you quite all right?'

''Ere, guv. Take it easy.'

Quinn looked down at his hands. They were formed into a tense circle, as if gripping an imaginary neck to strangle it. He breathed out slowly and noisily. It was a moment before his fingers began to relax. 'Is that not so, Mr Spiggott?'

'I confess, I wanted to kill Blackley. Wouldn't you, in my position?'

'Your own father.' Quinn's tone was almost

awed as he took in the implication of Spiggott's admission. 'Do you still want to kill him?'

'Do you want to stop me? Bring him to justice. Prove that he killed Amélie. Get the rope around his neck, Inspector.' A tremor of emotion passed over Spiggott's face as he finished his exhortation. He drew his head up to an angle of challenge.

'You may trust me to do my job. In the meantime, may I trust you not to do anything reckless?'

Spiggott looked down, without meeting Quinn's eye.

Father Thomas placed a hand on Spiggott's shoulder. It was as if the priest's touch had transmitted a jolt of electricity.

Spiggott looked up and nodded.

A Confrontation

Macadam leapt to his feet as soon as Quinn and Inchball returned to the department. It was clear he was pleased to see them. Desperately so, it seemed. The time spent in DCI Coddington's exclusive company had evidently taken its toll on him. But Quinn also sensed that Macadam was eager to share what he had learnt.

'How did you get on in Lambeth?'

Coddington assumed the privilege of answering for Macadam. 'Sergeant Macadam has made a significant breakthrough in the case, Quinn. I think it's fair to say it has changed my thinking entirely.'

Macadam gave an eager nod; his eyes shone with the certainty that Quinn would not be disappointed. 'I managed to track down Alf Spiggott to a disreputable public house that seems to pass for his place of work. You won't believe what I learnt, sir. As DCI Coddington said, it puts the case in a whole new light.'

'Alf Spiggott is not Spiggott's real father.'

Macadam was crestfallen. 'That's right.'

Naturally Quinn felt sorry for his sergeant. But he was merciless towards Coddington, determined to prove his superiority. 'His real

250

father is Benjamin Blackley.'

Macadam was shaking his head in bewilderment. 'How did you know, sir?'

'Spiggott told us.'

'You've spoken to Spiggott?' DCI Coddington's moustache convulsed in agitation.

'Yes, sir,' said Quinn.

'I see. I see. Right. I see. Very good. Good work. Spiggott. You found Spiggott. Good. Did you not arrest him?'

'On what charge, sir? I thought your view was that the monkey caused Amélie's death and there would be no point in pursuing the rape charge.' Quinn kept his expression impeccably deadpan.

'That's ... that's right. But this new evidence of a connection between Spiggott and Blackley? We had not expected that, I think.'

'And therefore? Because we hadn't expected something, does it mean we must arrest someone? Isn't that rather a knee-jerk reaction, if I may put it like that, sir?'

'Well, yes, of course. Provided you satisfied yourself, Quinn, that Spiggott had nothing to do with either crime?'

'I cannot be *satisfied*, sir, until I have proof one way or the other.'

'Of course, proof. That's what we need.' Coddington became suddenly charged with energy, if the animation of his moustache was anything to go by. Only to collapse in disappointment. 'Do you have anything?'

'We have nothing to place him at the mannequin house on Tuesday night. On the other hand, he doesn't have a definite alibi. And we simply do not know how skilful he is at picking locks. Possibly he could have let himself into the house without anyone seeing him. I think there are grounds to suspect him still. From a psychological point of view, I think it is possible to come up with a plausible motive for him. He was disappointed in love with Amélie. Perhaps he killed her to punish her, or to punish Blackley. Or perhaps his thinking was, if he couldn't have her, no one else would. It wouldn't be the first time I have encountered that convoluted mental process, sir.' For a moment, Quinn's focus was directed inwards.

'Punish Mr Blackley? What do you mean, Quinn?'

'It seems Blackley and the girl were *lovers*. If that is the right word. Certainly he gave her gifts and in return, she granted him sexual favours.'

'No, no, no ... this can't be true! Mr Blackley is a respectable citizen. You heard this from that Spiggott fellow, did you? He's obviously lying to divert attention from himself.'

'You may be right, sir. Spiggott was very quick to point the finger at Blackley. However, Blackley's son, Benjamin Blackley Junior, believed that Blackley was having an affair with one of the mannequins. Well, the impression I got was that he rather worked his way through them. Blackley has access to the mannequin house and keeps a room there. The gossip is he treats the place as his own private harem.'

'This is ... this is ... Good God ... We can't ...

My wife shops at Blackley's!'

'Welcome to Special Crimes, sir.'

'This sort of thing happens a lot, does it?'

'There's always something, sir. Something different.'

'I see. And so ... We should ... we should ... what we should *do*...' Coddington nodded vigorously, as if in agreement to something one of them had said.

'If I may make a suggestion, sir?'

'Go on, Quinn. You interrupted my train of thought, but never mind. What's your suggestion?'

'I think we should put a watch on the mannequin house. I am more than happy to volunteer to run the operation.'

'Good idea. Yes, I like that. A watch. Surveillance. Good.' Coddington made some strange rapid movements with his mouth, the sole purpose of which seemed to be to make his moustache jump around in a novel way. 'Why are we doing that exactly? I mean, I understand, of course, but let's just talk it through. To be clear.'

'Blackley,' began Quinn, speaking with slow, deliberate emphasis, 'is a man of prodigious sexual appetite.'

'He is? How do you know?'

'I sense it. You can almost smell it when you're standing close to him.'

Coddington was not the only one to fidget uneasily at the strange tone in which Quinn had made this assertion. 'Do you have anything else to base it on?'

'There had been a family meeting in which he was prevailed upon to rein in his appetites, because of the trouble Spiggott was making. It seems his wife and grown-up children know all about his peccadilloes. He made a promise to stop. I'm sure he meant to keep that promise. But he simply couldn't. He is a powerful, domineering man. And one of the ways he exerts his power is to force these girls to have sex with him. He is the rapist, I'm sure. On the morning her body was discovered, he sent a messenger around to the house with a contrite message for Amélie. He was sorry. He begged her forgiveness.'

'Have you asked him about this? He may have some perfectly reasonable explanation.'

'I am sure he will have.'

'But I thought you said he and the girl were lovers? That she gave herself to him in return for all those presents. That implies consent on her part, Quinn.'

'Yes. She had consented. She did consent. Before she knew about the connection between Blackley and Spiggott. Then she withdrew her consent.'

'I see. So ... we watch the place. Because?'

'Because he will not be able to keep away. He will move on to the next girl.'

'What? So soon?'

'There is something missing in Mr Blackley's character, sir. What you and I might call common decency. He is the most immoral man I have ever encountered. His heart is made of ice.'

'And if we see him return to the house, what then?'

'We do nothing. Our objective, at this stage, is simply to gather intelligence. To build up a picture of Blackley. It will be interesting to see if any of the other residents testify to his presence there. If not, it shows that we cannot trust their denials regarding his absence on Tuesday. And we may also be able to catch him in a lie, if he denies going there.'

'But it's not proof, Quinn. Is it? Blackley has admitted to keeping a room at the mannequin house. We know he has a key. He could simply argue that he was working late and availing himself of the facilities of the house, facilities put in place for his own convenience.'

'What we need is someone in there. Someone on the inside. Someone we can trust. So that, if we know from our surveillance that Blackley was in there, we can find out from our source inside exactly what he got up to.'

'Who do you have in mind?' wondered Coddington.

'Macadam, bring the car round to the front, will you?'

The girl's eyes were open but she didn't look up as he came in. She was still on the bed, lying on her side in her dressing gown, staring at nothing. She was not crying any more, though her eyes were rimmed with a red rawness, as if she looked out at the world through twin wounds.

'Edna?'

She lay unmoving. Not the slightest flicker to show that she had heard him, or was aware of his presence in her room.

'Edna, love? It's me, Silas. We had a chat yesterday. Do you remember?'

A slight movement of her head from side to side. Did she really not remember him, or did her feeble denial have a wider significance? Was she, perhaps, refusing to speak to him?

'You don't remember me? Surely you do?'

At last, her eyes swivelled to fix on him.

'Not Edna.' It evidently took a great effort for her to say this. Her head fell back on to her pillow and she closed her eyes. 'Albertine.'

'Ah, yes, of course. Albertine. Forgive me, Albertine. How are you feeling today, Albertine?'

He saw the bulge of her tongue move beneath her closed lips as she licked the inside of her mouth away from her teeth. This seemed to rally her energy. Her eyes sprang open once more, and she heaved herself upright into a sitting position. 'I must go back to work.'

'I'm sure Mr Blackley will understand...'

'No, I must go back, otherwise I'll lose my position...' She sprang to her feet with a speed which seemed to take even her aback. It certainly surprised Quinn when she tottered and fell into his arms. He was shocked by how little there was to her. He could feel her skeleton through the dressing gown. It was barely more robust than a bird's.

Quinn thought of the photographs of Amélie and the medical examiner's report. He looked

256

down at the crown of Albertine's head. Her hair was wispy and fine. It would not be going too far to say it was beginning to thin.

How easy it would be to crush her, he thought. *What little effort it would take to squeeze the life out of her.*

He was not proud of such thoughts. But he would not evade them either. He had to look upon them as part of his method. If he thought this now, looking down at Albertine, it was reasonable to speculate that Amélie's killer had entertained similar thoughts.

'Careful, now. My ... look at you. When was the last time you ate something, my dear?'

'I ... I've been too upset.'

'Of course. But we don't want...' Quinn stopped himself. He had been about to say, *the same thing happening to you as happened to Amélie.* 'We don't want you getting ill, do we?'

'I have to go back to work.'

'Not today, Albertine. I'll square it with Mr Blackley. Don't you worry.'

Albertine looked up at him with an expression of simple awe. 'How?'

'I'm a policeman. If he gives me any trouble, I'll ... lock him up!'

Despite her frailty, Albertine managed a sweet complicit giggle at this. It was a hint of the spirited girl she had once been – as recently, perhaps, as a few days ago. The energy drained from her as quickly as it had entered into her. She closed her eyes in defeat. 'You can't lock up Mr Blackley.'

'Why not?'

'Because without Mr Blackley there'd be no House of Blackley, and then what would we do? We'd all ... be out on the street.'

'I don't believe that's true, Albertine. Is that why people are afraid? Why no one will tell the truth about Blackley?'

'Mr Blackley looks after us. *You* can't look after us.'

'Mr Blackley didn't look after Amélie, did he?' For a moment, Quinn thought he had gone too far. He felt a tremor of suffering pass through Albertine. 'I want you to do something for me, Albertine. I want you to get your strength back. You have to be strong for me, Albertine. It's what Amélie would want too. You have to be strong for Amélie. So you can help us find out what happened to her. In a moment we'll go downstairs and see if Miss Mortimer has anything for you to eat. Then I'll explain what I want you to do.'

Quinn took hold of Albertine by the shoulders and held her away from him so that he could look at her. 'You need to be very strong, Albertine. For Amélie. Can you be strong?'

But it took all her strength for her to lift her head and open her eyes. And when he looked into those eyes, Quinn could not be sure he saw the answer he wanted. He could not be sure he saw anything at all.

'Think she'll do it, guv?' said Macadam from the driver's seat as Quinn settled into the back of the department's Model T. The car vibrated noisily, as if the stress of remaining stationary with the engine ticking over would be enough to shake it apart.

Quinn shrugged. 'Any sign of Inchball yet?'

'No, sir.'

'How did you get on, Macadam?'

'We're all set for tonight, sir.' Macadam gave a wincing smile. 'What happens if Blackley don't show, guv?'

'We have to make sure that he will. Apply a little pressure. Make him feel vulnerable and weak. He won't like that. Given the kind of man he is, his natural response will be to assert his power. Which, for him, means a visit to the mannequin house.'

The back door opened and Inchball got in alongside Quinn. 'Ain' much of a plan, if you ask me,' he grumbled. 'With respect and all that,' he added after a moment.

'But you've spoken to him? He will do it?' demanded Quinn.

Inchball consulted a fob watch. 'He'll be at the front in ... three minutes.'

'We'd better get round there too, then, Macadam.'

Macadam wrenched the gears with a grinding of metal and the car lurched forward. The engine misfired once but settled into an eager thrum, as if it was relieved to be on the move at last.

As they drew up along Kensington Road, Quinn saw Benjamin Blackley in place once again, cheerily greeting customers as they returned to his store. It seemed that the collective mood of restraint that had been in evidence in the immediate aftermath of the riot had now passed. An advertising campaign promising substantial discounts had no doubt helped the public overcome any qualms they might have had.

'Blimey, don' he ever let up?' wondered Inchball. 'I mean, ain' he got better things to do?'

'What could be more important than bringing customers into his store?' said Quinn.

At that moment Spiggott emerged from the entrance of Our Lady of the Sacred Heart Church and strode purposefully towards Blackley.

Inside the car the vibrations were deafening. Every piece of metal seemed to be grating against its neighbour. Quinn felt an angry throb in his pelvic bone. He had an image of bolts spinning loose from their nuts. The car seemed minutes away from falling apart around them.

As a consequence, it was impossible to hear what passed between Blackley and Spiggott. Fingers jabbed the air. Mouths were contorted to form inaudible shouts. The crowd parted around them, as shoppers decided for once to give the usually genial and approachable celebrity a wide berth.

It was safe to say that Quinn had achieved his objective of putting Blackley under pressure.

'Right,' said Quinn. 'That's enough.'

The three policemen sprang out of the car. Spiggott caught sight of them and ran off, disappearing into the crowd. Quinn put on a spurt to cross the road and approach Blackley. 'Everything all right, sir?'

'Thank God you've arrived, Inspector. That man ... you must go after him and arrest him.'

'Why's that, sir?'

'Slander! He committed slander. And made all manner of threats. Against me and my family. He's trying to blackmail me. And extort money. He's attempting to perpetrate a wholesale fraud!'

'Chip off the old block, is he, sir?'

'What did you say?'

'He is your son, isn't he?'

'Of course not! You've been listening to his lies as well, have you? Don't you understand? A man like me is vulnerable to this kind of attack.'

'I have to say, sir, I've spoken to Mr Spiggott and he seems quite sincere in his beliefs.'

'He may be sincere or he may not be. That doesn't make a blind bit of difference. It's simply not true.'

'It's not true you seduced his mother when she was a shop girl here?'

'Does *she* say that?'

'She's dead, as you well know, sir.'

Blackley looked surly rather than ashamed at being caught out. 'The point is, surely, that it's his word against mine. And he only has it on the word of his mother, allegedly. But, as you say, she is dead, and so can't back up the claim. And from what I hear, while she was alive, she was something of a lush. Certainly, she overlooked the courtesy of ever informing me of the boy's existence. You might presume she would have done, if what Mr Spiggott claims is true. And so, in short, Inspector, you can hardly blame me for being sceptical now.'

'You maintain that you are not his father?'

'My word is my bond, Inspector, and you have my word upon it.'

'But what of Amélie?'

'What do you mean?'

'Did she believe you?'

'What has this got to do with her?'

'Everything. It's her death we're investigating, after all.'

'I don't understand your insinuations.'

'When Spiggott told Amélie that you are his father...'

'Which is a lie – I thought we had established that!'

'If it is a lie, it is one she believed. She decided to break off with you, did she not?'

'Break off? Break what off? What are you talking about, Inspector?'

'Oh, come now, Mr Blackley, we know that you were having an affair with Amélie. The message you sent when she went missing. *I'm sorry. Forgive me.* The words of a lover to his mistress. Not of an employer to an employee. What was your offence, Mr Blackley? Why did you need to beg Amélie's forgiveness?'

'The previous day ... I had been a little harsh with her during the rehearsal for the fashion parade. She'd been slow and clumsy. Not her usual self at all. I lost my temper with her. Hooking Lady Ascot meant a lot to me. Everything depended on how the mannequins performed. Amélie had felt the rough edge of my tongue. And so I was worried that was the reason she had not put in an appearance. I should have been more patient. The mannequins are our prima donnas, Inspector. You have to handle them with kid gloves.'

'You would know everything about handling mannequins. You had affairs with others before her. Your son has admitted as much.'

'How many times do I have to tell you: Spiggott is not my son!'

'Not Spiggott. Benjamin Blackley Junior.'

'Our Ben?' It was a rare lapse into his native, northern vernacular, which perhaps showed how rattled he was. For one instant his expression was panic-stricken. 'What did our Ben say?'

'We know that he was inside the mannequin house on Tuesday night. He says that he was there to spy on you on his mother's behalf. Apparently he didn't trust your protestations of reform.'

Blackley's brows dipped sharply but he made no comment.

'And so, he secreted himself in Monsieur Hugo's room in order to keep watch on your ... comings and goings.'

'How could he, when I wasn't there?'

'He clearly expected you to be there.'

'And does he say that I was there?'

Quinn avoided meeting Blackley's glowering stare.

'I take it by your reticence that he does not.'

'Be under no illusion, Mr Blackley, the girls upon whom you prey feel only revulsion and contempt for you. They may accede to your demands, but only because they value the gifts your favour brings. It is all they can do not to vomit in your face when they bestow their kisses. You flatter yourself, no doubt, that women can't help falling at your feet. But half of them are terrified of you and the other half are using you. The one thing that unites them all is hatred. Of you.'

'You don't have much luck with the ladies, do you, Inspector?'

'How did you feel when Amélie told you it was over? It's not for her to say, is it? You'll decide when it's over, not her, the bitch. Is that why you decided to teach her a lesson?'

Blackley remained calm, chillingly so. His affable smile was once again back in place. 'You cannot say things like this and get away with it, Inspector. I don't care who you think you are.'

'Don't you see it in their faces, Mr Blackley? The disgust?'

'Good day, Inspector.'

'Did she tell you that she loved *him* not you? Or that she'd slept with both of you? Was that the straw that broke the camel's back? You're not one to share your pleasures with any man, are you, Mr Blackley? Let alone your son!'

Blackley shook his head and moved away from Quinn. He threw back his head and began to cry, like a market hawker, 'Welcome to the House of Blackley! Step inside and enter a world of provision. That's right. A world of provision! That's what we say on our advertisements, because it's true! Goods from all over the world, lacquered knick-knacks from Japan and China, cinnamon and turmeric from the Spice Islands, cotton from America, rubber from India, French fashions, lace from Madeira, the darkest molasses from Jamaica ... Whatever in the world you're looking for, you'll find it inside our doors. Welcome to Blackley's ... a world of *provision*!' Blackley clenched his fist and waved it high in triumph on the last emphatic word; he met Quinn's gaze with a defiant gleam.

A Watch

A drab mansion block occupied most of the south side of Caper Street, across the road from the mannequin house. Macadam had secured the cooperation of an austere middle-aged couple, Mr and Mrs Thomas Sledge, who had rooms at the front.

The Sledges had faces the colour of parchment. They dressed in black and spoke only in whispers, as if they were conversing in a public library. Perhaps the clandestine nature of the operation had some influence in this. Mr Sledge conveyed his thoughts to Mrs Sledge, who then communicated them to Macadam, who would in turn share them with Quinn. For some reason Macadam had also taken to speaking in whispers.

It was perhaps as well that Sergeant Inchball was not there, thought Quinn. He could imagine how he would react to the strange game of Chinese Whispers.

The Sledges kept their apartment dimly lit. Perhaps Macadam had briefed them to do so, but Quinn suspected this was how they preferred to live, in shadows and whispers. He saw no direct lights in the places he was admitted to, just soft flickering glows seeping out from half-opened doors.

After the whispering Mr Sledge took himself off and played no further part in the dealings with the police. He left it to his wife to show them to the room they were to use. Mrs Sledge walked with a stiff upright bearing, her step heavy and slow, as if she was leading a procession, or trudging through deep sand. It was almost as if she had to overcome a great reluctance, or force of resistance, to move through her own home.

She led them to a child's bedroom. The curtains were open, light from the street dappling the pink of the Empire in a framed map of the world on one wall. A toy sailboat rested on top of a bookcase, ready to be snatched up and run with to Hyde Park. *Boy's Own* adventure stories showed their spines on the shelves below. On a desk, a microscope and slides waited for a boy's eye to examine them. A child's sailor suit hung on the back of the door.

Mrs Sledge whispered something to Macadam. It was a long and intense communication. She waited for him to repeat it to Quinn. 'She says it was her son's room. He's dead. Snatched on his way home from school. Sexually molested and strangled. His body dumped in a dust heap. He was eleven. The police never caught his murderer.'

The woman watched Quinn's face as he took this in. Her expression seemed recriminatory, as if she held Quinn responsible for that earlier police failing. He nodded solemnly. 'Tell her we're very grateful to her and her husband for being allowed to use it.'

Macadam conveyed the message. Mrs Sledge seemed satisfied and left.

Macadam had brought a brown leather travelling bag from which he took a pair of binoculars.

'I'll take the first hour,' said Quinn. Macadam handed him the binoculars; he then took out a roll of carpet and a blanket from the bag and spread them out on the floor. 'Aren't you going to use the bed?'

'Mrs Sledge requested that we didn't.' Macadam took off his jacket. 'In fact, she would rather we didn't touch anything.' He seemed at a loss what to do with his jacket now that he had relayed that information. He settled for draping it over the back of the chair that was tucked into the desk.

Quinn sighed deeply. He looked at the model yacht, its string rigging and handkerchief-thin sails heartbreakingly frail, but they still had the power to dredge an ache of emotion into his throat. He was momentarily paralysed by a stab of grief for his own lost boyhood, and for all the innocence that had vanished from the world. Inevitably he thought of his father, remembering the great, good hero he had once been, a man of enthusiasms and optimism. The kind of father who could goad his son to delight, and share in it.

Quinn positioned himself to one side of the window frame and lifted the binoculars to his eyes. The entrance to Seven Caper Street was well-illuminated by a street lamp. There would be no difficulty in observing the comings and goings at the house.

Ten minutes into the watch the door to the mannequin house opened and Sergeant Inchball emerged. He looked up briefly, a minimal signal to Quinn that everything was ready. All the mannequins were inside the house, together with Monsieur Hugo and the domestics.

But no one else: Inchball had been instructed to make a sign if Blackley, or another interloper, was inside. As Inchball headed off down Caper Street, Quinn thought he detected in his gait the self-consciousness of someone who knew he was being watched. His step seemed deliberately jaunty, as if he was making the point that he was finished for the day, whereas whoever was watching him had a night of discomfort and boredom ahead.

Caper Street was a quiet turning, haunted by prowling cats. There was some pedestrian through-traffic, as well as one or two residents returning late from work, or setting out on a Friday night's entertainment. The public house on Abingdon Road, near where Caper Street came out, was one lure; though to judge by the evening dress of some of those leaving their houses, they were headed into the West End. As the first hour progressed, the passers-by grew noticeably more lively. One group of staggering men shouted boisterously, evidently on a pub crawl.

Quinn found his thoughts drifting back to his father. How could it be possible that such a man could take his own life? That was the question that he had never been able to get beyond. A respected family doctor with a good practice, he had somehow managed to run up debts that left his wife virtually destitute as well as widowed. What was it that had drained the family's coffers? A secret vice? Quinn had never detected the slightest whiff of alcohol on his father's breath. Was it something worse than drunkenness?

The last time he had pondered these questions, in the immediate wake of his father's death, his mind and nervous system had shattered. He had tried to imagine the worst that his father might be capable of. Each potential crime or depravity that passed through his mental review twisted and corrupted his idea of his father. He felt him gradually but perceptibly turn from a paragon to a monster.

To imagine his father in this way was, of course, an act of gross disloyalty. Quinn saw that he himself was the monster, the grotesque, craven, spiritually ugly fiend. It wasn't his father who was capable of any evil, it was Quinn himself.

When he emerged from the breakdown this had precipitated, he set himself consciously to be on his guard against his own worst propensities; to police himself, in other words. But the door had been opened: an awareness that he was capable of something mutated into a compulsion to do that very thing. By a fortuitous twist (or had he planned it like this all along?) he found himself in the one job where he could act on this compulsion, with the minimum risk of repercussions.

In other words, as a police detective, from time to time, it happened that he killed people.

The tiny chime of Macadam's pocket watch signalled nine o'clock. He sat bolt upright. 'Anything, sir?'

'No sign of Blackley yet.'

Macadam rose to his feet and took the binoculars. 'I'll wake you in an hour, sir.'

Quinn lay down on the rug. There was no comfort in it at all. He felt the floor's uncompromising rigidity squeeze his bones. He pulled the blanket over him and looked up at the toy boat on the bookcase. He thought about the boy that Mr and Mrs Sledge had lost, dressed in his sailor suit, laying his model boat down on the surface of the water. For a moment, he was that boy. But then he was the dark, shadowed stranger watching, waiting for the perfect moment to make his move.

A patchwork of difficult dreams. Long, slow minutes of numbing tedium. At times it felt as though he was keeping watch on his soul, rather than on the house opposite. But somehow the night passed.

The first leavening of the darkness came on his watch. Grey spectral forms gathered substance, like ocean liners nosing through fog. The houses opposite took shape, colours summoned by the birds' clamour. A whole street formed itself. The sprays of yellow light cast down by the lamps were left enfeebled and looking a little foolish. A moment ago, they had held all there was of the world.

Macadam stirred. 'Did he show?'

Quinn shook his head. It was the story of the night.

'What do we do now, sir?'

Quinn consulted his watch. 'We keep up the pressure.' He nodded his approval of his own plan and kept his gaze fixed on the door to number seven. After a moment he raised the binoculars sharply, as if some detail on the paintwork had suddenly aroused his suspicion.

Father and Son

Macadam drove Quinn round to the front of the store. Blackley was already in place, just as the store was opening, in anticipation of a busy Saturday morning's trade. He tipped his bowler at Quinn and even dared a wink as the Ford shuddered past.

'Pull up, sergeant,' said Quinn.

Blackley drew himself up, bristling at Quinn and Macadam's approach. His smile was cranked up a notch. It did nothing to mitigate the aggression of his stance. In fact, Quinn realized that the smile was itself an act of aggression, Blackley's assault on the forces set against him. At its mildest, it was an assertion of Blackley's indomitable will. But that will – and that smile – could not exist without the seam of hard, mineral ruthlessness that ran through Blackley's soul.

'What can I do for you, Inspector?'

'It's not you we want, Blackley. It's your son. Benjamin Blackley Junior. I take it he's in his office?'

The defiance fell away from Blackley. The smile flexed and sharpened. It must have been a strain now to hold it. 'Ben? What do you want with Ben?'

'By his own admission he was at the manne-

273

quin house on Tuesday night, the night Amélie was raped and murdered. He was the only male – apart from Monsieur Hugo – there. There are discrepancies in your son's account which we are forced to regard with suspicion. At first we thought he was covering for you. But the more obvious explanation is that he is himself the murderer. And the rapist too, of course.'

'Ben? No, not Ben. You're way off the mark there, Inspector.'

'Am I? Do you know something about what transpired in the mannequin house on Tuesday night that could bring me back on target?'

'I only know that my son is not a killer.'

'I'm afraid that's not good enough. We'll have to take him in for questioning. DCI Coddington is anxious to bring this case to a conclusion as quickly as possible. I'm sure that's what you want too, Mr Blackley, so that you can get on with your business. I imagine that we will charge your son later today. We'll hold him over the weekend and have him before the magistrates on Monday morning. The evidence is circumstantial, but in the absence of anything else we're confident it will secure a conviction. At the very least, it will go to trial.'

'You can't do this. It will break his mother's heart.'

'Have you nothing else to offer that might weigh in his favour?'

Blackley shook his head. There was no smile in place now. He stood to one side and allowed the policemen to pass.

You can never tell, thought Quinn. Never tell in advance how they are going to react. The hardened criminals expect it. And being ready for it, they are quick to break loose. The guilty sometimes almost seem to welcome it.

But the fear and bewilderment that showed in Benjamin Blackley Jr's face now – it was hard to see it as anything other than a sign of genuine innocence. His eyes were wide with dawning terror; his mouth gaped in speechless incomprehension.

'What is this?' Although he resembled his father physically, Blackley Jr lacked the older man's bluff confidence. Blackley Sr was a self-made man; he stood squarely up to the world, knowing what it expected from him and what he could demand in return. By the time his son was born he was already a successful business-man. His son, therefore, had had everything handed to him on a plate. He'd never had to prove himself, let alone make himself. The business his father had built up through the exercise of initiative, energy and sheer will-power would one day simply fall into his lap. In place of his father's hard-earned, hard-edged self-confidence, there was a thin and brittle arrogance. The slightest touch and it shattered.

Young Blackley shrank back in his seat, as if hoping the expanse of his desk would be enough to protect him. It was all he had, after all.

'You're under arrest.'

'For what?'

'On suspicion of murder. And rape.'

'You can't be serious.'

'Oh, I assure you, sir, I am in deadly earnest. Now then, you can either come quietly, or we can put the cuffs on and drag you out through the store. Which will it be?'

'My father will have something to say about this!'

'Your father? We have already spoken to your father. We told him of our intention. He stood aside. Waved us through. "He's all yours," he as good as said. "Take him away." '

'He didn't say that!'

'Not in so many words. But you know as well as I do, there was something he could have said. A few simple words that would have prevented us coming down here to arrest you. He chose not to. He chose to sacrifice you, Ben. Your father's thrown you to the wolves!'

Ben Blackley's head swung to the side as if he had just been slapped across the face. 'He wouldn't do that,' he murmured. But the hurt in his expression belied his assertion.

'You know what he's like. All he has to do to save you is tell the truth. But it's more important to him to be outside the store touting for business. He has hardened his heart to you, Ben. He doesn't care what happens to you so long as he can save himself and his own reputation.'

Ben Blackley shook his head.

'It's hard for you to accept the truth. It feels like you're betraying him. I know. I know what you're going through ... My own father...'

Ben looked up sharply. 'What?'

'...killed himself.'

'What's that got to do with anything?'

'You remind me of the young man I was at the time. I couldn't accept that my father would do such a thing. That he would leave me. That he would choose self-annihilation. Did he have so little love for me? And what of my mother? How could he do that to her? He was not there to see the pain that he inflicted. No. The man that my father was, the loving, loved, husband and father – he would not, could not do such a thing. I was incapable of imagining what could have driven him to the act. So I refused to believe it. Oh, my mother believed it. She had no choice. She was the one left penniless. Destitute. How she turned against him! And how I hated *her* for that. Not him.'

'What is your point, Inspector?'

Quinn thought for a moment. 'Why do you think my father killed himself?' His voice was low, but intense, as if everything was hanging on young Blackley's answer.

'I have no idea.'

Quinn nodded. 'I don't know either. I have never been able to find out. But I have come to the conclusion that he must have done something so shameful that he simply could not live with himself.'

'You don't know that,' said young Blackley.

Quinn shrugged. 'What I would say to him, having lived the years I've lived, and having committed a few sins of my own, what I would say to him now is, "Whatever you have done, you're still my father." '

'So, you had a father who killed himself. I don't see what that has to do with me.'

'You have a father who may have done far worse.'

'How can you be so sure he has done anything?'

Quinn looked down at Ben Blackley. 'You know your father is no saint.'

'He's not a murderer.'

'Perhaps not. The only way we can establish that for certain is if you tell us the truth.'

Ben Blackley put a hand to his forehead and hid his gaze from Quinn.

'Do you know the one and only thing that your father said to try and stop us taking you away? "It will break his mother's heart," he said.'

A muffled sob came from Blackley Jr.

'Listen, my young friend, I know you're not lying to protect your father. It's for your mother, isn't it? She didn't send you to spy on him. *You* needed to know for yourself the true depth of his depravity. What was your plan? To use what you discovered for your own purposes? Were you worried he was going to crack over the Spiggott affair and recognize him as his son? You wanted some leverage to make sure that didn't happen. Or perhaps you simply needed to know the truth about your father.'

Ben Blackley rubbed his face vigorously with both hands. When he looked up at Quinn his expression had a fearful, chastened quality to it. The young man seemed suddenly and profoundly uncertain, as if he had been subject not simply to a passing doubt, but to the fundamental upheaval of his core beliefs.

'I can understand that. But the truth is a terrible thing, is it not? Once you know it, you cannot un-know it. The man your father once was is gone forever from you. A monster stands in his place.'

'I saw nothing. I know nothing.'

'I understand why you say that. You're determined that your mother should never know the true nature of the monster she has devoted her life to. You even swore on your mother's life that your father was not in the mannequin house on Tuesday night! It is psychologically interesting that you should choose such an oath – interesting, but plausible. It shows you were thinking of your mother. The lie needed to be sworn on her life to make it believable. You justified it to yourself because you were doing it for her sake. You saw it as the lesser of two evils. To find out the truth about her husband would destroy her. What then will it do to her to see her first-born son hanged for a murder he did not commit?'

'If I tell her that I didn't do it she'll believe me, no matter what anybody else says.'

'You're prepared to swing on the gallows for your father?'

'My mother will believe me. A jury will believe me.'

'You never can tell with juries, son. All right, Macadam. Get the cuffs on him.'

'There's no need,' said Ben Blackley, rising. 'I'll come of my own free will.'

Macadam began to back off.

'Cuffs, Sergeant Macadam.'

'That's not fair! You said...'

'I don't care what I said. I've changed my mind. We can't take any chances with the likes of you.'

Macadam nodded and closed down young Blackley by the speed of his attack. He was well-practised at apprehending trickier customers than this. He turned him deftly, gathering up his wrists and snapping the handcuffs around them. A sharp wrench of the arms upwards produced a cry of pain. Macadam began frogmarching him towards the door, steering him by his arms.

'You can't do this!'

Quinn mimed for Macadam to give the young man's arms another tweak. He was not a sadist. But he needed to make an impression, and not just on young Blackley.

They dragged him screaming in pain through the back-room offices. Quinn was gratified by the cowering looks they drew from the staff they passed.

Macadam drove Ben Blackley forward, using his cuffed arms like a tiller. Blackley stumbled several times, giving a fresh scream each time Macadam yanked on his cuffs to keep him upright.

'Bastard!'

'Don't want you having an accident, do we?' said Macadam.

The stairs were a struggle. Blackley Jr fell out of Macadam's grip at one point, to lie sprawling across a flight of steps.

Quinn signalled for Macadam to go easy. He wanted to put pressure on the young man but not to injure him.

They proceeded more patiently from then on, the policemen pausing at each step for young Blackley to catch up. At last they reached the ground floor. Ben Blackley nodded towards a side exit. 'We can get out this way.'

'No. We want the front exit, son,' said Quinn.

They stepped into the store. It was still early. Not quite as busy as Quinn might have hoped for on a Saturday morning. However, he made sure that their progress did not go unnoticed by those who were there. 'Make way,' he shouted. 'Police coming through. Everyone out the way, please. Thank you.' This was despite the fact that they had a clear way across the floor.

Just as they were about to go through the front door, Quinn leant towards Ben Blackley and whispered something into his ear. The young man appeared startled by it. He frowned as he considered what Quinn had said, as if trying to make sense of it.

They pushed out on to the street. Macadam hoisted the young man's arms up his back once more. The cry that this prompted turned Benjamin Blackley's head. The smile froze on his lips when he saw his son cuffed and manhandled.

'You're making a big mistake, Inspector.' To his son, he added: 'Don't worry, Ben. We'll sort

281

this out. These fools will have to let you go.'

'We can let him go here and now, sir, if you like. It's up to you. All you have to do is tell us what happened in the mannequin house on Tuesday night.'

'I wasn't there. Does Ben say I was there?' Blackley asked the question with complete confidence in the answer.

'Oh, don't worry. He hasn't revealed your secret. Yet.'

'Well, then...' said Blackley.

'Well then,' echoed Quinn, 'if you weren't there, he certainly was. Which means, by a process of elimination, that he must be Amélie's rapist. Unless you expect us to believe that it was Monsieur Hugo.'

Blackley looked uneasily at the gathering crowd. 'Keep your voice down, Inspector. Is it really necessary to bandy such terms around on the public highway?'

'Is it really necessary to rape young girls to whom you stand *in loco parentis*?'

There was a collective gasp from the onlookers.

'No, no, no. You can't get away with this, Inspector. Your incompetence is breathtaking. While you're here dragging off my son and making wild accusations, the real killer is going free. I shall complain to the highest authorities. The highest authorities, you hear!'

Quinn nodded as if this was no less than he expected; as if, indeed, it was strangely satisfying to hear Blackley make the threat. He turned to young Blackley. 'Do you have anything you wish to say to your father, Ben?'

Macadam released his hold on Ben Blackley so that he was able to stand upright and look his father in the eye. With the two of them face-to-face, it was easier to see the differences, as well as the similarities, between the two men. They were from the same pattern, no doubt. But if the father's face had been carved from granite, the son's was barely formed, the features thumb-pressed into a mound of grey putty.

'Whatever you have done, you're still my father.'

Benjamin Blackley the elder frowned as if what his son had said was beyond mortal comprehension.

'And I'm still your son. I always will be ... whatever happens.'

'There's no need for that kind of talk, Ben. We'll get this sorted out, you'll see. You can trust me. I'll get the best lawyers available. I'll talk to Yeovil now. He'll know what to do.'

It was perhaps not surprising that a mood of nervous excitement had taken hold of the small crowd gathered around them. But it became clear that the growing commotion was not entirely due to what had passed on the pavement outside the House of Blackley. A stream of shoppers coming out of the store seemed ominously on edge too. Quinn was reminded of the hysteria that had caused the stampede two days ago.

Blackley had noticed the change in mood and was distracted by it. Quinn saw his son's body sag with disappointment. It seemed that what Quinn had insinuated earlier was true. Blackley would always care more about his store than his family.

At that moment Yeovil pushed his way through the crowd, as if he had heard Blackley's call and rushed to answer it. 'Mr Blackley, sir!' Quinn was struck by how wide the man's eyes were open. He had the thought that Yeovil was not a man to surprise easily. Consequently, when he was surprised, he experienced the emotion to a more extreme degree than others. 'Mr Blackley, sir,' he repeated. 'She's dead!'

'What do you mean? Who's dead? What are you talking about, man?'

'She's in the window. Dead.' Yeovil turned to Quinn, as if he was seeing him for the first time. 'Someone's killed her and put her in the shop window.'

A Striking Window Display

'Take him to Brompton nick,' said Quinn to Macadam. 'And raise the local bobbies. Then you'd better get word to DCI Coddington, if you can. He needs to know about this. You'd better get him to bring Inchball along too. We're going to need everyone on this.'

As Macadam led Ben Blackley away, Quinn turned to Yeovil. He still had the dazed, appalled face of a man to whom the unexpected was inconceivable. 'Now, sir, what's all this about?'

'It's the Summer Fashions window display.'

'And where will we find that?'

'It's in the Grand Dome. In the Costumes Salon.' Yeovil glanced back uneasily at the entrance to the store. It was clogged with two competing streams of foot traffic: those fleeing the new horror, and those rushing to find it.

Quinn took out his whistle and gave three sharp blasts. The noise caused a momentary relaxation in the jam, as at least some of those trying to force their way through thought better of it. Clearly their instinctive reaction to the presence of the police was that they ought to make themselves scarce.

Among those peeling away, Quinn noticed the back of a head that he thought he recognized.

'Spiggott!'

The young man picked up his pace but Quinn caught up with him, laying a hand on his shoulder.

'What are you doing here?'

'I have a perfect right to be here.'

'I rather suspect you've lost your position at the House of Blackley.'

'I'm entitled to come here and shop. The old place offers a *world of provision*, don't you know.' Spiggott quoted Blackley's advertising slogan with a bitter emphasis. He tapped a small white cardboard box that was tucked under his arm.

'Were you trying to get in or out?'

'I heard that man. What he said. Someone else has been killed.' As an afterthought, Spiggott added: 'He was the one who was spying on me, you know.'

'So you thought you'd go and take a look?'

'Why haven't you arrested Blackley? It's not Ben Blackley. It's his father. *My* father. He's the monster.'

'You'll have to let me decide whom I arrest and whom I don't.'

'He's grinning ... Look at him grinning. Two dead now, and all he does is grin!'

'Go back to the church and stay with Father Thomas. Don't do anything rash. Leave it to me.'

Spiggott walked slowly backwards, away from Quinn. 'Two dead. How many more will it take before you stop him?' He spun on his heels and broke into a half-run. Just as he reached the entrance of the Sacred Heart, he paused and turned as if to shout something else back to Quinn. But evidently he thought better of it and disappeared into the church precinct.

Quinn marshalled a still-stunned Yeovil inside. He could not prevent Blackley from tagging along.

Despite what Spiggott had said, the great businessman's smile had vanished utterly from his face. Quinn had seen it slip briefly once or twice, but this was the longest Blackley had been without his trademark expression in place. His face was like thunder, in fact. 'This is an outrage,' he declared. 'That they could do this...'

Quinn regarded him quizzically.

'To bring something like this inside the House of Blackley ... it's ... it's...'

'Sacrilege?' prompted Quinn.

Blackley's cursory nod suggested that Quinn's assessment went without saying. 'This is a blow against me, Inspector. An insult to me. This is my enemies at work. They're trying to destroy me. First the fire, then that girl at the mannequin house. Now this. Someone is trying to ruin me, Inspector. That's what this is all about. That man Spiggott, for instance. Why did you let him go?'

'He rather thinks I should have arrested you.'

287

'But that's preposterous. Why should I attack my own interests?'

It was immediately apparent that the Costumes Salon was the scene of a tragedy. Shrieking mannequins prowled aimlessly about; sometimes, animated by brief bursts of energy, they broke into a run. But what they were running from, or to, was unclear. Monsieur Hugo tried to restore calm but the tears were streaming down his face. Arbuthnot was nowhere to be seen, though several other sales assistants stood in a sombre head-shaking cluster.

Yeovil led them towards an ancient commissionaire who was standing by a closed blank door. The store's green livery and top hat gave him the glamour of authority, which he took every bit as seriously as if he were a serving policeman.

'She's through there,' said Yeovil.

Quinn approached the door but the commissionaire raised his hand to prevent him. 'Shtop right there, shonny.' The man's dentures whistled alarmingly.

'It's all right, Dresden,' said Blackley. 'He's with the police.'

The door led into the display window, a raised platform facing outwards and screened from the interior of the store by a partition wall. A space hardly bigger than a cabinet in a museum, it was crowded with clothing dummies in summer fashions. They lurked gracelessly around an open picnic basket which was brimming with wax food.

288

She was lying awkwardly on the ground, as stiffly as the dummies were standing. It didn't look like she was there for any picnic. Her body position was all wrong – arms by her side, legs straight out, head back. Besides, she was still wearing the dressing gown that she had had on the day before, when Quinn had spoken to her.

'Edna,' murmured Quinn.

An audience was gathering on the other side of the glass. Those looking in behaved entirely without inhibition, seeming to have no sense that they themselves could be seen by the man in the window. Either that or they believed his gaze was unimportant, as irrelevant to them as that of an animal from another species.

The onlookers pointed out the dead girl to one another and shared grim *aperçus*. They shook their heads, affronted. He could almost hear them declaring it was a *disgrace* that such a thing could happen on their doorstep, in the store they frequented daily. If they looked at Quinn at all, it was to flash him a look of angry recrimination, as if they held him to blame for the outrage.

Quinn called out: 'Mr Yeovil, can I ask you to go out there and disperse those people?'

Yeovil answered with something vaguely affirmative. As Quinn waited for him to appear outside, he heard the thud of clambering feet as he was joined in the window. 'Oh, God. No. Not this.'

'Do you have any idea who might have done this, Mr Blackley?' It was clear that the identity of the dead girl came as a considerable shock to Blackley. A blow, even.

'My enemies. My enemies have done this.'

Outside, Yeovil was shooing away the inquisitive. He glanced in anxiously. Quinn nodded his approval and signalled for Yeovil to stay where he was to deter any further interest. It also suited him to have Blackley separated from his 'legal adviser'. 'And who are your enemies, would you say? Leaving aside Mr Spiggott. We know all about him.'

'You could start with that papist priest...'

'Do you mean Father Thomas?'

'He's the ringleader.'

'You have a *ring* of enemies?'

'I am under no illusions. There are many men who would like to ruin me. When there's a winner – like me – there are always losers. I have forced more than one business to the wall, I admit it. It's the law of the jungle in commerce. Survival of the fittest. I can't help it. It was their fault they couldn't compete, not mine.'

'Where does Father Thomas fit into it? Surely you don't see the Catholic Church as a business competitor?'

'Isn't it?'

'And isn't this...' Quinn gestured down towards the dead girl. 'Isn't it a somewhat extreme tactic for a disgruntled competitor?'

'I wouldn't put it past them. They'd stoop to anything if they thought it would hurt me. Well, I've survived worse than this. This won't hurt me.' Blackley was quick to correct himself. 'I mean, it won't hurt my business. Obviously

290

I'm deeply pained at the girl's death.'

'Have you ever had sexual relations with Edna Corbett?'

'Who the bloody 'ell's Edna Corbett?'

'She is.'

'I thought her name were Albertine.' Blackley's voice was suddenly almost tender. His soft Yorkshire vowels had a plangent rhythm.

'Yes, she's known as Albertine here. But her real name is Edna.'

'I never knew.'

'So ... Have you?'

Blackley stared at the body on the floor, his eyes bulging from his head. 'No. I can honestly say that I haven't. *Hand ... on ... heart*, Inspector.' He enunciated the words deliberately, slamming his palm against his breast. 'Hand on heart.'

Blackley seemed at pains to impress Quinn with his fidelity on this particular issue. Naturally this led Quinn to suspect that the same could not be said for any of the other mannequins. 'Was she the only one you hadn't slept with?'

Blackley turned sharply towards Quinn. 'I believe that's what's known in legal circles as a leading question, Inspector.'

'What had stopped you? Was she not your type? Or was it simply because you hadn't got round to her yet?'

'This is outrageous!'

'Two girls have been killed. If as you assert, these crimes have been committed to injure you, it is essential that I understand, as well as

291

I can, the relationship between you and each of the dead girls. Therefore, I implore you to be honest with me.'

'I don't know what you're talking about. The only relationship I had with either girl was that they worked for me. I was their employer. That's all there is to it.'

'Where were you last night?'

'I was at home. With my wife and family.'

'Was your son with you? Ben.'

'Ben?'

Quinn noted the suppressed alarm in Blackley's voice. It was enough to tell him that Ben Blackley had not been at home the previous night.

'He's a young man. He has friends. And interests of his own. It doesn't signify if we don't bump into each other of an evening. I believe he may have gone out to the picture palace. I recollect that's what the wife said.'

'Of course, I shall talk to him about that myself. We have him in custody, as you know.'

'I may have that wrong,' said Blackley nervously. 'It may not have been the picture palace.'

'You don't know where your son was last night, do you, Mr Blackley?'

'Why should I? He's old enough and daft enough to do what he wants.'

'Even if it includes murder.'

'He didn't do this, Inspector. He's not a murderer. You know that.'

'I'm afraid that, apart from you, he's the only plausible suspect we have.'

'And that's enough? You don't need evidence, for example? Or witnesses?'

'In some cases, a confession is enough.'

'Has Ben confessed?'

'Not yet. But one of my men, Sergeant Inchball, is very skilled at extracting confessions.'

'You don't really believe this?'

'I don't know what to believe, Mr Blackley.' Behind this guarded statement was Quinn's uneasy realization that he and Macadam had kept watch on the entrance of the mannequin house all night; they had seen neither Blackley nor his son enter.

There was no easy solution to that particular conundrum. But Quinn was distracted from contemplating it further by the siren bell of an approaching police vehicle.

The Door that Led Nowhere

Macadam returned with detectives and uniforms from the local station. Remembering the
panic that had ensued from the false fire alarm
two days ago, Quinn was reluctant to order a
sudden evacuation of the premises. However,
the whole building had to be considered a
crime scene. Who could say what evidence
might be contaminated by the through traffic
of customers?

He decided to proceed discreetly but determinedly. The urgent priority was to seal off the
Costumes Salon. He also sent Blackley off to
find a sheet that could serve as an improvised
screen for the window. Blackley had under-
taken the commission with enthusiasm, apparently relieved to be distancing himself from the
dead girl.

At the same time, he positioned policemen at
all the entrances, turning new customers away.
Those that were already inside Blackley's
would be allowed to leave in their own time,
without panic.

Of course, the possibility had to be considered that the murderer was still inside the store. But it was unlikely. The body must have been put in position before the store opened; otherwise whoever put it there would have been seen carrying it.

Macadam had in tow a short, corpulent man introduced to Quinn as Dr Prendergast. There was something rather seamy, if not unhealthy, about Prendergast's appearance: a sheen of perspiration over his olive-tinged complexion; a rash of angry red spots around his nose and above his collar. He breathed heavily through an open mouth, wheezing asthmatically. Quinn felt he was one of those men who could only be improved by bathing. A pungent masculine odour emanated from him.

The good doctor looked down at the body and sighed. 'Another skinny one.' He glowered out at the street, where Yeovil was negotiating with a fresh group of sensation-seekers.

'I have asked Mr Blackley to fetch a sheet to rig up over the window,' said Quinn.

This prompted an approving grunt from Prendergast as he lowered himself to peer into the dead girl's face. 'Petechial haemorrhaging once again, Inspector. And this time I see we have ligature marks around the neck. Accompanied by deep, but very narrow abrasions. This one was strangled too, but with more force than the other girl, I would venture. Something sharper and more aggressive than a silk scarf caused these marks. If I had to hazard a guess, I would say ... a wire of some kind, the way it has cut into her skin. I suppose you'll be wanting a time of death. It always seems so important to you policemen. Impossible to be absolutely accurate, of course. Cadaveric rigidity is such an unreliable indicator.'

'We know she died sometime last night, or in the early hours of this morning. I spoke to her myself yesterday afternoon.' Quinn winced his eyes shut at the memory of the discussion that had taken place between them. He sniffed noisily and continued, 'And her body must have been placed here before the store opened. Do you think you will be able to give us a more accurate time than that?'

'Probably not.'

'In which case, I am more interested to know whether there is any evidence of recent sexual activity and whether it was consensual.'

'How typical of you policemen. Always thinking the worst of people.'

'I am only influenced by your report into Amélie Dupin's death.'

'*Touché*, as the French say. Though I hope you won't mind if I wait for the modesty drapes before I go peering up her dressing gown?'

'Yes, of course. Please do.'

Prendergast continued his examination of the disposition of the body. 'At least we know with this one that it wasn't the monkey. That is to say, it's hard to imagine how a macaque monkey could have conveyed her body here. Unless it had an accomplice.'

Quinn said nothing. He found the doctor's jaundiced flippancy uncongenial. It jarred with his dismay at Albertine's death. He had to admit that he had not seen it coming. He was struggling to understand it as an event, let alone as a mystery to be solved. An uncomfortable question suggested itself to him: had his attempt to recruit her assistance somehow caused her death?

Quinn had no doubt that it would be held against him by his enemies. But in truth he cared little about that. He was haunted more by the sense that he had failed Edna. He should have done more to protect her. It seemed obvious now, in retrospect, that her closeness to Amélie would have placed her at risk. But from whom? He was no nearer to answering that question than he had been when he first set foot in the mannequin house two days ago.

He found Macadam taking a statement from the mannequin known as Marie-Claude. She had a guarded expression, as if she was trying to remain aloof from what had happened. From death, in other words. She watched Quinn closely as he approached. Her posture tensed as she realized he was about to speak to her.

'Did you see or hear anything unusual in the mannequin house last night?'

'Your pal's already asked me that.'

'And what did you tell him?'

'Nothing. Not a dicky bird. I slept like a log.'

'You didn't see anyone in the house who shouldn't have been there?'

'No.'

'It's the same with all the others, sir.' Macadam shook his head glumly. 'No one saw anything.'

'All right, Sergeant. Let the local boys finish off here. I need your help with something.'

Quinn led Macadam out of the Costumes Salon and through the door that led to the warehouse. A motor lorry was backing into the loading bay, its engine over-revving, exhaust fumes filling the brown gloom.

Quinn felt moisture brimming in his eyes. He put it down to exhaustion, after a night spent on surveillance. Or perhaps it was the pungency of the fumes, in which was mixed a tang of raw petrol vapour.

The cheery whistle of a workman drew a knot of emotion to his throat. It seemed an inhumanly callous sound. Like birdsong, incapable of conceiving of suffering.

'Are you all right, sir?'

'We must take care, Macadam. This latest ... spectacle is designed to confuse us, I think. Designed to present a greater mystery than is actually there. But it is not a mystery at all. It is simply an outrage. We must not be distracted by the outlandish aspects of the case. There is a very simple explanation to all of this, I am sure. People are lying to us – that's to be expected. That's why we must concentrate on the evidence. The facts. The facts are all there. Like the coloured fragments in a kaleidoscope. We must twist the kaleidoscope until a pattern appears. A pattern that makes sense.'

'And what are the fragments we have so far, sir?' Macadam gave an encouraging smile.

They had come out into the dispatch yard. Plumes of stinking black smoke rose from a brick-built incinerator. Next to it a heap of rubbish was accumulating, ready for burning. Mostly broken crates and crumpled boxes, together with their discarded metal bindings. There was waste from the various workshops that were housed in the store, carpentry off-cuts, oddments of carpet and sundry rags. Scraps from the kitchens gave it the characteristic ripeness of a rubbish heap. There was a large willow-patterned teapot on the summit of the heap. Quinn picked it up because at first he could see nothing wrong with it. Closer examination revealed that the tip of the spout was chipped. The teapot looked as though it had seen many years' service; the inside was stained with tannin. He placed it carefully back on the pile of rubbish, in exactly the same place from where he had taken it.

A high fence ran along the side of the yard next to the incinerator.

'No one entered or left the mannequin house through the front door. We can be *sure* of that, can't we, Macadam?'

'Of course, sir,' Macadam answered forcefully, as if he was affronted at the very voicing of such a question.

'So, it's obvious that the body must have been brought out through the rear of the house. No mystery there. It's simply a matter of deduction.' Quinn walked over to the incinerator. He scanned the fence, craning his head back to take in its full height. 'The back garden to the mannequin house adjoins the yard somewhere along here, does it not?'

Macadam nodded and pointed upwards. 'You can just see the top branches of the tree in the garden there. The one that blasted monkey jumped from.'

'Ah, yes, the monkey. I can't help thinking that the monkey holds the key to this mystery, after all. Just as DCI Coddington first suspected.'

'Do you really think so, sir?'

'What was it doing in her room? How did it get there from the Menagerie without the salesman knowing? There's no mystery to this, Macadam. It's simple enough. Glaringly obvious, if you subject the facts to rigorous deduction.'

Macadam frowned deeply, as if willing himself to a point of understanding.

'Naturally, the eye is drawn to what is most ... eye-catching. We are overwhelmed by the sensational. It is a technique employed by stage illusionists. I believe it is known as misdirection. The secret, from our point of view, is not to be bamboozled. In terms of finding a solution – or of working out how the magician has pulled off his trick – the sensational aspects are the least important. And the least interesting.' Quinn began to feel his way along the fence with both hands, applying varying degrees of pressure as he went. His manipulations resembled those of a doctor making a tentative examination of a patient's abdomen. 'There must be ... some way...' Quinn felt a panel of fencing shift beneath his fingers. He tensed his fingers and kept up the gentle movement. All at once, the panel swung stiffly away from him, revolving on a central upright axis. The climbing plants on the other side of the fence gave some weak resistance to the movement. But Quinn was able to push it open far enough to step through into the garden of the mannequin house. He had the sense that the plants had been loosened by many previous passages.

The grass had still not been cut and was meadow-lush in places. The tallest stems had seeded. The border plants sprawled with a wayward abundance. The camellias were already out: great wads of pink littering the ground. There was a sense of wildness barely held back.

Macadam joined him. 'If Blackley knew about this...'

Quinn nodded grimly. 'Of course he knew about it. That's how he came and went as he liked. He never used the front door. No wonder we didn't see him last night.'

'He claims he has an alibi.'

'His wife, you mean? His wife and children ... I dare say they will confirm it. People lie to us, Macadam. You know that.'

'So how did he get into the house? Through the scullery?'

The two of them looked up at the house. Glancing sunlight flared in the windows, shimmering blinds of soft fire suddenly drawn.

Quinn's curiosity was snagged once again by the door that went nowhere. One storey up, with no way of reaching it, since the steps that had once led down to the garden had long ago been dismantled and never replaced. 'They said there wasn't a ladder. Do you remember? When the monkey was in the tree? Blackley and Miss Mortimer both claimed to know nothing about a ladder. But there must be one here.'

Quinn had the bit between his teeth now. He scanned the garden with a methodical rigour, seeking out irregularities, chinks in the innocent screen of appearances. But it was a strange regularity that caught his eye.

Along a strip of the sprawling border the long grass presented an abrupt and very straight edge.

Quinn got down on his knees, feeling the moisture of the grass through the material of his trousers. 'They lied to us.' He pulled it out – a simple wooden ladder that had been hidden away beneath a line of rampant shrubbery.

At first sight it seemed too short to provide access to the door on the first storey. But Macadam helped him set it upright against the wall of the house. Quinn climbed to the top rung. Standing on that and leaning into the wall to keep his balance, it was just possible to reach the handle of the door that went nowhere. It could certainly be opened from the ladder. One energetic hoist up would be enough to get inside.

Quinn nodded to Macadam with satisfaction and climbed down. 'I think this proves Blackley had the means. But we must be careful not to jump to a premature conclusion. He may not be the only one who knew about the gap in the fence and the ladder.'

'He may not have known about them at all,' Macadam pointed out.

Quinn gave his sergeant a startled, indignant look. 'I have no doubt he will deny all knowledge of them.'

He retraced his steps to the back of the garden and led the way back through the revolving fence panel into the dispatch yard.

'If you wanted to dispose of a body, the means are here. That is the normal instinct of a murderer – or any criminal – to destroy the evidence. Not to flaunt it in the most public of places. If Blackley is the murderer ... that aspect of the crime simply doesn't make sense. His outrage at the presence of the body in his precious store appeared genuine. I am not sure he is such a proficient actor. That damned smile of his ... He manages to hold it in place, but the effect is hardly natural.'

'You are inclining to the view that someone else is the killer, sir?'

'Regrettably, yes.'

'Why regrettably, sir? Surely it makes no difference to us who the killer is, provided we catch him?'

'I don't like him. I have never liked him. Not from the first moment I saw him. I don't like the way...' Quinn's words trailed off. He had caught sight of the warehouseman coming out from the loading bay. The man fixed him with a sullen glower as he hunched over the lighting of a cigarette. The still-burning match was thrown without regard to where it landed.

The warehouseman lifted his head defiantly as Quinn approached. 'You have a habit of throwing lighted matches around, don't you? I saw you do that once before. It's a rather dangerous habit, is it not? It could easily spark a fire.'

The man blew out smoke. He stared Quinn in the eye without flinching.

'What's your name?'

''Oo vants 'a know?' Quinn remembered the man's accent, the strange mangled growl of Cockney and something even more eastern, more exotic.

'Kaminski, isn't it?' Quinn remembered now the exchange he had heard between the warehouseman and the driver. 'Good day, Mr Kaminski. I am Detective Inspector Quinn of the Special Crimes Department.'

'You looking for dat monkey? I ain' seen 'im.'

'No, I'm not looking for the monkey. I'm interested in the fence. Did you know about it?'

'Vot abou' da fence?'

'There's a way through to the house.'

The man shrugged.

'Have you ever seen anyone go through there?'

'I ain' see nobody.'

'Mr Blackley? Did you ever see him go through this way?'

The man spat.

'How about his son? Mr Blackley Junior? You do know who he is, don't you? Did you ever see him cut through here?'

'I never see nobody.'

'Any of the other men from the store?'

The man's expression remained blank. He did not seem dismayed or even surprised by Quinn's persistence. He simply shook his head with detached patience.

A sudden thought occurred to Quinn. 'What about you? Did you ever go through there?'

Kaminski evidently found this a hilarious suggestion. His laughter struck Quinn as somewhat forced.

'What's so funny?'

'Vy I vant to go in dere?'

'Do you know who lives in that house?'

'I know.'

'The mannequins.'

'I know.'

'You know then that a girl was murdered there on Tuesday night. You may have heard that another girl has been killed now. We believe her body was brought through here. Through your yard. Through your warehouse.'

'I ain' seen it.'

'You must have seen something. What time is the yard opened?'

'Depends.'

'This morning, for example.'

'*Dis* mornin'?' The emphasis suggested incredulity that Quinn should be interested in this particular morning.

'Yes.'

'We open early dis mornin'. Saturday, ain' it? We go' a van in early, ain' it?'

'Early being...?'

305

'Seven.'

'You were here at seven?'

'I was.'

'Was anyone else here then?'

'I'm always first.'

'So you were here on your own?'

'I ain' see nothin'. I ain' see nobody.'

'Where do you come from, Mr Kaminski?'

'Come from? I come from Whitechapel.'

'No. What's your country of origin?'

'Polska.'

'How long have you worked here at Blackley's?'

'I work 'ere ever since I come over. Thirty years now I've been at Blackley's.'

'Any complaints in that time?'

Kaminski's expression darkened. 'Wha' do you mean?'

'Does Mr Blackley treat you all right? I've heard he can be something of a tyrant.'

Kaminski concentrated on his cigarette, which for some reason had become suddenly fascinating to him. His expression was distracted when he met Quinn's eye again, as if he had forgotten the question.

'Well? I'd be grateful if you'd answer my question.'

'You speak to anyone here. Dey all got complaints. Wha' you gonna do?'

'I don't know, Mr Kaminski. What are you going to do?'

Kaminski's gaze became inward-focused. Then he looked up, startled, at a sudden cry that came from the entrance to the loading bay.

'Ah, Quinn, there you are!' DCI Coddington, in his herringbone Ulster, stalked across the dispatch yard. His face was set into what he no doubt imagined was that of a stern, implacable authoritarian.

Kaminski took the opportunity provided by the interruption to squeeze out his half-smoked cigarette and tuck it behind his ear as he slipped back inside.

'This is a bloody mess, Quinn!' Coddington did his best to maintain his angry martinet persona.

'Yes, sir.' All at once, Quinn was overwhelmed by exhaustion. He found he had little patience for Coddington's charade. Edna's death was simply too upsetting to indulge in games. And if anyone had a right to take Edna's death badly, Quinn felt it was he. 'We didn't see it coming, sir.'

'You can say that again, Quinn. This doesn't look good for you, you know.'

'But no one saw it coming, sir,' Quinn insisted. 'Did you?'

'Don't be impertinent. I should never have let you talk me into the surveillance operation.'

'The surveillance operation didn't kill Edna.'

'Can you be sure? What if the murderer got wind that he was being watched?'

Quinn felt the same stab of self-reproach that had pained him earlier. He had set up Edna, or Albertine, to be his source on the inside. The killer, or someone linked to the killer, could conceivably have overheard him talking to her. The conversation had taken place in her room.

But it was not unknown for people to listen at doors. He had to accept that there was some truth in what Coddington said.

'You're finished, Quinn. Finished. Do you hear?'

'I see.' Quinn felt strangely liberated. He realized how physically tired he was after a night divided between the floor and the window. Suddenly all he wanted to do was to go home and sleep. He had felt he was getting somewhere with the case, that a solution was within his grasp. But now he was not so sure. No matter how much he twisted the kaleidoscope of fragments, he could not form them into a pattern that made sense. 'So you will be taking over the case completely?'

Coddington's eyes stood out in panic. His moustache was convulsed with twitches. 'No, no ... What I mean is, you *will* be finished. Just as soon as you've wrapped things up here.'

Quinn almost found the energy to smile. 'I see. I'm to solve the case for you, and then I will be dispensed with.'

'Don't flatter yourself, Quinn. There's any number of officers who could solve this case. It's simply that you've been working it from the beginning. It doesn't make any sense to replace you at this stage.'

'Not quite from the beginning, sir. You were working it to begin with. I was brought in on the second day.'

'Just get on with it, Quinn. And no more bloody mistakes, hey?' Coddington began to turn away.

'Is that it, sir?'

Coddington faltered and cocked his head expectantly. 'What?'

'Don't you want to know what I've discovered, sir? So that you can direct the future progress of the case? That is your job, after all – is it not, sir? You are the officer in charge. I am merely executing your orders. That's been the case since yesterday morning.'

'You won't bring me down with you, Quinn. If that's what you're trying to do.'

'I'm not trying to do that, sir. All I'm trying to do is find out who killed Amélie Dupin and Edna Corbett.'

A vindictive twist of the mouth animated Coddington's drooping moustache. 'Got you stumped, has it?'

'There's something vital that I'm missing, I will give you that. As yet, I only seem to hold a tangle of loose ends. I can't quite seem to tie them together.'

'And you the great detective.'

'I never claimed to be a great detective. If you remember, sir, you foisted that accolade on me.' It was perhaps a mistake to remind Coddington of the admiration he once professed towards Quinn.

'Go on then. Tell me. What marvellous breakthrough have you made?'

Quinn gestured to the gap in the fence. Coddington frowned. His moustache twitched impatiently. 'And what's the significance of that, pray?'

'It means that on Tuesday night, when

309

Blackley said that he was not observed going out through the front of the store, he could easily have slipped out the back unnoticed and gained access to the mannequin house through this aperture. And last night, granted we didn't see Blackley, or anyone, enter the mannequin house by the front door. He could easily have got in this way.'

'But if you didn't see him, it's immaterial. You have no proof. He could have got in. So could anyone else. You'll need more than that, Inspector Quinn.'

'Yes, I know. And I intend to discover more.'

Inchball joined them in the yard, firing the barest, tersest of nods in Quinn's direction. It was a minimal gesture, but eloquent of so much. 'Has he told you?'

Quinn looked inquiringly at Coddington.

DCI Coddington shifted in embarrassment. 'I was just about to.'

Inchball rolled his eyes for Quinn's benefit. 'Two things. She was a virgin. Edna. Prendergast has just confirmed it. He asked DCI Coddington to pass on the news.'

Coddington's moustache gave a defiant jump. 'There were other important matters to be dealt with first. I would have got round to it.'

But Quinn remembered that Coddington had turned away.

Inchball sniffed noisily in contempt. 'Second thing: we heard back from the forensic boys.'

Macadam pressed forward eagerly. 'Good old Charlie. Come up with something, did he?'

Inchball's face was set in a resentful glower. '*I* don't know. '*E* wouldn't show me what it said.' Whenever Inchball was in a temper, his aitches fell by the wayside more than usual.

'It was not necessary for you to see it. I passed on to you everything that you needed to know.' Coddington stuck out his moustache self-righteously. 'The wooden hairpin we recovered from beneath the bed ... He found traces of silk fibres on it. Red silk, matching the scarf around her neck.'

Quinn nodded to Macadam with satisfaction. 'Our kaleidoscope, Sergeant. I believe one fragment has just been shaken into place.' He turned to Coddington. 'And the key? Did he have anything to say about the key?'

'Nothing significant there,' said Coddington, though his eyes avoided Quinn's. 'Nothing very remarkable at all. It was just a key. An ordinary key. No hidden trickery.'

'It would be helpful to see Cale's report.'

'I don't have it on my person, naturally. But you may take it that I have communicated all the salient details.'

'In that case, I think I can say with some confidence how Amélie Dupin met her death.' But Quinn felt far from confident; he felt tremulous and queasy. His exhaustion had reached the point that he felt at odds with the solidity of his surroundings. He wanted to sleep so much that it would have been easy to persuade him that he was walking through a dream.

Ascending the Dome

'If you don't mind me saying, guv, with respect and all that.' Inchball's brow was cross-hatched with lines of concern. 'You look like shit.'

Quinn gazed distractedly back. There seemed to be something of a lover's awe in his fascination for his sergeant's eyes. 'She wasn't murdered, after all. The wooden hairpin was a tourniquet. Remember the bruise; the elongated bruise near her jawbone. That was caused by the pressure of the pin as it held the scarf in place. She had twisted it tight herself, giving one last turn that she was unable to undo. Suicide by strangulation is very rare. But it is not impossible. All that's required is for the victim to create a fatal situation which the organism's natural instincts for self-preservation are unable to undo. She was weak – half-starved, according Prendergast. She suffered from a debilitating nervous condition. She had used up all her strength to fasten the tourniquet, jamming the pin tight against her jawbone. She had none left to undo it.'

Coddington made a disparaging yelp. 'Is that it? Is that the great mystery unravelled? She killed herself? Is that the best you can come up with? That's your answer to the locked door mystery? I must say, I'm disappointed, Inspector. You didn't even solve it yourself! Doctor Prendergast first raised the possibility in his report. And now the forensics lab has provided you with confirmation. You've done nothing.'

Quinn frowned at Coddington, unable to understand his petulance. Coddington's strange mood was a kind of angry, jealous antagonism, mixed with a sense of vindicated disdain. It wearied and depressed Quinn unspeakably; there was simply no time for it. 'My job isn't to come up with a startling solution. It is to examine the evidence and draw the most likely conclusion from that. And besides, the mystery isn't solved yet, sir. For now there is a greater mystery. Why? Why did she do it? And why this particular method? Is it not a strangely technical means of self-dispatch for a young girl to choose? A tourniquet around the neck? Someone must have put the idea in her head, surely. And if she was aided and abetted in her suicide, that makes whoever is responsible for that at the very least an accessory in the commission of a crime. Someone, I believe, put the pin in her hand, as well as the idea in her head. That individual is to all intents and purposes her murderer.'

Coddington shook his head impatiently. 'Nonsense! You cannot persuade another person to kill themselves against their will.'

'Perhaps not,' conceded Quinn. 'But aren't we all, from time to time, enticed by the idea of self-annihilation?' Quinn searched Coddington's face for a hint of understanding. Perhaps it was the fact that he didn't find any – not the least trace of human sympathy – that provoked him to go still further. '*I know I am.*' He made the admission in a husky whisper, his voice in awe of the words it uttered. He cleared his throat, to say more definitely: 'And certainly, my father was.'

Coddington shook his head despairingly. It seemed that he was beginning to pity Quinn, which was perhaps the surest sign possible that it was all over for him. 'I hate to ask, but what has your father got to do with this?'

It was a reasonable question, perhaps. Quinn found it difficult to articulate the connections between the case and his own personal history, but he sensed them nonetheless. The dark, groping tentacles of the past were pulling him back down to an unfathomed abyss. As a child he had been terrified by talk of a 'bottomless pool' which was rumoured to exist in a scrap of wasteland near his school. He had taken the figure of speech literally, and imagined a body of water extending downwards infinitely. A number of local children had apparently fallen into it over the years, their bodies never recovered. According to the popular account, the police, with their nets and dragging chains, had never been able to plumb the depths of the pool. He had imagined himself diving into it and plummeting down to explore its infinite mystery. He had no doubt that he would encounter the other children who had dared to plunge beneath its surface. Perhaps this was how it claimed its victims, by exercising a fatal fascination over their childish minds? They did not fall in; they threw themselves in willingly.

One summer he set out alone to find the pool. It was perhaps as well for him that he failed. But the idea of it stayed with him over the years. Every time he began a new case, it felt in some way as though he was diving into a similarly bottomless pool, its depths swirling with the pallid bloated corpses that his investigations disturbed. One of those corpses was invariably his father's.

'My father killed himself. I think I speak with some authority, then, on the subject of suicide. Most of the time we fight against it. The death-wish. And our friends, our true friends, will strengthen us in that fight. So that the part of our will that wants to live wins out over the part that wants to die. But what if there is a man capable of exploiting and magnifying the negative, self-destructive part of our will? He does not have to be in the room at the time the victim dies to be guilty of causing her death. He could have planted the seed earlier. And if that man, in perpetrating such an event, is executing the wishes – the orders, we might even say – of another individual, are they both not guilty of a conspiracy to murder?'

'This is all very well,' said Coddington. 'But you'll have a hell of a job proving it.'

'Another thing, guv.' Inchball's tone was surprisingly gentle. He showed himself capable of tact and compassion, as well as the casual brutality for which he was better known. 'Something that's botherin' me. How did the

315

hairpin find itself on the floor under the bed?' Inchball grimaced regretfully, as if it pained him to point these things out. 'If she killed herself, the tourniquet should still have been in place when she was found.'

'We don't have all the answers, I admit. But we do have a few more questions to put to certain individuals. Blackley, for instance. I want to talk to Mr Blackley one more time. Also, I want you to find that man Yeovil.'

'Yeovil?' Coddington's moustache rippled with distrust.

'Mr Yeovil is Blackley's creature. I believe he has certain exceptional talents which he is prepared to put to use unscrupulously on Blackley's behalf.'

'What about Blackley's son, sir?' wondered Macadam. 'What do we do with him?'

'Leave him to sweat a little longer. If we can at least get him to confirm that he saw his father in the mannequin house on Tuesday night that would be something. The main thing is, find Yeovil. That's what I want you men to do.'

Inchball, Macadam and Quinn nodded once in perfect unison. A moment later DCI Coddington attempted a nod of his own. He evidently felt it somewhat lacking, to judge by the anguished wince that came immediately after.

Coming back through the Menagerie, Quinn caught sight of the older salesman, Kenning. 'Have you seen Mr Blackley?'

Kenning seemed to have aged since Quinn had last seen him, just two days ago. But that had been at the time of the panic over the false fire alarm. His face had slumped into an expression of permanent defeat, his gaze blank and unfocused. 'He made me kill her.'

Quinn felt the hammering of his pulse in places where he had never experienced it before. It was a throb inside his right bicep, a ripple through his thigh, a tensing in his throat. 'What did you say?'

'He made me kill her,' repeated Kenning. The man was half in a trance.

'Who are you talking about? Who made you kill whom?'

'Blackley.'

'Mr Blackley made you kill ... Amélie? Albertine? Which one?'

Kenning frowned in confusion. 'No. Miranda. He made me kill Miranda. He said it was all her fault.'

Quinn sighed. Then frowned. One aspect of this trivial revelation intrigued him. 'How do you kill a parrot?'

'The same way you kill a chicken.' Kenning made a sharp twisting movement with his hands. 'You break its neck.'

'I see.' Quinn could not say that he was upset by the parrot's death. However, he wondered facetiously if this would be another fatality counted against him when the reckoning was done. 'Do you know where he is now?'

But Quinn did not need Kenning to answer. An explosion of angry shouting in Blackley's distinctive Yorkshire accent had him running through the police cordon back into the Costumes Salon.

Quinn scanned the floor but Blackley was nowhere to be seen. 'Where is he?'

Monsieur Hugo gestured upwards, a queasy expression on his face.

Quinn looked up to the first-floor gallery. His eye was drawn to a flurry of activity. Blackley was beating one of his staff with a furled umbrella. The man brought his arms up to cover his face and hunched himself over protectively. But otherwise he took his beating without resistance.

The gated lift was decorated ornately in a distinctly French style: all art nouveau cast-iron curlicues and elaborate gilded mouldings. These features did little to mitigate the brutal functionality of the caged shaft. If Quinn hadn't felt himself once again overwhelmed by exhaustion, he would have taken the stairs. But the lift car was waiting.

As soon as he stepped on board, he regretted it. The lift attendant in a green top hat and tailcoat had something of the manner of a spider welcoming a fly. The car shook precariously under Quinn's weight. A warning screech echoed ominously as the attendant slammed the latticed gate shut behind him. The exertion caused further tremors. The tang of oiled machinery was the only comfort afforded.

'Floor?' The attendant's haughty demeanour was to be expected. It was his mission to pilot the craft that ferried customers to the various floors of the House of Blackley. His was a noble calling; his skills arcane. It was understandable if he wished to impress his passengers with the importance of his office, and to remind them with a raised eyebrow that their lives were in his hands.

'First.'

The attendant pursed his lips as if he were a connoisseur of floors; it seemed that his willingness to take Quinn where he wanted to go would depend on whether, in his considered opinion, the floor in question passed muster.

He pressed the appropriate button. A moment later the suspended car juddered into motion with a chthonic rumble.

Quinn felt a mixture of apprehension and impatience; the typical emotions of a lift passenger, perhaps, but they were compounded by a definite sense of impending crisis. Until now, in public at least, Blackley had managed to maintain his act of imperturbable calm. But now he had allowed himself to be witnessed violently assaulting a member of his staff. It was a sign that he was beginning to feel the pressure Quinn had been applying.

That made him unpredictable. And therefore dangerous.

The lift car quaked to a halt. The attendant slid open the latticed gate, fixing Quinn with a regretful look. 'First floor. Umbrellas, parasols, canopies, tents, pagodas. Walking canes, shooting sticks, sword sticks. Diverse concealed weaponry.'

In response to Quinn's incredulous stare, the man added: 'Articles of protection and defence.'

Quinn hurried along the gallery to the umbrella and parasol area. Blackley was no longer there. The man who had endured a beating from him was flexing his back tentatively. The bent wreck of an umbrella lay discarded on the floor. 'Where is he? Blackley?' demanded Quinn.

The man's eyes oscillated nervously, avoiding Quinn's. 'H-he's gone.'

'I can see that. Why was he beating you?'

'I think you must be mistaken.'

Quinn picked up the broken umbrella.

'There was an accident.'

'Listen, man, I'm a policeman. I can help you. I saw it. He has no right to treat you like that. It was common assault.'

'I don't know what you're talking about.'

Quinn threw the umbrella back on the floor in frustration. 'Where did he go? Up? Or down?'

The salesman shrugged.

Quinn's gaze was drawn upwards by the great luminous floating disc of the dome's stained-glass roof. He was reminded of the visual analogy of the mystery that he had discussed with Macadam: the small coloured panes were arranged in a pattern of multiple symmetry, suggesting the haphazard designs thrown up by shaking and twisting a kaleidoscope. He imagined some unseen giant hand rotating the Grand Dome of Blackley's so that the countless *tesserae* of the roof shifted to form new patterns, firing and flaring as they performed their complex choreographies in the sunlight. He willed them towards meaning. Like the patterns in a kaleidoscope, they always seemed to be on the verge of a figurative representation. Yet, however pleasing the patterns were, there was always something elusive about them.

Quinn tried to put himself in Blackley's shoes. The cupola represented the high point of Blackley's achievements, as well as literally being the highest point in his building. Was it fanciful to speculate that at a moment of stress he might want to reassert his dominion over his commercial empire by ascending to its summit?

In the event, it was all Quinn had to go on.

The green-liveried lift attendant welcomed him back with a knowing leer.

The idea of the bottomless pool came back to Quinn. He imagined the lift shaft plunging endlessly downwards. Not to Hell, beyond Hell. He decided not to get back inside the lift car.

He felt the rigours of the night in every step he took. He took consolation in the thought that his career would, in all likelihood, soon be over. Coddington had meant it as a threat. It seemed like an enticement now, one which he could hardly wait to be fulfilled.

He was tired. Physically tired. But tired, too, of the corpses, of so long an acquaintance with the dead.

Tired of the killing.

He had always believed that he had needed his job to make sense of his life, to give it purpose. He had met the chaos and violence of existence with a constant search for rational explanations. He wondered whether, paradoxically, it was this very search that had prevented him from finding meaning, and therefore peace. Was the secret instead to embrace the mystery, to surrender to it?

Quinn thought of Father Thomas and the consolations of religious faith. He wondered if he himself had the courage to surrender himself to that particular mystery, perhaps the greatest of all. For some reason he took comfort in the idea of entering the church of the Sacred Heart again after the case was over. He was not a Catholic, but he craved the redemption offered by the confessional.

He was so tired that if the next floor had been Beds he would have simply thrown himself down on to the first inviting mattress he came to. He emerged instead on the Floor Coverings gallery. Turkish rugs were draped over the balcony, advertising to the floors below their crimson richness. Quinn inhaled the distinctive smell of new carpets: strangely inviting, almost intoxicating.

He hurried along the gallery, stumbling more than running, weaving in and out of the piles of rugs like the shuttle on a giant loom. The patterns on display progressed from the traditional to garish sprawls of colour no doubt influenced by the latest movements in art and

322

theatre. Out of the corner of his eye he caught sight of a black and white rug cast haphazardly on the ground. The pattern snagged on his consciousness; he had the feeling that he had seen it somewhere recently. More distractingly still, he couldn't help thinking that whoever had left it there was in danger of a reprimand – or worse – from Blackley. But fortunately for the staff on this floor, Blackley was nowhere to be seen.

The next floor up was the Drapery Gallery. Bolts of iridescent silk flowed down over the balcony into the chasm of the Grand Dome, like multicoloured waterfalls frozen in mid-cascade. There was no sign of Blackley amid the forests of upholstery fabrics or gardens of curtain material. Silent birds stretched their wings without moving, as if they had been startled and petrified by his passing.

Upwards, then, to the Haberdashery Gallery. At some point, Quinn's exhaustion began to play tricks on his mind. He was suddenly unsure whether he was in pursuit or in flight. The further he ascended, the greater the sense that he was escaping the tentacles of the past. But he also knew that he was forcing this confrontation not simply for the good of the case. There was something in it for him too. Something linked to his past.

Blackley, he realized, had become a proxy for his own father. When he confronted him, he would put to him the wrongs that he had committed against his son – or sons if Spiggott was to be believed. He would charge him with abandonment and betrayal. It was hard not to be aware of the correspondences with his own predicament.

The very top floor of the Grand Dome was taken up with a tea room and restaurant, as well as a Ladies Lounge and lavatories for both sexes.

On this floor weary shoppers could come to restore their energy while looking down on the fray. No doubt this was why Blackley chose to place these facilities at the top of the store. Quinn had noticed that the higher he ascended the fewer customers he encountered on each floor. This may have been the result of the gradual evacuation of the store. However, he felt that there was a commercial principle at work. Anyone who was sitting down was necessarily no longer shopping. Their purses were resting as well as their legs. Blackley would understandably wish to discourage any respite at all from consumerist activity. If you were determined to sit it out for a period, however briefly, he would make sure you worked hard for that privilege, having first dragged your bones up the full height of his Grand Dome. And from the tea room there, you would have a tempting view of the Costumes Salon, the beating heart of the House of Blackley. This view could not but be of interest to you, for you were more than likely to be a woman. Quinn accepted that you might possibly be a man accompanying a woman, in which case, he speculated, Mr Blackley was probably not very interested in you at all.

He saw Blackley patrolling the tables of the tea room, his affable smile once again back in place as he charmed and chatted to the ladies taking refreshment.

To confront Blackley in front of an audience of adoring females would inevitably place him at a disadvantage. Quinn seized his moment.

'Mr Blackley! May I have a word?'

'Can't you see I'm busy?' Blackley squeezed out the words through gritted teeth.

Quinn looked around at the handful of middle-aged to elderly women scattered around the tea room. Their faces were turned in fearful interest towards the two men in their midst. 'Busy? Here?'

'You have no conception what it takes to make a business concern like the House of Blackley function smoothly. Every department places equal demands upon my attention. Regrettably I am unable to be in more than one place at once. There is only one of me.'

'Why have you abandoned your son?'

'What are you talking about?'

'Ben. Does he not need you more than the store does?'

'Ben will be all right. You've got no reason to hold him. You're just fishing. As soon as your fishing expedition comes up with nothing you'll be forced to let him go. In the meantime I have alerted his mother to his predicament. She is at the station where he is being held with our family lawyer. Everything that can be done is being done.'

'If I were you, I wouldn't be so sure. You

think you can rely on him because he's your son. But you ought to know that a son's feelings for his father can be ambivalent in the extreme. It can turn from admiration to contempt overnight. The truth can change everything. What truth did Ben discover on Tuesday night, Mr Blackley?'

'Fishing again! You won't catch me out that way, Inspector!' Blackley almost seemed to be enjoying himself.

'You should know, we found the way through. The way to the mannequin house. The swivelling fence panel. That's how you are able to come and go without anyone knowing. You climb up the ladder to open the door to the spare room that Miss Mortimer keeps in readiness for you.'

'Why do I need to go to such lengths when I have a perfect right to stay in that house any time I like? I own it, for God's sake!'

'Sometimes it suits your purpose to keep your visit secret.'

'Now listen to me, Inspector. You cannot come here, in my place of business, in front of my customers, making your nasty insinuations. I will not stand for it, do you hear?'

'Why did Amélie kill herself, Mr Blackley?'

'What do you mean? How could she kill herself? I thought she were strangled?' His Yorkshire origins came through with sudden force. *A sign of stress?* Quinn wondered.

'She was. But we now believe that she engineered the circumstances of her death herself.'

'So you can let Ben go!'

'She may have killed herself, Mr Blackley. But she didn't rape herself.'

There was a gasp from the tea-sipping ladies, who were enrapt by the men's exchange. Blackley regarded his audience with a sheepish look. 'Ben had nothing to do with that.'

'Is that an admission, Mr Blackley?'

Blackley flashed a complex look towards Quinn. It was a look that seemed to confess to every crime that could be imagined, let alone committed. But there was contrition in it too.

And – for the first time – fear.

Less than Perfect Fathers

'What is it you want to tell me, Mr Blackley?'

Quinn sensed the attention of all the tea room ladies focused intently on them. Blackley must have felt it too.

'Nothing. I have nothing to tell you. Except...'

'What?'

'The last thing I wanted was Amélie's death.'

There were sympathetic noises from the ladies.

'We can't always control the consequences of our actions.'

Blackley's eyes narrowed. The thought had evidently never occurred to him before.

'You felt bad, didn't you, about what happened? That's why you wanted to put the new pictures up in the hall. Scenes of Paris. You had never seen her so upset. It shocked you. Your monstrous egotism meant that you couldn't possibly understand that you were the cause of her distress. You thought perhaps it was because she was feeling homesick. So you endeavoured to make her feel at home. To try to make amends.'

'No, you're wrong. It wasn't like that. I already had the pictures.'

'Before you raped her, you mean?'

'Come now, Inspector. You won't catch me out like that.'

'You sensed her moving away from you and thought that the pictures – and the monkey – would buy back her affections?'

'I was worried about her. Amélie meant a lot to me. She was my best mannequin. Naturally it upset me to see her upset. As it would any caring employer.' A wistful expression passed over Blackley's face. 'If she had only seen the pictures ... they might have cheered her up ... she might still be alive.'

Quinn was having none of that. 'Did Yeovil hypnotize Amélie? Did he plant the seed of suicide in her mind?'

'Why would he do that?'

'Because you told him to.'

The suggestion drew a gasp from the audience.

Blackley shook his head vigorously, as much for his ladies as for Quinn. 'No. You're barking up the wrong tree there, Inspector. If Yeovil did hypnotize her – and I don't believe for a minute that he did – it was not at my request.'

'Why do you have Mr Yeovil in your employ, sir?'

'He has certain skills that are useful to me.'

'He has been spying on Spiggott?'

'Yeovil has been helping me with that particular problem, yes. That young fellow Spiggott has been causing me a deal of trouble. Despite what I might wish, I cannot be everywhere. I have to trust men like Yeovil to be my

329

eyes and ears.'

'Do you know anything about the theft of Shizaru from the Menagerie? Did Mr Yeovil help you with that too?'

Blackley seemed taken aback. A mask of indignation settled over his features. But he could not prevent a glimmer of amusement showing through. He might even have winked at the ladies. 'It's not a crime. Everything in the store belongs to me. I cannot steal from myself. I merely wished to take the monkey without the men in the Menagerie realizing.' He drew closer to Quinn and lowered his voice confidentially. 'I knew that Amélie had a soft spot for the little fellow. But discretion ... discretion was important. I can trust Yeovil to be discreet.'

'But Mr Yeovil can be more than discreet. He can ensure that others are discreet too.'

A smile of grim acceptance flickered on to Blackley's lips. 'You've worked so much out, Inspector.' He fixed Quinn with a steady, pleading look. His voice was once again raised. He was playing to the gallery. 'Can you not work out who is doing this to me? Who is attacking me in this way? Not even you can believe I was responsible for putting that girl in my own shop window.'

'To be frank, Mr Blackley, the difficulty I face is that you have made so many enemies. I just now saw you assault a member of your staff in Umbrellas and Parasols. There have been others, I believe. Didn't I once read about you taking a cane to a man for yawning?'

The ladies tut-tutted their disapproval at this.

330

One or two cried *'shame!'*.

Blackley grew irritable, sensing that he was losing their sympathy. 'My people know where they stand when they enter my employ. There are rules. The rules must be obeyed. They sign a contract to that effect. I cannot be blamed if I hold them to it.'

'They don't sign up to being beaten, I rather suspect.'

'I am firm but fair!' protested Blackley. 'And even if what you say is true, does that really give some bugger the right to do this? To murder a poor defenceless girl, just to get back at me for a little heavy handedness? Is that what you're saying happened, Inspector?'

It was a point well made. Blackley had won his audience back over. Quinn sensed heads bobbing in approval around them.

Quinn's shrug was more of a convulsion of exhaustion, as if he was trying to slough off the worries of the case. 'I am beginning to fear that we will never know the truth of what happened.' His words sounded defeated even to his own ear.

'Remember my offer, Inspector.' Blackley drew himself up as if he had sensed the issue swing in his favour. His old confidence seemed to return to him, along with his habitual smile. 'Yeovil ... Yeovil can help you.'

'Don't worry. I shall be speaking to Mr Yeovil soon enough.'

The ladies of the tea room seemed satisfied with the outcome of the exchange. They were more intent now on their own chatter, which was no doubt energized by the scene they had witnessed. They had experienced a frisson of outrage, the hint of scandal, but somehow the universe had been restored. When it came down to it, it seemed that most of them approved of Blackley's approach to staff discipline; or at least did not object to it strongly enough to forgo the privilege of shopping at his store.

Quinn could not help but feel a strong sense of anticlimax. The brief look of contrition that Blackley had let slip was the closest he would come to an admission of guilt over the rape. A guilty look was not enough to secure a conviction in a court of law. In such crimes it invariably came down to a question of the man's word against the woman's. Even if Amélie had lived it would have been difficult enough to prove, especially with a man of good standing and character such as Blackley. Furthermore, given Blackley's power over her, there was no guarantee that Amélie would have made an accusation; far more likely, in fact, that she would have kept quiet. Despite what Dr Prendergast had said in his report about the association between rape and murder, the motive for Blackley to kill Amélie simply wasn't strong enough.

It was not only Blackley's failure to own up to his misdeeds that frustrated Quinn. His disappointment went deeper than that. He remembered the idea that had come to him as he had ascended the floors of the Grand Dome: that he was chasing not Blackley but another less than perfect father.

'What is the matter, Inspector? You look as if you have seen a ghost.'

'My father killed himself, you know.'

'What has it to do with me?'

'You think that you are protecting yourself when you hold on to these secrets of yours. But it's quite the opposite, Mr Blackley. Secrets put you at great risk. They expose you to blackmail and extortion. And they drive a wedge between you and those who could love you, and whose love could truly save you. My father was killed by his secrets. I'm imploring you not to make the same mistake that he made.'

'I am not your father.'

'I don't care whether you tell *me* the truth or not. I'm used to people lying. But please, I beg you, be honest with Ben.'

'Have you quite finished, Inspector? I am a busy man.'

Quinn nodded a reluctant release. Whatever resolution he had hoped for, it was clear that Blackley would not provide it.

The lift attendant pulled the latticed gate to with a nod of satisfaction. 'Find what you were looking for, sir?'

Quinn ignored the question. He looked the man squarely in the eye but could not penetrate his permanently ironic manner. He became convinced the man was another of Blackley's spies. And so he couldn't help feeling that he was now Blackley's prisoner; in other words, the prisoner of the man he had set out to catch.

'Which floor?' said the attendant, holding and reciprocating Quinn's steady scrutiny.

'Ground.'

The attendant nodded and pressed a button. Somewhere wheels shifted, machinery rumbled. The lift shuddered and sank. Quinn's sense of confinement intensified.

He could not help voicing his thoughts. 'How do you bear it, just going up and down all day? Do you not feel caged in?'

The man shrugged. 'It makes me appreciate the horizontal all the more when I am able to enjoy it.'

They picked up more passengers on the next floor, a young couple with a gaggle of children of various ages. They filled the lift car with noise and heat. Quinn looked up at the empty shaft above, concentrating on the greased cable and grimy brickwork to take his mind off his present discomfort.

As the lift shuddered into descent, he became aware of a series of sharp blows dealt repeatedly to his shins. He looked down to see one of the children, a boy of about seven, determinedly kicking at his legs. The boy was looking up at Quinn to monitor his reaction. Quinn couldn't help noticing that he was wearing a sailor suit that reminded him of the one hanging in the dead child's bedroom at the Sledges'. He wondered if the Sledges' son had been a shin-kicker, and whether that had contributed to his early, violent death in any way.

Quinn tapped the boy's father on the

shoulder. 'I say, your son is kicking me in the shins.'

The man's expression was doleful, but not apologetic. 'Well ... he doesn't mean any harm.'

'Can't you get him to stop?'

The man sighed. 'Archie, do you mind awfully stopping that for a moment, old sport?'

'For a moment?' Quinn was incredulous. 'I rather want him to stop it for good.'

'Stop it, Archie. There's a good fellow.'

Archie gave one final crack with his shoe, just on the edge of the bone. When Quinn looked down, the boy's expression was utterly un-abashed; it seemed to suggest that the blow was no more or less than Quinn deserved.

At last the lift attendant drew back the gate on the ground floor. Quinn's torturer and his innumerable siblings burst out with an explosion of screams. Their mother called after them ineffectually: 'Children! Children! Oh, do be careful.'

Quinn was glad to see Macadam bounding towards him with an eager, excited step. He knew what his sergeant was going to say before he opened his mouth: 'We have him, sir. Yeovil. He's in the back of a Black Maria outside.'

'Good work, Macadam.'

Less enthusiastically, Macadam added: 'Sergeant Inchball is with him. He seems to think that he can soften him up in anticipation of your interviewing him, sir.'

'Take him round to the mannequin house. Mr Blackley has offered us Mr Yeovil's services. I see no reason not to avail ourselves of them.'

'Sir?'

'I'm interested to see just what he is capable of. How great his powers really are. That will allow us to form an opinion on a crucial head.'

'What do you have in mind, sir?'

'An experiment, Macadam. To find out whether Yeovil is capable of persuading a young, impressionable girl to take her own life.'

'Are you sure this is a good idea, sir? I am afraid it may end unhappily. Perhaps we should wait to talk to DCI Coddington...'

'It's all right, Macadam. I know what I'm doing. You'll need to gather up the rest of the mannequins too. They should still be in the Costumes Salon. You can bring them round in the Black Maria with Yeovil. I shall see you there, at the mannequin house.'

It was unfortunate that at just that moment Quinn's exhaustion from the night's surveillance operation got the better of him, causing a violent and prolonged spasm to ripple the soft sac of flesh beneath his eye.

Macadam's expression clouded with dismay.

The Experiment

Quinn crossed the dispatch yard, watched all the way by Kaminski. He pushed the swivelling panel and emerged in the garden of the mannequin house.

A shape moved in the small window of the rear room, someone backing away as soon as Quinn came through. The flare of sunlight on the glass made it difficult to identify who had been looking out. It was enough, for now, to know that someone had.

They had been watching from the spare room. Blackley's room.

Quinn entered the house through the scullery. Kathleen was at work, wringing damp clothes through a mangle. She rubbed at an itch on the side of her nose with the knuckle of a red raw hand.

'Where's Miss Mortimer?' said Quinn.

The maid seemed to shrink into herself, cowering away from the question.

Quinn went through into the kitchen. Miss Mortimer wasn't there either. He met her in the hall. She was coming downstairs.

'What do you want?' demanded the housekeeper.

'Has anyone told you about Edna?'

337

'We use their French names in here. Mr Blackley insists on it.'

'Albertine.'

'What about her?'

'She's dead.'

Miss Mortimer showed no sign of emotion. Quinn wondered if she had heard.

'I said she's dead. We found her body in a shop window at Blackley's.'

Now the colour drained from her face. She seemed to lose her balance for a moment, reaching out a hand to the wall to steady herself. Quinn had never seen a more spontaneous – and, it seemed to him, unfeigned – display of shock.

'No! But that's not possible!'

'I'm afraid so.'

After a moment's more consideration, Miss Mortimer seemed to regain her composure. She was able to stand up without support. 'Does Mr Blackley know?'

'Yes.'

Quinn was surprised by the vehemence of the sob that escaped from Miss Mortimer at this point. Even more surprised when she put a hand to her mouth and fell to her knees. 'Oh ... this will break him.'

Quinn's natural instinct was to recoil from the unexpected display of emotion. At the same time, it fascinated him. Reluctantly, as if he feared that emotion could be communicated by touch, he approached her and helped her to her feet. 'On the contrary, Miss Mortimer. He claimed it would take more than this

338

to hurt him.'

Miss Mortimer looked at him sharply.

'Now, I need to look in Albertine's room.'

'In Albertine's room?' The woman had reverted to the obstructive repetition of questions that Quinn had noticed the first time he had interviewed her.

He gestured impatiently for Miss Mortimer to lead the way upstairs.

The door to Albertine's room was locked. Miss Mortimer produced her great fob of keys from her housekeeper's apron. Quinn half-expected the keyhole to be blocked by a key on the other side, but Miss Mortimer was able to unlock the door without any obstruction.

There was something very different about the room, but Quinn couldn't, at first, work out what. Undoubtedly it had a forlorn, abandoned air to it. But there was more to it than that.

Was it just his sense of loss at Edna's death? Or was there something else missing from the room, other than a girl's life?

Quinn breathed in deeply through his nostrils, as if he believed he would be able to sniff out the solution to the mystery. Did he half-expect to inhale the smell of death there? He detected a far sadder scent: the sickly mixture of stale perfume and unwashed body odours that formed Edna Corbett's ghost. The image of the grieving girl on the bed came back to him, her last days both unhappy and unhealthy.

Quinn was aware of Miss Mortimer watching

him. He held a challenging finger towards her. 'I saw you. At the back of the house just now. Looking down from the spare room. From Mr Blackley's room. Why were you in there?'

'I go in all the rooms. It's my job. I have to tidy them up. Get them ready.'

'Did someone sleep in that room last night? Was Mr Blackley here?'

'I have to go into all the rooms.'

'Why were you watching from the window? Who did you expect to see come through the fence? Mr Blackley? Were you expecting Mr Blackley to sleep in the room tonight, perhaps? You were getting the room ready for his visit tonight?'

'I've seen that monkey again.'

Quinn frowned at the abrupt change in the conversation. 'You have?'

'I've put poison out for it.'

'Is that strictly necessary?'

'Dirty little beast. We can't have a monkey running wild.'

'Where did you see it?'

'On the fence. Looking at us. Cheeky bugger.'

'Just now?' Quinn had not noticed the monkey when he came through. Perhaps the woman was deluded.

'Before.'

'You hoped to see it again? That's why you were watching?'

'I want to see it eat the poison.'

Quinn began to feel sorry for the animal. 'Why do you want to kill it?'

340

'Hasn't it done enough harm?'

'Why do you say that?'

'There was no trouble here before it came along. Never should have been in the house in the first place. Mr Blackley wouldn't have allowed it.'

'Would it surprise you to learn that it was in fact Mr Blackley who gave Shizaru to Amélie as a gift?'

'He shouldn't have done it. It's against the rules.'

'But doesn't Mr Blackley make the rules? He can do what he wants, surely?'

Miss Mortimer shook her head emphatically. 'No he can't.'

'You're not frightened he might be cross when he finds out you've put poison out for the monkey? I remember he was cross with you once before.'

'He has to learn to obey the rules like everyone else.'

'And you will teach him?'

Miss Mortimer was prevented from answering by the sound of the front door bell.

'I believe that will be my colleagues with Mr Yeovil and the other mannequins. Could you please let them in and ask them to wait downstairs. Perhaps you could serve tea for everyone?'

'What do you think this is, a Lyons' Corner House?'

'The girls who are in your care have had another very unpleasant shock today. Do you not wish to make sure they're all right?'

'Oh, I'll look after my girls, don't you worry about that. It's all these policemen and the like that I object to.'

'I'm afraid that is an inevitable consequence of murder, Miss Mortimer. Once one starts killing people, one does tend to draw the attention of the police.'

Quinn heard the front door open downstairs. Presumably either Kathleen had answered it or one of the mannequins had produced her own key. In contrast to the mood in the garden a couple of days ago, there was no boisterous shrieking as the mannequins came in. Evidently it required two fatalities to impress them with the chastening gravity of death.

Quinn smiled and nodded to dismiss Miss Mortimer. She took her leave, frowning at his words.

Now that he was alone, he could begin his examination of the room in earnest.

Somehow it made sense to start with the place where, in Amélie's room, he had found the vital clue of the wooden hairpin, under the bed.

His own body felt heavier than he had ever known it to be; the core of the weight was a knot where he suspected his heart to be. The floor seemed to pull him down.

The bare boards bit into his knees with merciless rigidity.

The gloom beneath a dead girl's bed is laden with its own quality of despondency. Staring into it, he was faced with a granular blankness. He caught sight of a small object nestling

342

among the fluff clumps at the far side of the bed. It was just beyond his reach.

A strange dread took hold of him. What he feared was not that the solution would remain beyond his grasp, but that in discovering it he would be left staring into an emptiness more terrible than the one he glimpsed now. His job, he had always believed, was to effect restitution on behalf of the dead. But what if restitution was not possible? Certainly it was not possible if he was denied his usual recourse to the law-enforcer's privilege of violence.

He realized that the killing habit that his superiors lamented was not, as he had so often protested, the result of any number of regrettable accidents; it was the only thing that made sense of it all.

His shins ached, the after-throb of the torment inflicted on him in the lift. He felt it as the focus of the pressure that always built in a case. The pressure that could only be released in one way.

He flattened his chest to the floor and stretched his arm out, fingers splayed to retrieve the object. The first touch sent a jolt of recognition back through his fingertips. Immediate, unmistakable. It was the same kind of cloth-covered box as he had found in Amélie's room. The same kind of musical box as was on sale in the Locks, Clocks and Mechanical Contrivances department where Spiggott worked.

One more stretch and he locked a pincer of fingers and thumb on to the musical box. He teased it closer so that he was able to strengthen his grip and retrieve it.

His joints creaked as he hauled himself to his feet. He tried to turn the key that was projecting from the side but it was jammed. When he sprang the lid, no sound came out. The tiny ballerina had been snapped off her base.

It was at that point that he realized what was missing from the room.

Sergeant Inchball was waiting for him as he came downstairs. He held out a slip of paper. ''E 'ad it on 'im all the time, the lyin' bastard.' The preponderance of dropped aitches was again an indication of Inchball's emotional state.

'What is it?'

'Charlie Cale's report. I thought you ought to see what it said about the key. Coddington couldn't make head nor tail of it. That's why he wanted to keep it from you, I'll warrant. Didn't want to make himself look stupid in front of you.'

Quinn took the paper and unfolded it. 'How did you get this?'

'I have my methods.'

'Does he know you have it?'

'Give me some credit.'

Quinn glanced down at the paper. His gaze went immediately to a scaled-up sketch of the trapezium-shaped bow of the key. Charlie Cale had drawn a number of short, horizontal marks coming in from the sides, more or less at the centre of the bow. These marks were continued in drawings of the side sections. He had written

344

the word *striations*.

'Maybe it don' mean nothin',' said Inchball. 'But I thought you should see it so you could decide for yourself, guv.'

Quinn read through the notes that Charlie Cale had appended to the sketch. The scientist offered no opinion as to what had caused the marks. His account was technical and almost incomprehensible to Quinn. As far as he could tell, Cale had discovered some loose grains of brass in the microscopic grooves indicated. It seemed to be noteworthy that two types of brass were recovered, each with different proportions of copper and zinc. One formulation matched that of the key itself. The other represented an external source. No explanation for the discrepancy was given.

'Why would he keep it from me?'

'Because he wants to be the one who cracks the case. Either that, or he's too stupid to understand what it means.' Inchball nodded emphatically, to indicate he tended towards the latter explanation. Then a pall of confusion came over his expression. ''Ere, what *does* it mean, guv?'

'It means ... at least I think it means ... I know who killed Amélie.'

'I thought she killed herself, guv?'

'That's what I thought too. But this evidence changes everything. If only he had told me.' Quinn folded and pocketed the sheet.

The surviving mannequins, Marie-Claude, Giselle, Minette and Michelle, were huddled together on a chaise longue, heads bowed towards a centre of intense whispered communion. It seemed to Quinn, as he entered the drawing room, that Marie-Claude was hissing out instructions.

It was hard to know what to make of this, except that the four hard and heartless girls were at last beginning to feel some measure of guilt for all the misery they had inflicted on their two weaker fellows, both now dead.

The homeliness of the drawing room struck Quinn as a sham; as false as the vignettes presented in the store's windows. Everything in the room came from Blackley's, of that he had no doubt. The japanned table, the oversized vases that looked like they had been grown in some kind of ceramic forcing house, the chaise longue that served as a mannequin perch, the deep brown leather armchair into which the mountainous Yeovil was pensively sunk. All of it was, in Quinn's eyes, contaminated by its source.

Of course, Coddington was there. He strode up to Quinn and led him back out of the room. Just before he left, Quinn caught Macadam's look of contrition.

'What's this all about, Quinn?'

Quinn decided against challenging Coddington over the withheld forensic evidence. There would be time for that later. Besides, he wanted to enjoy the reciprocal pleasure: to experience for himself the obscure sense of power that came from holding back all that he knew. He did not believe that DCI Coddington would have been able yet to reach any meaningful conclusions regarding the forensics report. If he had, he would have hardly refrained from showing off his brilliance and wrapping up the case without Quinn's involvement. But it was clear that Coddington was very far from putting the pieces together.

In fact, given the evidence Inchball had just shared with him, the experiment Quinn had had in mind was no longer strictly necessary. But he did not, as yet, want to show his hand to Coddington, so he decided to stick to his original plan. At the very least, it would serve to throw Coddington further off the scent. At best, it might provoke a crucial revelation.

'I want to test a theory.'

'What theory?'

'I think these girls know more about what has been going on in this house than they have told us. I think Mr Yeovil can help us to get it out of them. He has certain talents, which Blackley is experimenting with in order to control his staff further. How much more obedient they would be if he could bend their individual wills to his own. Beyond that, perhaps, he may also be interested in influencing the minds and decisions of his customers.'

'And what has all this to do with the case?'

'When I was in the garden the other day, Yeovil tried to hypnotize me. He failed, of course. Nevertheless, I believe he may have greater success with more impressionable individuals.' Quinn refrained from adding: *such as yourself.* 'I believe he may have hypnotized

Amélie. Blackley denied it – or at least he denied it was anything to do with him. I want Yeovil to hypnotize one of the other girls.'

'To what end?'

'To get her to do something that she would naturally be extremely opposed to – consciously, at least.'

'Why should he? Won't he be helping you to build a case against him?'

'I believe the man's vanity will not be able to prevent him from doing it.'

DCI Coddington's moustache jutted forward aggressively. 'Sergeant Macadam warned me that you were planning something like this.'

'Oh, he did, did he?'

'Now don't go blaming Macadam. He's only trying to do what's best for you, believe it or not. He's trying to protect you.'

'Protect me? From what?'

'From yourself.'

Quinn squinted in disbelief. 'What could possibly go wrong?'

'Is it really necessary for me to answer that?'

'We'll make him think he's helping us in the case. Perhaps he will be. As I said, these girls are not saying everything they know. I'm damn sure there's some piece of this jigsaw that I'm missing. Everyone I speak to is holding something back.'

Coddington said nothing. His moustache wriggled uncomfortably.

'All I'm proposing is that he gets one of them to reveal some detail that she wishes to keep from us. I'm not suggesting he tries to induce her to commit suicide.'

'I'm very glad to hear it.'

'We need to make a breakthrough in this case, sir. And we need to make it soon. I think Yeovil can help us.'

Coddington sighed heavily. The question of urgency clearly carried weight with him. 'Which of the girls will you use?'

Quinn suppressed a smile. For all Coddington's hobbled indecision, he was as capable of being reckless as Quinn. All that was required was a little prodding. 'I'll let Yeovil decide that, I think.'

When they returned to the drawing room, Miss Mortimer was there, distributing cups of tea from a tray of rattling china held by a trembling Kathleen. The mannequins held on to their cups and saucers as if their lives depended on it.

Quinn noticed that the china was the same blue willow pattern as the discarded teapot he had seen on the rubbish heap. It was a common enough design.

'Mr Yeovil.' Quinn called the name firmly. A hush settled on the room. But Yeovil didn't look up. He appeared lost in a trance.

'Yeovil!'

The second, sharper cry drew his attention. A frightened child – admittedly a very large frightened child – peered up at Quinn, one eye obscured by the white glare in the monocle lens.

'It's all right, sir. No need to be alarmed. I didn't mean to startle you. It's just that I need your help with something. Mr Blackley has offered your services to the police. The time has come, I think, for us to avail ourselves of them.'

Yeovil had the mannequins stand in a line. He walked from one to the next, staring fixedly into each girl's eyes. Nothing was said. But as a result of that inspection he tapped Marie-Claude on the shoulder. 'Not her.'

'Wha's wrong wiv me?' Marie-Claude's wide face seemed to open up further with injured vanity.

'Please sit down,' said Quinn.

Yeovil conducted a second pass along the remaining girls. This time he held up a hand in front of their faces, murmuring something that Quinn could not make out. When he came to the third girl in the line, she leaned forward slowly, until her forehead touched Yeovil's palm. 'Her,' said Yeovil.

The other two returned to the chaise longue, shaking their heads uncomprehendingly. Even Marie-Claude's belligerence was subdued.

Yeovil looked to Quinn for direction, his face meek and submissive. Since the time he had spent in the back of the Black Maria alone with Sergeant Inchball, the confidence had drained entirely from Mr Blackley's special legal adviser. Quinn didn't know what had passed between the two men. And he preferred to keep it that way.

Quinn nodded for Yeovil to continue.

Yeovil removed his monocle and polished it

in his handkerchief for some minutes. When he returned the lens to his eye, it seemed that more than just its glassy gleam had been restored. The old Yeovil had snapped back into place.

'What's your name, my dear?'

'Giselle.'

'Giselle. What a lovely name.' Yeovil pointed to his newly polished monocle. He shifted the position of his head minutely so that the sunlight constantly flared and vanished, flared and vanished, setting up a regular pulse of light. 'You see my eyeglass? We call it a monocle, don't we? Look at the surface of the glass. Can you see how smooth and bright it is?' The sunlight continued to flicker. 'Keep your eye focused on my monocle. Don't look through the monocle. Look at the surface of the monocle. Let your gaze slide unimpeded over the surface of the monocle. Round and round it skates, like a skater on an ice rink. Your gaze skates over the round rink of my monocle. And as you circle the surface of my monocle you fall into a deep, deep, deep trance. You remain awake. You're able to keep your gaze skating over my monocle, you're able to hear my words, and at the same time you're aware of a wonderful feeling of peace and calm and well-being. Can you hear me, Giselle?'

'Yes.'

'You're skating over the gleaming surface of my monocle, skating back, back in time, to last night. It's Friday night, Giselle. Do you understand? You've skated over the surface of my monocle back in time.' Yeovil allowed the glinting monocle to hold her for a few moments in silence. 'What day is it Giselle?'

'Friday.'

'That's right. Friday. Where are you?'

'Home.'

'You mean here, at the mannequin house?' Giselle's eyes were fixed on Yeovil's flashing monocle. Her head swayed constantly. The motion seemed to resolve itself into a nod.

'What can you see, Giselle?'

'It's dark.'

'It's night time, is it? Are you in bed, Giselle?' The girl's nodding grew more defined.

'But you're awake? Did something wake you, Giselle? A sound?'

Her nods were more vigorous, more anxious, now.

'What can you hear, Giselle?'

The girl's mouth fell open, and to Quinn's astonishment she began to sing. Her voice had a cracked, lilting quality, as frail and uncertain as an echo in a dream. At the same time he was intensely aware of the physical mechanics of how that sound was produced; of the quivering membranes within her throat. Somehow, that made it seem all the more fragile. He knew full well the transience of flesh; how much more ephemeral were the by-products of its vibrations.

She sang a wordless melody, her *la-la-las* faltering at times, her voice falling short of the note, flat like a child's. Despite her flawed delivery, Quinn was able to recognize the tune.

It was the theme from *Swan Lake*.

Unprompted by Yeovil, Giselle raised her hands above her head, forming a loose circular shape with her arms. She crossed one leg in front of the other and began to rotate slowly on the spot, keeping up her melancholy singing.

There were sniggers from one or two of the other mannequins, but Marie-Claude hushed them sharply. It seemed she was interested to see how Giselle's performance played out. To judge from her grim expression, she was resigning herself to the possibility that this would not end well for any of them.

Quinn's attention was divided between the pirouetting Giselle and the other mannequins. So the disruption, when it came, took him entirely by surprise. It came from a source he had ceased to notice, but she was still there, at the edge of the room, holding the tray of tea things.

'I don't like it! It's not right! It's the Devil's work!'

Quinn turned just in time to see Miss Mortimer slap Kathleen across the face, causing the maid to drop the tray. The teapot, sugar bowl and milk jug crashed to the floor.

'Look what you've done, you careless girl!' Miss Mortimer flashed a sly look around the room as she tried to put the blame entirely on the hapless maid. 'Pick it up now.' To Quinn, she added: 'She's an ignorant Irish girl. She doesn't understand.'

The outburst was enough to break Giselle's trance. She frowned in confusion at her own arms held above her head, before slowly lowering them.

'I understand well enough,' protested Kathleen. 'I understand that every time he gives one of them a music box, I have to wash the blood out of the sheets.'

'That's quite enough of that filthy talk!' Miss Mortimer stooped down to pick up the tea things, her sly glance encompassing the room. 'Look at the mess you've made. That's the second teapot you've broken in as many days.'

Kathleen held up the detached handle. 'You can stick it back on, Miss Mortimer. You're ever so good at mending things.'

'It's never the same. Now go and get a cloth from the kitchen, you clumsy girl.'

Kathleen slumped from the room.

Quinn intercepted her in the hall on her return. 'Did you know there's a way through to the yard at Blackley's? You can get through the fence. Do you ever go through there? To put out rubbish, perhaps? Like the last teapot you broke?'

The maid shrugged. It was the closest Quinn was going to get to a confirmation.

Kathleen made a move to get past him, but he held on to her arm. 'Who were you talking about? Who gives them the music boxes?'

'Who do you think?'

'Mr Blackley?'

'That's right.'

'And have all the girls here received a music box from him?'

She nodded unhappily, once.

'And they were all virgins before the gift?'

'Virgins.' She nodded fiercely.

'But not after?'

A look of distaste came over her.

'What about Edna? I mean Albertine.'

'He hadn't got to her yet.'

'I found a music box in her room. It was broken.'

'Someone got to her. Saved her.'

'Is that how you see it?'

'From a fate *worse* than death.'

'It's still murder, Kathleen.'

'It wasn't me!'

'Do you know who it was?'

'I cannot say.'

'What happens when he has slept with all the mannequins in the house?'

'The eldest is moved out, in order to bring in new blood.' Kathleen cast an uneasy glance in the direction of the drawing room. 'I have to go now. Miss Mortimer will be wondering where I got to.'

And indeed, at that moment, Miss Mortimer appeared at the door. 'There'll be a stain in the carpet if you don't hurry up.'

Kathleen hurried past Quinn.

'Miss Mortimer,' said Quinn, 'I'd like to take a look in the spare room again. I hope you have found the key to the wardrobe there.'

'The spare room?' The echo of his request was charged with indignant bemusement, as if looking in the spare room was an idea so out-landish it topped even the strange sequence of events that had just occurred.

An Interest in Keys

Quinn followed the housekeeper up the stairs, addressing thoughts to her back as they occurred to him.

'You're not really deaf, are you, Miss Mortimer? It's an act. Not an affectation – no. There's more to it than that. A necessity, I would say. A psychological necessity. You've turned a blind eye and a deaf ear to all that's gone on in this house over the years. Everything he's done. The girls that have come and gone. You've heard nothing. Seen nothing. The whole time. What a strain that must place upon you. Why do you do it? Why do you put up with it? Put up with him? Were you a mannequin once yourself? And when you got too old – and too fat, let's face it – when his fancy turned to younger, slimmer girls, instead of casting you out he set you up to run the house. Is that what happened? He must have held some genuine affection for you at one time. He must have held you in high esteem, to make an exception of you and keep you here in the mannequin house. And so you felt you owed him a debt of gratitude? Is that why you tolerated his behaviour? Or was it more than that? You actually helped him. You prepared the girls. You talked them into it, if necessary. You were their confidante. They trusted you. When you told them to accept Mr Blackley's gift, they complied. You could talk them into anything, couldn't you?'

Miss Mortimer had reached the top of the stairs. She turned and waited for Quinn. Quinn felt suddenly vulnerable. For once, the housekeeper loomed over him, her solid bulk blocking his way. It would have been an easy matter for her to push him in the chest and knock him down. He imagined himself toppling backwards in a neck-breaking reverse summersault. Given the bone-weary exhaustion he was suffering, the slightest shove from her would have been enough.

He stopped two steps below the landing, their eyes level. She did not blink. He felt the blepharospasm start up again, running riot through the soft flesh beneath his eye.

She gave no indication of having heard a word of what he had said. 'What are you doing down there?'

'You're rather blocking my way, Miss Mortimer.'

The housekeeper seemed poised on a fulcrum of decision: either she would push Quinn down the stairs or step back to let him pass.

In the event, she stepped back. Quinn would never know if she had even considered the former option. Perhaps she had simply wanted to keep him, for a moment, on the same level as her.

'Who took the rug out of Albertine's room?'

357

'The rug?'

'Yes. The black and white, zebra-striped rug. It's gone from her room.'

'Is it?'

'Yes. And here's something ... I saw it in the Rugs and Carpets gallery at Blackley's. The very same rug. I'm sure of it.'

'How did it get there?'

'That's very much what I would like to know.'

'I'm sure I don't know.'

'No. Of course not. How would you?'

'Do you know?'

'I have an idea. I have ideas about a lot of things, Miss Mortimer.' Quinn felt a strange tense rippling in his heart; it was a stern sensation, a reminder of his mortality, of the excitement inherent in his own impermanence. He felt on the brink of something momentous: the cataclysm of discovery.

He decided to delay the moment of crisis, as if doing so would prolong his life, as well it might.

The room was cast in a shadowed chill. The window of the door that went nowhere afforded a dour light. Quinn crossed to the wardrobe.

'So do you have it?'

'Have it?'

'The key for this.'

'Mr Blackley has it.'

'I see. That's not what you told me before. Before you said it was missing. Now you are quite definite that Mr Blackley has it. Something has changed, I think. Once, you were willing to protect him. Now...?'

'I looked for it, and then remembered.'

'It was when we were in the garden, wasn't it? When the monkey was in the tree. He shouted at you. Worse than that, he humiliated you. That's when everything changed.'

'You asked for the key. And I'm telling you ... Mr Blackley has it.'

'What will I find inside the wardrobe, Miss Mortimer? Do you know? Of course you know. You know everything. He has never hidden any of it from you, has he?'

Some flicker of acknowledgement passed across her face. It was transient in the extreme but it was all Quinn needed. 'Come now, Miss Mortimer. Are you sure you don't have a key to this wardrobe somewhere on that wonderful housekeeper's fob of yours? You have an interest in keys, don't you, Miss Mortimer? You like keys. You like collecting them. And you like wielding them.'

The housekeeper puckered her lips as if in reaction to a sharp taste. With a sudden flurry of decision she produced the fob from her skirt pocket. 'There's no big secret. You know it all anyhow, thanks to that stupid Irish lump.' Miss Mortimer found a small key and opened the wardrobe door. She removed the key and backed away so Quinn could look inside.

The wardrobe was empty apart from a square box about two feet high. Quinn lifted the cardboard flaps and peered in.

The store of cloth-covered musical boxes was

359

down to about half now.

Quinn reached in and took out one of the musical boxes. It was, as he had expected, identical to those he had found in Amélie's and Edna's rooms. He wound the key and lifted the lid, releasing the pirouetting ballerina and the tinkling melody. The theme from *Swan Lake*.

He watched as the mechanism wound down and the ballerina spun to a halt before closing the lid.

He turned and looked at Miss Mortimer. 'Do you still have the one he gave *you*?'

'No. You're wrong about that.'

This was a surprise. 'What do you mean?'

'My love – our love – was different.'

'Never consummated, you mean?'

'Of course not!'

'But you thought perhaps one day ... You were saving yourself for him?'

'His wife didn't love him. And all those silly girls – none of them loved him. Least of all Amélie. They didn't make him happy, not really, not deep down. I was the only one who really loved him. Who would allow him to be ... the man he was, without judging him. I was the only one who could have made him happy. If only...'

'If only he'd given you a chance.'

She looked searchingly into Quinn's eyes, a look that wondered if it really was possible that he understood.

'How must you have felt, to be installed in that house, looking after all those girls? His harem.'

'I was happy. I knew it made him happy.'

'I understand,' said Quinn. 'I understand more than you can imagine. I once loved someone and would have done anything for them. Yes, even that. I would even have killed, if I thought it was what my love wanted. I think I'm beginning to understand why Amélie had to die.'

Miss Mortimer's brows descended in a troubled frown, as if to be understood was the one thing she feared.

'It wasn't because of the trouble she was threatening to make,' continued Quinn, his voice still sympathetic. 'No. It was because she was the only one he ever loved, wasn't it? All those girls, in all those years. None of them counted for anything. But she ... She was loved. *She* was the one he loved. Not you. Not any of them. Amélie. And what did she do? Refuse him! How dare she?'

The dip of her head, the tremor of her lips ... it was all he needed to know he had fathomed the mystery of her lonely heart.

Suddenly she lifted her head and let out a howl of anguish. 'The things she was saying! Wild, vindictive accusations.'

'She confided in you about the rape?'

'Rape?' Miss Mortimer screamed the word back at Quinn. In the sudden violence of her paroxysm he had an intimation of her insanity. 'There was no rape. There couldn't be any question of rape. Mr Blackley had a right to expect...'

'My dear Miss Mortimer, what are you

361

saying?'

'She was threatening to make trouble. We couldn't allow it.'

'You couldn't allow anything to harm Mr Blackley?'

'He was so good to us all. A father. Better than a father. Was it so much that he asked of her? Could she just not give him that? Something she had already given him ... He deserved a treat now and then.'

'And so you killed her. She didn't kill herself. You killed her.'

'She told me she couldn't bear to go on living. Not after what had happened. I helped her. I held her in my arms. I stroked her hair. I took the hairpin from her hair and stroked and stroked and stroked her hair.'

'And then you used the hairpin to twist the scarf around her neck?'

'It was what she wanted. She didn't fight it.'

'How did you manage the door? It was very clever of you to lock it from the outside, with a key on the inside.'

'You're the detective. You work it out.'

'Oh, that was never any great mystery, as far as I was concerned. There are countless ways to achieve it, given the simple locks on the doors here. We were confused by the monkey. I dare say you were too, as you weren't aware of its presence in the room when you killed Amélie. But the monkey, if I may say so, was always a red herring. The monkey had nothing to do with Amélie's death. In fact, the poor fellow may even have tried to save her life, snatching the hairpin out of the tourniquet and throwing it on the floor. But it was too late by then. She was already dead.'

Miss Mortimer said nothing. Quinn looked over her shoulder. Coddington, Macadam and Inchball were at the door. Quinn held his finger up to his lips to silence them.

'Do you have it in your pocket still?' he whispered to Miss Mortimer.

'What?'

'The picture wire. The picture wire that you used to hang the prints in the hall. And also used to wind around the bow of the key so that when you pulled it from the other side of the door the key would turn and trip the lock. The wire unwound as you pulled it and you were able to draw it out through the gap between the door and the jamb. Isn't that so?'

'I read about it in a detective story. I didn't believe it would work. But it did.'

'It was the same picture wire you used to strangle Albertine – is that not so? But this time it was to punish him, wasn't it? For the way he treated you in the garden. Oh, yes, you were going to make sure he didn't get his hands on the next girl. You were going to break his toy before he had a chance to play with it. Just like you broke the music box he gave her.'

'I saved her from him.'

'Perhaps. But she paid a terrible price for her salvation.'

'I hear they found her in a shop window. That's what the girls are saying. How did she get there?'

363

'You really don't know, do you? Let's try and recreate what might have happened. You killed her and rolled her up in the rug, then carried the rug outside, through the gap in the fence. It was easy enough. There was hardly anything to her, after all. She was another one who had half-starved herself, just like Amélie. What did you do then? Place the rug, with Albertine wrapped up inside it, into the incinerator, confident that the evidence would be destroyed next time the fire was lit?'

A slight pucker of Miss Mortimer's lips suggested that Quinn was on the right lines.

'You didn't count on the workman looking inside and taking a fancy to the zebra-striped rug. Imagine his surprise when he found a corpse wrapped up in it. What kind of a man – you have to ask yourself – what kind of a man, upon making such a grisly discovery, does not immediately raise the alarm, but instead decides to – what? How can we describe what he does? Play a practical joke? Was that it, do you think? How much hatred, how much pent-up bitterness and hatred must have been required for him to seize that opportunity in that particular twisted way? To carry the rug with Albertine inside it through the store and dump her body in a shop window, before discarding the rug in the Rugs and Carpets gallery of the House of Blackley? Can you imagine how much he must have hated Mr Blackley?'

'Yes. I can.'

Quinn signalled to Macadam and Inchball. One sergeant gently took each of her elbows and steered her round and out of the room.

'So,' said Coddington. 'You worked it out at last. Not before time.'

'At least I have delivered the suspect into custody alive. Indeed, I do not think that the deaths that have occurred in the course of this investigation can with any fairness be blamed on me. I wasn't responsible for the riot at Blackley's. And Edna Corbett was not, it turns out, killed because I had involved her in the investigation.'

Coddington seemed dissatisfied with Quinn's justifications. Or at least his moustache made its dissatisfaction felt.

'What shall we do about Blackley, sir?' asked Quinn.

'What do you mean?'

'The rape.'

'We can't prove anything there, Quinn. It's her word against his, and she's dead. It's hard to make a rape charge stick when we don't even have a complainant.'

'Amélie confided in Miss Mortimer. Mortimer killed her *because* of the allegations she was making against Blackley.'

'Water under the bridge now. We'd better let his son go too, pronto. Big mistake you made there, Quinn, picking young Blackley up. He had nothing to do with any of it.'

'He saw his father in the house. I believe he may have overheard the rape. Possibly he heard Amélie weeping afterwards.'

'You can't expect him to testify against his own father.'

365

'I think the pressure of being detained, the possibility that he might be charged with the offence himself ... these may weigh upon his mind. He might be persuaded ... We should at least talk to him.'

'Let it go, Quinn. I'm sure Mr Blackley has learnt his lesson. He'll be more careful now in his dealings with his young female employees, I'm sure. I'm more concerned about this workman who put the body in the shop window. Why the hell didn't you arrest him when you had the opportunity, Quinn?'

'In all honesty, I have only just now worked out his involvement in it all. My priority was to pursue the murderer.'

'We can have him for Perverting the Course of Justice, at the very least. What's his name?'

'Kaminski.'

'Foreigner, is he?'

'A Pole.'

'Agitator, no doubt. I'll get one of the uniforms to pick him up. As for Mr Blackley, you'd better get round there right away and apologize in person for all the inconvenience you have caused. You can tell him that he is no longer under suspicion and that we are releasing his son from custody forthwith. I hope you know how to grovel, Quinn. The last thing we need is Blackley coming after us with some kind of writ for wrongful arrest or police harassment.'

'Perhaps it would be better coming from you, sir?'

'Not likely. I don't want to be anywhere near

the firing line when Blackley finds out what a monumental cock-up you've made.'

'I understand, sir.'

'And I shall expect your report on my desk first thing in the morning.'

'Tomorrow is Sunday, sir.'

'Yes. First thing Sunday morning. Criminals don't rest on the Sabbath, Quinn. We can't afford to either. You should know that.'

Quinn looked down at the music box in his hand, before unconsciously pocketing it. 'Very well, sir.'

'How did you...' Coddington cleared his throat, swallowing back the question that he had been about to blurt out. It obviously cost him too much to voice it.

Quinn looked up enquiringly. 'How did I work it out?'

'What made you suspect *her*? If I hadn't heard her confess, I wouldn't believe it, I have to say. That trick with the key was quite ingenious. I wouldn't have believed a woman capable. Not a woman of low intelligence such as Miss Mortimer.'

'Miss Mortimer is not as stupid – or crazed – as she pretends to be. She has quite a practical bent. You heard what Kathleen said about the broken teapot. And when Arbuthnot came round, she was in the middle of hanging pictures on the wall. When I found out about the—' Quinn broke off. He had been about to mention the striations on the key that had figured in Charlie Cale's report. 'Again, it was a question of deduction. When I tried to think of how one might trip a key on the opposite side of a closed door, it occurred to me that one possible method might be to wind wire around the bow, or handle, so that it would turn when the wire is pulled through. The fact that Miss Mortimer had been handling picture wire at around the time of the murder naturally brought her under suspicion. If there had been scratches around the bow of the key, I might have got to the solution quicker. I would also have expected Cale to have found traces of a second type of brass on the key – most hanging wire is made from brass, I believe, but it is of a more flexible consistency than the brass of a door key.'

Coddington's moustache gave an uneasy twitch. 'Was there nothing else?' he asked quickly, evidently keen to steer the conversation away from Cale's report.

'When I learnt that she had put poison out for the monkey, I realized she was a woman capable of anything. You may remember that time in the garden, how violently Shizaru reacted to both Miss Mortimer and Blackley. I had always believed that the monkey's significance would be as a witness, rather than a perpetrator. I think that Miss Mortimer's desire to kill the monkey was a belated reaction to that incriminating outburst. You will remember how delighted she was that the monkey got away. But she also feared its return, I think.' Quinn moved to the window at the back of the room. 'She was watching for it earlier from this very window.'

Quinn half-expected to see a flash of grey moving through the branches of the cherry tree. But, of course, he did not.

'And the monkey? Where is the monkey now?' Behind him, Coddington's voice was sharp and insistent.

Quinn shrugged. 'He remains at large. We have to accept that some loose ends simply cannot be tied up.' He continued to stare at the top of the fence, where Miss Mortimer claimed to have last seen Shizaru. But despite the fixity of his wishful concentration, the monkey refused to materialize.

A World of Provision

Quinn blinked in the sunshine, feeling like some subterranean creature bursting unexpectedly out of the ground. The sudden pulse of birdsong struck him as angry and raucous. So much that he had not noticed until now: that the sky was a veil of fine thin blue, smeared here and there with the sparsest of chalk thumbprints. That he was hungry. Devilishly hungry.

He discovered he was in no hurry to let Blackley off the hook. So he took the long way round to the store, stopping off along the way at a cheap restaurant on the Earl's Court Road for a very late and hearty breakfast: eggs, bacon, sausages, liver, black sausage, fried bread and endless cups of tea. The feast restored him. He was nearly ready for his meeting with the great commercial genius.

First, however, there was one more restorative visit that he wished to pay.

Sunlight flooded into the little yard, to be caught and refracted in the leaves of the lime tree; the full force of the light, however, fell squarely on to the front of the church, setting the honey-coloured bricks aglow. It was a benign effect, as if the building was beaming with pleasure at the sight of him.

He pushed the door open and voiced a soft 'hello?' that reverberated shockingly in the empty church. He followed the call with echoing footsteps. He had reached halfway down the aisle when the door to the sacristy opened and the cassocked figure of Father Thomas emerged.

'Oh, it's you.'

'Yes.'

'Lovely day, isn't it?'

Quinn nodded vaguely.

'How may I help you, Inspector?'

'How do you manage to believe ... to continue to believe...?'

'My goodness, I wasn't expecting that particular question!'

'In the goodness of God. In God. Can you know anything of what really goes on in the world? If you had seen what I had seen ... would you be able to believe?'

'I know more of the evil that men – and women – are capable of than you imagine. Far from undermining my faith, that knowledge is what makes faith essential to me. Without a belief in God, I would be overwhelmed by the chaos.'

'At times, I am.'

'Then I feel deeply sorry for you, Inspector.'

'As I came up to the church, I had the feeling that it was smiling to me in welcome.'

'Perhaps it was.'

'It was just the sunlight playing on the front of the church.'

'You will always be welcome in my church, Inspector.'

'I'm not a Catholic.'

Father Thomas gave an unconcerned shrug. 'These things can be rectified.'

Quinn was more explicit: 'I don't believe in God.'

'Don't worry. He believes in you.'

Quinn was disappointed in the priest's answer, which struck him as glib. 'He has no idea who I am and of what I am capable.'

'He knows you are a man, and therefore capable of anything.'

Quinn grimaced his dissatisfaction.

'It would help you to open your heart to Him. To confess your sins. You will find that He will not turn from you. He will continue to believe in you. Continue to love you. No matter what you confess to. And then you will find it impossible not to believe in Him. That is the great beauty and strength of the Catholic Faith.'

'The idea of confession does have its appeal. Is Peter Spiggott here?'

'What do you want with him?'

'We've made an arrest. The housekeeper at the mannequin house, Miss Mortimer. She has confessed to killing Amélie Dupin, and another girl too. A friend of Amélie's called Edna Corbett.'

'What about *that man*?'

'Mr Blackley?'

The priest nodded, evidently unable to bring himself to say Blackley's name.

'He had nothing to do with either death.'

'But he raped her?'

'We believe so. We cannot prove it.'

'And so he is getting off scot-free?'

'There is not sufficient evidence to secure a conviction. No one will testify to his presence in the mannequin house that night. There is no complainant to press charges against him. We have no choice.'

'You had better let me break it to Peter.' Father Thomas was for a moment lost in his own thoughts. 'He will take it badly.'

'Men like Blackley always come up smelling of roses.'

'The Devil looks after his own.'

'Doesn't it shake your faith in God a little?'

'You must understand, Inspector, if I entertain, for one moment, the possibility of a godless universe, then I am lost. I would be part of the chaos. The chaos would enter into me. There would be nothing to prevent me – any of us – from committing the very worst of crimes. We would all be as black as Blackley.'

'I hope, then, that you continue to believe.'

The two men shook hands. The priest clung on to the policeman's with both of his, as if he feared what would ensue if he let him out of his sight, out of his church.

Blackley was outside the store, announcing its reopening. DCI Coddington had no doubt given his approval – presumably caving into Blackley's pressure – once the body had been taken away. It seemed that the news of Miss

Mortimer's arrest had already reached him, no doubt through Yeovil.

'Everything half price today!' he was announcing. 'To celebrate the sensational arrest of the mannequin house murderer!'

'You heard then?'

'Indeed, I have, Inspector.'

'And you are turning it to your commercial advantage, I see?'

'After Thursday's bloody disaster, I have a lot of ground to make up.'

'Your son, Ben ... he should have been released by now.'

'That's as it should be.'

'You haven't seen him?'

'He hasn't come back to the store as yet.'

'I wonder if he ever will.'

'What is your point, Inspector? Your case is over. Do you have something else you wish to say to me?'

'I have been ordered to apologize to you.'

'Is that so?'

'Yes.'

'Very well then.' Blackley nodded for Quinn to go on.

'I am therefore obliged to apologize for any inconvenience you may have been caused. You must understand, however, in the course of a criminal investigation, we have a duty to consider all the evidence that comes to our attention. However inconvenient it may be for those concerned.'

A spark of genuine amusement kinked Blackley's grin. He seemed to regard Quinn with something like admiration. 'Is that it? It hardly qualifies as the most sincere apology I have ever heard.'

'It is the best you'll get from me.'

'Perhaps you're right. In some ways I blame myself for all this mess.'

Quinn was astonished. 'You do?'

'Aye. It were me who set her up in the mannequin house in the first place. I put her in charge of them poor girls.'

Quinn felt something sharper than disappointment. He remembered the musical box in his pocket. He took it out and wound the key. 'Do you feel no other responsibility for what happened?' Quinn released the lid and let the ballerina dance. He held it out towards Blackley, an eloquent enough accusation.

'Pretty,' said Blackley, as if he had never seen an object like it before.

Perhaps he had intended to say more, but he never got the chance.

'Blackley!'

The cry came from the direction of the entrance to the Sacred Heart. Spiggott was striding purposefully towards them. In his hands was the white cardboard box that Quinn had seen him carrying earlier that day. It bore the legend, 'A world of provision'.

Spiggott opened and discarded the box in one smooth motion. The same motion continued to a terrible conclusion: his right arm extended out towards Blackley. In his hand the contents of the box: a revolver.

'Spiggott! Don't be a fool!' cried Quinn. But

even as he shouted the words, he knew he didn't mean them. Wasn't this, in fact, the very event that his visit to the church had been intended to precipitate?

The shot, when it came, was the most absolute and appalling sound imaginable. Quinn had heard guns discharged before, of course. Often when they were held in his own hand. Or in the hands of those who were directing their fire towards him.

But somehow the sound of a gun is always more shocking to a bystander than to anyone directly involved in an exchange of gunfire, even if that bystander is a seasoned police detective. There can be no sense of control over or responsibility for what is happening. One is overwhelmed instead by a haphazard and profoundly inimical world.

This was the chaos of which Father Thomas had spoken.

Blackley fell to the floor. Blood pooled around his head. The gasps and spasms of his dying held them fascinated. Then it was over.

The people on the street were screaming. They had probably been screaming for some time. But this was the moment that Quinn became aware of it. It needed the reverberating punch of the gunshot to die before he was able to process any other sounds.

He noticed too that the musical box had not yet reached the end of its melody.

Spiggott kept his right arm outstretched, as if he wanted to hold the gun as far away from him as possible. Smoke curled up from the tip of the barrel.

There was a strange blankness in his eyes. Whatever combination of rage and hatred had caused him to fire the gun had been expelled along with the bullet. 'I loved her.' His voice was quiet but strangely firm, as if this was the only explanation necessary for what he had done.

The hand holding the weapon began to shake. Slowly the direction of the barrel rotated. Quinn held up one palm as if he believed he could fend off a bullet with it. But it was soon clear that Spiggott did not intend to shoot the detective. Instead he inserted the barrel of the revolver into his mouth. A moment later there was a bloody mess where his head had been. The force of the gun's explosion threw his body backwards on to the pavement.

'I ought to have seen that coming.' The ballerina in Quinn's hand finished her final pirouette. He pushed her down and fastened the lid.

Quinn stayed late at the department that night to write the report that DCI Coddington had requested. It was worth it for the privilege of watching the evening form in the attic window. The sky's twilight transformations took him to a place above the fray. The death of Blackley in particular would not play well with his superiors, he knew. But as he glimpsed the vast, subtle shifts of colour in the square panes it was hard to care.

The hammer was about to fall. Let it fall.

He wrote the report by longhand on carbon-backed papers, producing one copy for Coddington, another to be delivered directly to Sir Edward, and a third which he kept for himself.

At last, it was done. The full weight of dusk gathered at the window – one final transformation away from night.

Quinn left Coddington's copy on his own desk, which Coddington had appropriated. Not for too much longer, he hoped. He had not been able to keep Coddington's withholding of vital forensic findings out of the report.

He donned his bowler, shrugged himself into his herringbone Ulster and headed out with the other two copies under one arm. It felt as if he was leaving the department for good.

He could still feel the weight of the musical box in his pocket. He knew it could be considered evidence but he doubted anyone would miss it. And he had plans for it.

She was not at her desk, of course. Her typewriter squatted beneath its dust cover, the surface of the desk scrupulously cleared.

He placed the musical box where she could not miss it, right in front of the machine at which she spent so much of her day working. But he was immediately dissatisfied with the positioning. There seemed something obstructive about it. He tried balancing the gift on top of the typewriter, but that looked too ostentatious. Putting it behind the typewriter ran the risk that she would not notice it.

At last, he went back to his original choice,

on the edge of her desk, just in front of the typewriter.

He knocked on Sir Edward's door. There was no reply and when he tried the handle it was locked. He wanted to be sure that Sir Edward read his report, so he pushed the single sheet of paper under the door. He folded the other copy and placed it in the inside pocket of his Ulster.

On his way past Miss Latterly's desk, he snatched up the musical box and slipped it back into his pocket.

What on earth had he been thinking?

He sat on the top deck of the number nine omnibus, up in the open night. Around him the lights of Piccadilly hung like fallen stars. He was part of the darkness he had earlier seen forming. Under its influence, he allowed himself to entertain impossible dreams: that tomorrow he would find his nerve and give her the musical box in person.

Some part of his rational faculty was not yet obliterated by exhaustion. And so he ultimately accepted that this would never happen. But he was only able to replace one preposterous fantasy with another. In short, he imagined himself giving the musical box to Miss Ibbott.

He justified this to himself by arguing that there would be nothing meant by it. It would be seen as the disinterested gift of a grateful lodger for his landlady's daughter, a way of showing his satisfaction with his accommodation. A gift, effectively, from an adult to a child, comparable perhaps to a fond uncle treating a favourite niece. It was patently not the gift of an admirer to a lady about whom he entertained hopes; no one would be able to construe it in that way, except perhaps Messrs Timberley and Appleby, and they would only do so ironically, to make mischief.

Of course, he realized that the best thing to do with the cursed object was simply throw it away. But he could not quite bring himself to do that.

It was approaching eleven o'clock as he walked the last stretch of his journey home. The night was warm. He was glad to be out in it. He saw more people in the quiet residential streets of South Kensington than were usual at that time. The balmy weather after so much rain drew them out. He had the sense of something lively at large. But then his recent experiences made it hard for him to believe in the good-natured fellowship that seemed to be communicated in these strangers' glances.

Perhaps it was the policeman in him. He couldn't help suspecting that they were up to no good.

He couldn't help speculating, too, about the lives that were lived in the houses he passed. Outwardly so respectable, just like the mannequin house, the flat, stuccoed facades repelled him. In contrast, Quinn found the warmth of the night welcoming.

Mrs Ibbott had left a light on. A soft glow seeped out from the semicircular window above the street door, dispensing a gleaming edge on to the area railings.

Waiting for him on the front step was Mr Percy, the cat whose complacent air of prerogative had come to mind when he had seen Blackley in the garden with the mannequins. The cat sprang to his feet and preened demandingly around Quinn's ankles, mewing his complaints. Sleek, black and overfed, the animal was like a small bundle of the night that had come to life solely for the purpose of importuning Quinn.

As Quinn opened the door Mr Percy slipped in through the smallest possible gap. The cat shot off, his self-importance reflected in the pertness of his tail; Quinn was utterly forgotten now, having served his purpose.

Closing the door behind him, he felt a chill weight settle in his heart. His life closed down to what it was – no more, no less. Whatever potential he had possessed in the night was lost to him.

He was Silas Quinn. A man approaching middle age. A bachelor. Possessor of certain talents and uncertain qualities. In his professional life a fearless – some might say reckless – pursuer of dangerous criminals. In his private life, in the pursuit of his own happiness, he was an abject failure. A coward.

It was that failure that he was coming home to.

He would never give the musical box to Miss Latterly. And he realized just in time what a terrible mistake it would be to give it to Miss Ibbott. But he wouldn't throw it away. He would keep it hidden in a drawer, a secret reminder of – what? He could not say *of what might have been*. More accurately, *of what never could be*.

At the very least, it would serve as a reminder of his emotional cowardice.

For once, he didn't worry about making a noise coming in. The door hinges screeched a gleeful mocking chorus. He hardly heard it.

The other occupants of the lodging house had evidently already retired for the night. No one came out to quiz him on his late return. That's to say, his landlady, Mrs Ibbott didn't; it was invariably she who sought to involve him in the life of the house.

As he reached his landing he heard the tread of someone coming down from the floor above. He turned to see Miss Dillard in her nightie and dressing gown. A faint whiff of sherry preceded her.

'Oh, Mr Quinn, it's you.' Miss Dillard looked down in embarrassment. 'I left my novel downstairs.' She evidently felt her presence was something that needed to be explained.

She kept her eyes away from his out of embarrassment, but at that moment he found himself craving a glimpse of her irises. He needed to remind himself of the startling metallic clarity of their grey.

He reached out a hand and tilted her face up.

The colour was like a shot of fortifying liquor. It was objectively, absolutely beautiful. And so it made up for a lot.

'You have very beautiful eyes.' Quinn releas-

382

ed her jaw. She kept her gaze on him. He felt the spasm beneath his eye flare up again.

'Good night, Miss Dillard,' he said at last, turning away from her.

She made a small, disappointed sound.

Quinn broke off from opening his door with a self-conscious gesture. 'Oh, Miss Dillard.' He straightened up and pulled the musical box from his pocket. 'I was wondering ... I thought perhaps...' He thrust the gift towards her. 'It's a musical box.'

Her face lit up. Her smile was not beautiful like her eyes, but there was a wan sadness to it that touched him. She wound the key and opened the lid. The tiny ballerina danced in her hand. She turned her eyes on him in delight. And once again he was granted a glimpse of that beautiful clear grey.